THE GIRLS NEXT DOOR

THE GIRLS NEXT DOOR

PAT KELLEY

DEER LAKE PRESS
CLINTON, WA

Printed in the United States of America
by
Deer Lake Press
Clinton, Washington

For information contact Deer Lake Press
at kelley@kelleybarts.com.

Books may be purchased for educational,
business, or sales promotion use.

First edition

Cover Design by Terry Hansen

Identifiers
978-1-7358928-0-1 (printed)
978-1-7358928-1-8 (ebook)

Subjects: Pat Kelley, Sex Trafficking, Victims, Child Sex Trafficking, Exploitation, Prostitution, Abuse of Power.

Other books published by Deer Lake Press

POETRY FROM THE DESERT FLOOR
THE LAST CONFESSION
TO THE TOP OF THE TREE
SOLD BY DEER LAKE PRESS
MAKING FINE SPIRITS

DEDICATION

To all the girls who said "They didn't believe me."

CHAPTER ONE

Father Francesco rose from his chair and steadied himself. "Well, you two lovebirds, how are you feeling about being an old married couple of two months?"

Matthew laughed. "What a question. I never in a million years would have believed that I would be married, and married to the most beautiful damsel in the land."

"And, you, fair damsel?"

"Ecstatically happy. And, you, Father. Are you happy?"

"I cannot believe, how happy." Father Francesco donned his old panama hat. "I'll be down by the river among the rocks under the bridge. I want to check the pools between the rocks."

"The river's running low. You can probably see rocks, maybe some fish, and any debris that has been tossed into the river." Maggie said.

"Are there pools of life such as one finds at the ocean?" Francesco asked.

"Not really. The river is usually swift flowing. The Columbia is low right now because the dam has lowered the river level. You'll be able to see the bottom close to the shore."

"Oh, Maggie, I love this place. You know how much I love you two. I'm so happy you included me in your wedding plans." The old priest beamed. He had abandoned his retirement in Spokane and joined Maggie and Matthew in their new lives.

For twenty years he had written encyclicals for the Vatican on matters of the social issues of the church. Ironically, one of his last papers was on the need for priests to be allowed to marry. When he realized Maggie and Matthew were in love even before they knew it, he had written the Vatican asking that Matthew be allowed to marry and remain a priest. The "no" had been a cautionary note. Someday. We will think about it. Someday had been too late for them, so Matthew had called churches all over the northwest asking to be allowed to marry and serve God.

"Personally," Matthew said, "it's we who are profoundly grateful for your suggestion that we could marry. A married priest was not exactly what I expected my future to look like." Matthew grabbed Maggie's hand.

Maggie smiled, her cheeks glowing. "Oh, Francesco, can you imagine what the gossip is like in Grand Coulee? Their priest got married and invited the entire valley to attend. I'll bet Bishop Davis had a heart attack, but then I don't much care." She pulled back her mahogany curls with a broad sweep of her hand.

Father Francesco smiled. "My life would not have been much fun had I stayed in Grand Coulee or Spokane. I might have written more encyclicals, but nobody would have cared." He hugged Maggie and bid them a good afternoon. "I'm off to climb the rocks down to the mighty Columbia River. I'll be hunting for a story I can tell your children." In mock fierceness, he raised his arm as a challenge to the unknown.

Maggie and Matthew exchanged silent glances. A moment alone was a treasured moment. "And what will you do?" Maggie asked.

"Look in all the crevices between the rocks. Don't know what I'll find, but I'm off. I'll be back in an hour or two." Matthew and Maggie watched him slowly make his way down the driveway to the highway. "He'll enjoy a couple of hours by himself," Matthew said. "He'll probably bring back fish caught with his bare hands for dinner."

"You get to clean them," Maggie laughed.

"I thought you were the fisherman in this family. Suddenly you don't want to clean fish? What kind of a pioneer are you?"

"The kind who cleans out old, oily garages to make way for a mission. Changing the subject, do you think this clean-up will ever be complete? Sometimes I think Father Daniel never actually saw the condition of this building. And, we could use his seven-foot frame to clean the higher spots."

"I suspect he knew. He felt it was a freebee that we could use. We owe the man our best effort. After all, he's allowing me to remain as a married priest. There are few who could be progressive enough to let that happen."

"True. We owe him a lot. But I still think I'll ask him to come help."

"I'm sure he will be happy to help. Now, let's get back to work."

"Tyrant!" Maggie laughed as she picked up a small pry bar and began peeling off the siding. She gave him a wicked smile. "Instead of slaving, let's retire to the back room for a few minutes and hope no one shows up. I'm in need of an afternoon nap."

"I like your style," Matthew said, following her inside, then picking her up and carrying her to their make-shift bed. "I need more naps like this."

Father Francesco slowly walked down to the highway. Even with his cane for support, he took care not to fall. As he approached Dinty's Cafe, a small boy was throwing rocks into the street. Without looking up, he asked, "Who are you?"

"I'm Father Francesco," he answered. "Who are you?"

"I'm Toby."

"Are you practicing to be a baseball player, Toby?"

"Nah. My daddy won't let me throw a baseball. Says I'm too young, I might break a window or hurt somebody. But I'm not really young. I'm four."

"Well, young man, I believe all this practice will make you a fine baseball player."

"Thanks. Where are you going?"

"To the river. I've never walked on the rocks beside a fast-flowing river like the Columbia. I hope there are interesting things to see."

"What kind of things?" Toby asked.

"Perhaps small fish or rocks that might have come from historic lava flows."

Toby looked at Francesco and said, "Bye," then threw another rock at Francesco's back, hitting one shoe. Hmm, Francesco thought. This child is a bit of a scalawag.

Francesco crossed the highway and looked down at the mosaic of huge gray boulders, wondering if the Celilo Natives had ever fished in this exact spot. He knew they had fished at Celilo Falls, where the dam now stood.

As the old priest picked his way down under the bridge, he found what he'd really come for. In the bridge's shade, the sun's oppressive light and heat were gone and the air was a good ten degrees cooler. Traffic sounds from the nearby freeway and the bridge itself grew soft. The wind filtered a cadence of birdsong, rushing water, and bugs. Francesco heard the sounds and in the cool dimness marveled that God was with him and had brought him peace. Once near the water, he moved from pool to pool, moving deeper into the dim, cool, quiet under the bridge that connected Oregon to Washington.

The rocks were smaller, closer to the river and he wondered if they had been put there when road builders had dynamited the hill to build the bridge or whether they were natural deposits from the ice age. Probably rock haulers. He stepped carefully so as not to fall. Needing to rest he sat on a flat-sided granite rock shaped like a seat, and drew a deep, steady breath.

And then he saw it, a small skeleton in about a foot of water.

Bones? He lifted his ancient body and took a few steps forward. Definitely an entire skeleton and just as definitely a human. Out of habit he raised his arms towards the sky and then gestured over the bones, as he blessed them. I must bring Matthew and Maggie, he spoke softly to himself. He pulled a piece of paper from his pocket and put a small rock on it so he could identify the exact spot. He carefully picked his way straight up to the highway and walked as fast as he could back to the building. Exhausted, he labored inside, sputtering, "Matthew! Maggie!"

"What is it Father?" Maggie asked as she ran to him and carefully eased him onto an old folding chair.

"Body," he said. "I must take you now."

"What do you mean, body?" Matthew asked.

"Bones. I found human bones under the bridge. You must come. I'll show you, but we must drive. I don't think I can walk that far again."

"What kind of bones?" Maggie asked.

"Small human skeleton. Perhaps an older child."

"I'll get the keys," Maggie said.

"Wait," Father Francesco said. "I need my book and vestment." He raised himself from the chair and hurried into the back room, reappearing with both items. "I'm ready."

They drove the distance in two minutes. Father Francesco got out of the truck and motioned for them to follow him down the hill. Carefully navigating the rocks, they shadowed him until he found the tiny piece of paper. The water was clear enough that they could see a fully intact skeleton covered with bits of mud and river grass.

Matthew helped Father Francesco to sit. "We need to call the police immediately. Someone may know who this is and what happened. You two wait here while I climb up to Dinty's to find out where the police station is. It's unlikely that Bigg's Junction has one. Probably the closest sheriff is in The Dalles. I'll call and wait there for someone to come. While I'm waiting, I'll ask at the restaurant if anyone knows whose bones they might be." As a matter of practice, Matthew blessed the bones before he turned and climbed back up the hill.

Matthew entered the restaurant, looked at small groups seated at various small tables, and asked "Is Pauline in the back? I'd like to borrow the phone."

Pauline peeked up through the serving window. "Whatcha want, Father?"

"I need to call the police, or sheriff, or whatever you have here. I assume you don't have any police here."

"Yeah, we do. It's a sheriff's station. It's down in a little RV by the nearest silo. If nobody's there, you'll have to call Wasco County Sheriff or the state police. Come on back here. You can use my phone." As he walked toward the back room, a small child stepped in front of him.

"You aren't my father. There was another man said he was my father. I asked my real father and he said priests are called father. Are you a priest? What's a priest?"

"I am. I'll talk to you after I make a call."

Pauline asked, "What's going on?"

"Father Francesco found a small human skeleton in the river, under the bridge. The police need to know about it so they can call the medical examiner."

Pauline pointed to the wall. "All the numbers are there. I suggest you call the county sheriff. They can notify The Dalles police and the state police.

Matthew made the call. When he finished, Pauline asked, "Where did Father find the skeleton?"

"Under the bridge. Do you know anything about any missing kids?"

"Oh yeah. About five years ago two Native American girls, twins, disappeared down by the river. Never seen or heard from again. Might be one of them."

"I'll ask the police about them when they arrive. May I have a cup of coffee while I wait?" Matthew pulled a dollar out of his pocket and handed it to Pauline.

"Father, please, keep your money."

"Thanks." Matthew pocketed the money and walked back out front and saw the little boy standing next to a table with two men. He ran to Matthew and asked, "Now tell me what a priest is."

"It's a minister in the Catholic church."

Uninterested, Toby said, "Oh," and turned back to one of the men. "Dad, can I go back outside and throw rocks?"

"No. We're heading home." The man stood. Matthew didn't pay attention. He was focused on the child.

"Ah gee," the boy said as he pushed open the door and walked towards the truck, the two men following. Once in the truck one man said, "Oh shit." Without answering, the other man nodded his head in agreement.

Father Francesco and Maggie sat under the bridge without speaking, watching the river sweep by. Francesco held his head in his hands. He no longer heard the sweet sounds of the desert or the rush of the water. It was silent. Too silent. It was the silence of the dead.

Matthew waited outside the store, close to the highway exit. I wonder if this is another mission. Find missing children. Shades of Iraq. Who do they belong to? There's always a story. His six-foot frame stood straight, his short blond hair impervious to the blowing wind. He stood as if waiting for an order to commence an inquiry. He'd been in Army military intelligence, without the law degree. He'd been more interested in seeking out humanity in a war zone, talking to families, putting the pieces together after a tragedy. Thoughtful and persistent, he was always in the throes of completing an assignment. He was also an EMT. His fellow soldiers considered him the go-to guy when they needed emotional and psychological support, especially coming in from fire fights and long, stressful patrols. Those experiences had led him to the priesthood. He'd considered no other occupation until he met Maggie. Maggie, the alive, full of energy, happy woman. Then he wanted both.

Forty minutes went by before he heard the siren. A few minutes later, an Oregon state trooper pulled up to where Matthew waited on the I-84 exit. Matthew introduced himself to the officer, told him about Father Francesco finding the bones, and pointed to the rocks below the bridge. "One of the waitresses in the café said she thought it might be one of the Native American sisters who disappeared five years ago." As they descended through the rocks, an officer from The Wasco County Sheriff's Department arrived. He climbed down to join the group. "Whatcha got?" he asked.

"A nearly full human skeleton. Other than that, we don't know a thing," Maggie said.

The State Patrol officer, Ben Freedman, offered a suggestion. "Maybe it's one of the twins that disappeared a few years back."

"That's what I was told up at the cafe," Matthew said. "Who were they?"

"They were Celilo girls. Twins, maybe twelve or thirteen. Beautiful girls. Not the type to be in trouble with anyone. Well-respected girls. They were involved in school activities, got good grades. One day they just up and disappeared. Neither girl was ever found, so the case has been on hold for maybe five years."

The officer turned to the newly arrived sheriff and said, "Hi Rex." To the others he said, "This is Rex Tyson, Wasco County sheriff."

"Hi, how are ya Rex?" They shook hands around the group.

"You think maybe it's one of the twins?" Rex asked

"Could be. The skeleton is about the right size. Apparently the reason we never found it was because no one looked when the river was down," Rex said.

"You probably know more about this story than I do, Rex. What can you fill in?" Ben asked.

"Not much. We always wondered if somebody kidnapped them since we never found any sign of them. Lots of people called in clues, but most were hoaxes or people asking about a finder's fee. The only valuable clue was that someone had seen them heading to the river. We walked the river, but nothing ever surfaced that led us to any type of conclusion. If this is one of the twins, we'll be able to reopen the case. I'll call the medical examiner to come and collect the bones. It'll take a while, maybe three or four weeks, before we'll know anything. They'll have to send the bones to the state lab. Then they have to look at any clues they might have. Looking at the size of the skeleton, I'm gonna put my money on the idea that it is one of the twins." Turning to the four, he said, "Do you mind waiting until the ME arrives? I think it will take a good half hour to forty-five minutes to get somebody out here. You a priest?" The officer addressed Father Francesco, noting that he wore a purple vestment signifying a Christian burial.

"I am and so is Matthew," Father Francesco said pointing to Matthew.

"Well good. I'm Catholic. Have you blessed these bones?" Rex asked.

"Actually, we both have." Father Francesco said, moving to his sit-down rock.

"And who might you be, young lady?"

"Maggie Callahan," she replied. She and Matthew had agreed she would continue using her maiden name so as not to confuse his status as a priest. As they got to know people, they would let the truth slip out. "I'm helping the priests clean up a building so we can open a small church here."

"A church? I'm impressed. Sort of sounds like you're missionaries."

"I guess we are. We're doing this through St. Michaels in The Dalles," said Father Francesco.

"I hope you don't mind waiting," Ben said. "It will help us move this along. I'll call it in. Meanwhile," turning to Father Francesco, "I'll take your story about how you found the bones."

Father Francesco relayed the story of walking and finding the bones. "One thing I don't understand," he said, "is why the bones weren't found earlier. They are not in deep water and should have been easy to spot."

"This area is usually covered with water from the dam back-up, but when the water runs high, they control the flow at the dam. They also do it in late summer, to prepare for fall and winter rains. The river falls for a week or so. Father, you were simply in the right place at the right time. Tomorrow it will probably be flooded again." Rex's phone rang. He listened, turned to them and said, "Accident up the highway. I'll be back some time later to see you. Glad you found these bones."

After both officers were gone, the three sat silently and looked at the skeleton. Finally, Matthew broke the silence. "Have either of you ever dealt with a dead or missing child?" They shook their heads. "I did, "Matthew said. "When I was in Iraq, a child went missing in a small village. She was later found in a storage bin so we knew she'd been murdered. It was tough. It's different from when a child dies from disease or an accident. There is finality with that child. With a kidnapped or murdered child, there doesn't seem to be an end. The parents and friends live forever with a cloud hanging over them that tells them they will never know what really happened. They mourn the child as well as their own lives. The beauty of life leaves them like a wisp of smoke."

"Did they ever find out how she died?" Maggie asked.

"No, not really, or at least nothing that was provable. But you don't have to speak the language to know that the family's grief never goes away."

An hour later two vehicles arrived, one the medical examiner in an ambulance and in the other, a three-man forensic investigation team. Their first question, "Has anyone touched the bones?"

"No," the three responded in unison.

The medical examiner continued, "I'm going to make a suggestion. Please don't tell anyone about the bones. People who might be watching us lift the skeleton may make assumptions but won't think beyond that unless a story gets started. If it isn't one of the Native American girls, I don't want the mother to rekindle memories and then find out it's someone else's child lying under the bridge."

They all nodded their heads in agreement. "The only problem is that I talked to people at the café when I called it in. There weren't many people there, but they heard me call," Matthew said. "Will that be a problem?"

"I hope not. Okay let's do our job."

The trio waited while one assistant drew a picture of the bones, how they lay among the rocks, the direction of the head, and a general description of the rocks under the bridge. Pictures were taken. Two others waited and when signaled to go ahead, they carefully collected the bones, putting each piece in a bag and marking it with a number and the type of bone. The skull was the last to be bagged. It was carefully wrapped in paper and, almost lovingly, put inside a large, fabric bag. Nobody spoke until they finished.

"Thanks for calling this in," the ME said. "I can't speculate, but I suspect this is a pretty important find." The ME then shook each hand. "I understand you two are priests. Thanks, Fathers." He smiled at Maggie. "We'll treat these bones with care. When we're done, I'll let both police units know the results so they can let you know."

After the men left, Maggie said, "It's going to be tough waiting for answers."

"Yup, but wait we must," Matthew said.

"What's this yup about? You sound like a cowboy. You must be getting acclimated."

"Yup." Matthew sent her a teasing smile.

The three climbed out of the rocks up to the highway.

CHAPTER TWO

Thoughts about the medical examiner's report slipped to the back of their minds as they ran back and forth between St. Michael's in The Dalles and the Chinook and Paiute Confederated Tribes Center in Warm Springs. The center advised them with respect to where and how they might find an altar for the church. The three went to every used furniture and antique store in both towns, telling the owners that they were interested in an altar, pews, or comfortable folding chairs. They would also take small wooden tables that could be used for serving meals.

Once the news got out that there were two priests building a church inside the old garage at Bigg's Junction, people came to gawk and ask why they were working so hard on this particular building. A few said they would come to church once it was ready. A very few came to help.

When Officer Rex arrived three weeks later with news, Matthew and Francesco gladly set aside the tedious work of scrubbing down the exterior walls and motioned the officer to sit down and drink an iced tea. Glad for a reprieve from the back-breaking work, they pulled up camp chairs. "You two shouldn't be working this hard in the sun. Where are your parishioners ready to help?"

"Not open for business, yet," replied Matthew. "What were the results?"

"The bones do belong to one of the Celilo twins. Which one we don't know yet, but this finding allows us to reopen the case and see if we can figure out which twin is dead and search for clues as to what happened to the other one. Of course, the other twin might also be dead somewhere else, or may have been lost in the river, or may be alive and living in an unknown part of the country. In any case, it will take a long time to sort out what really happened."

"Does that mean you'll interview all the people you talked to five years ago?" Francesco wanted to know.

Rex rubbed his chin. "The problem is that some of the primaries may have moved out and we don't have the manpower to launch an investigation that might bring real answers. We'll appoint one detective to the case, but keep in mind that the detective will have other cases to work on. So keep your ears to the ground. You may be able to help figure this out." Rex looked at his watch and noted the time.

"Watch and listen. Sometimes people say or do things that they think are unimportant. They may be hiding something or don't know the impact of what they know. Also, try to take notes about everything that's said. Notes are essential to understanding what's happened. After a while your memory recalls that others have repeated the same idea. Eventually your logic kicks in. That's when you organize what you've learned into times and places things happened. Eventually you'll begin to think of different ways something might have happened. That's the five-minute lesson in police detecting. You all passed the course."

"Rex," Maggie said, laughing, "the three of us solved one of my family mysteries. We're pretty good at sleuthing. Could we be allowed to help?"

"A bit unorthodox, but it seems that having two priests and a young woman trying to follow the clues would be a good idea. To keep it legal, you'll have to write down everything that's said and share it with me. We'll talk as often as you need to."

"We're more than okay with that," Maggie said. "This place isn't ready yet for an altar plus tables and chairs. It will be a good way to learn to know the community and build a parish. Remember that movie, *Field of Dreams*?

Its most famous line was 'If we build it, they will come.' That's us. We'll talk to the community and they'll come."

"Exactly right, Maggie. I never saw the movie, but I agree with the notion." Francesco chuckled, shaking his head. "I need to get out more. I have no idea what's she's talking about."

"Here's my office phone, my car phone, and my home phone. Call me any time. I'm relying on you. I'm going to try to get Tom Marshall to take the case. He's a good man and he'll work with you."

"Before you leave," Matthew said, "what's the parents' last name? That's the place to start."

"I don't remember their last name. I'll have to look in the file. But the mother's name is Ananya. She's a tiny woman. Ask at the restaurant. I'll bet they know her last name. Ananya was the center of the search for her daughters. She had us going to everyone in the Bigg's Junction area. We gave up long before she did. I'll bet she's still looking."

CHAPTER THREE

The front yard looked like a dried mud flat. Maggie could imagine that when the rains came, they put down planks to walk across the yard. A tiny, falling-apart picket fence gave no feeling of beauty or security. An old arbor opened the path to the house, but it was bare of roses to add color and fragrance. The house was unpainted, weathered from years of cyclone winds blowing down the gorge. The windows were dark with dirt, as if they'd never been washed since the time of the flood.

The three climbed the steps and Maggie knocked on the door. Matthew tugged at his collar as if he wasn't sure he should be wearing it, but he found people weren't so intimidated when they saw it.

Silence hung in the air. No one responded. They started back down the stairs when a tiny woman peeked out the door. She looked to be in her fifties, straight black hair, no gray, and a woven bracelet on one wrist. "May I help you?"

"Yes. My name is Father Brannigan and these are my friends, Maggie Callahan and Father Francesco. If we may, we'd like to talk to you about your daughters. May we come in?"

Despite her size, Ananya did not appear frail. She, in fact, looked like she had the world under control. She opened the door without a word.

A single light bulb hung from a lone cord in the middle of the room. "How may I help you?" She pointed to the couch, indicating they should sit down. They sat on the old couch, broken on one end so Matthew sat askew. Ananya sat in the jacquard-covered chair, the flowers in the fabric faded from years of wear. On a side-table were pictures of two girls as they entered their teen years. Maggie guessed they were eleven or twelve, maybe thirteen. They both had the long, black hair and the high cheek bones of their Sioux Indian heritage. Both girls wore big smiles.

The lady caught her looking. "Those are my girls, twins."

"They are beautiful. What are their names?" Maggie asked.

"They are Lakota, daughter of the moon, and Dakota, friendly person." There was no emotion as she said their names. The woman simply stared at them waiting for Maggie to talk.

Matthew said, "I'd like to know what you know about what happened to your daughters."

The silence they'd felt outside hung in the room. They waited until Ananya finally sat up straight, looked at them, and said, "I don't know for sure what happened, and the cops have never been clear about it. I'm not bad-mouthing the police. I just don't think they know exactly what happened or who to blame. Wait, are you the priest who found the skeleton?" Ananya asked, looking at Father Francesco.

Not expecting her to know about the find, Francesco's voice warmed with sympathy. "I am."

The atmosphere changed immediately. "My name is Ananya. Their father's name is Jalen." She pulled her hair back, reached into her pocket and pulled a rubber band out and tied her hair in a ponytail.

"I've been in this house since I was a child. My twins were born here. This house and its memories are all I have left."

"May I ask where Jalen is? Is he at work?" Maggie's voice was soft.

"Jalen joined his ancestors about a year ago. He couldn't bear the thought that he couldn't find his daughters, and the police seemed indifferent to searching for them. I refused to give up. I'm glad you may have found one of them, but we still don't know what happened to them. Why did they die? How did they die?" She paused and then resumed talking, her voice on the verge of tears, but controlled. "It's always been my challenge to find out what happened. Unfortunately, nobody knows or if someone does know, they aren't talking. We Indians are a tight group. I believe that if someone knew, they would have told me. Since no one ever came forward, I searched on my own. I don't think locals were involved. They've been so kind and many of them helped out in the search. Anymore, I don't know what to think." She put her head down, tugged on the rubber band until her long black hair fell over her eyes.

"We'd like to help," Matthew said. "We can ask questions that perhaps the police are not able to ask. In fact, they have given us permission to ask questions. We'll approach everyone as priests asking questions. Father Francesco will keep the notes and Maggie will help any way she can."

"My help, if it's okay with you, will be to keep in constant communication with you," Maggie said.

Ananya's face clouded for a moment as she struggled with a decision and then her face cleared. She stood and smiled through quiet tears. "Please, please help me. I suddenly feel full of energy and hope." She grabbed Maggie's hand and led her to the kitchen. The kitchen was all hewn wood, orderly and spotlessly clean. Bottled spices, dried and canned foods lined shelves built strictly for that purpose, strong planks, attached to the wall by black iron braces. Ananya put water on the stove, pulled out dried herbs, black tea, and filled four tea strainers. "I don't use sugar," she said. "I hope it's not too strong." When the water boiled, she put a tea strainer in each mug and handed two to Maggie to carry back to the living room.

The four chatted. Father Francesco asked, "What happened to their father?"

"He was so broken by the loss of his girls. He blamed everyone, her school mates, his buddies, even the police. When neither girl was found, he became more and more depressed. I couldn't help him because I was depressed myself. I couldn't function much beyond cooking enough food to keep us alive." Ananya didn't speak for a few moments, as if she didn't want to be reminded of what happened to Jalen.

"Then one day, when he was at Dinty's café with a friend who was trying to help him, he got into a fight with a white man who was just passing through. He accused the man of murdering his daughters. According to the police report Jalen took out a knife and went after the man. The man defended himself by trying to dodge Jalen. Jalen went berserk and began flailing, swinging his knife around the man with no apparent effort to actually hit him. Eyewitnesses said Eugene, that was his friend, yelled at him many times but Jalen was like a mad man. Eventually the stranger landed a haymaker punch and Jalen fell down unconscious. By the time the police got there from The Dalles, Jalen was dead. They said it was an aneurysm. I believe he wanted to be killed. It wasn't like him to pick a fight, but he had lost all hope. It's been really difficult, losing all three of them." She put her face between her hands again. The silence of the dead again crept in to hold them captive. When Ananya lifted her head, her face was stained with tears. Getting control of herself, Ananya looked at the three and pleaded, "Please help me. Tell me what to do."

Maggie moved to Ananya and knelt beside her chair. "The police have offered Father Matthew and Father Francesco a roster of the names of people who might know what happened. You can help by identifying these people, where they live, what they do. They'll revisit each person and ask again what they remember. If one of the girls is out there, we'll find her."

Ananya smiled. "I have a list of about seventy-five people the police talked to. Excuse me, it's in my desk drawer in my room."

When she returned, she had a folder with five pieces of paper. She handed them to Maggie. Beside each of the names was an anecdote about the person and what that person may have contributed to the search.

"This is very impressive, Ananya. We'll call on each person. You can help us know how to speak to them."

"Thank you. I will help any way I can. I need to know what happened," Ananya said.

Maggie hugged Ananya. "We'll make copies so you don't lose these. We'll check it against the lists the sheriff and the state trooper have."

"Are the police really going to allow you to talk to people?" Ananya asked.

"They said unofficially we could, but we have to share everything we learn and they will check it against old records. Since this list of people came from you and not the authorities, we're okay. We'll approach it as two new priests learning about the community. We'll slip it into conversations," Matthew said. "I assure you we won't overstep our authority."

Ananya smiled. "Please, please find my daughter if she's still alive."

CHAPTER FOUR

"If we're going in two entirely different directions, do we need more than just the truck?" Maggie asked. "One for you two, the truck, and me a small car or you the small car and me the truck so I can pick up altars and pews. What do you think?"

"I agree on the need for another car." Matthew stood up and moved to his desk. "I don't want us forced to make car payments, but I also want each of us to be safe. We don't have to look for a junker." Father Francesco gave him a questioning look, half-bowed and trudged away.

"Where is the money coming from?" Maggie asked. "We barely have a nickel between us."

"Remember what I said when we married? I have a fund for emergencies. All I had to spend money on in Iraq was an occasional dinner out. I was able to save a substantial amount of money. This is an emergency. You need to have a reliable car."

Maggie kissed him on the cheek. He returned it with a passionate kiss. "I do hope our rooms are finished soon," he whispered into her neck.

"Maybe we should find a motel for the night. Father would understand."

"Yes, he would. He keeps asking me when we're going to take the night off." Matthew smiled.

"Then let's do it tonight. And, if you don't mind, not at the local motel."

"I don't mind at all." He smiled and kissed her again. "Perhaps we can find a car."

"Deal. The Dalles, it is. I'll pack us a bag." Maggie jumped up and began packing.

The next day Maggie drove home in her nearly new compact car, perfect for driving about the countryside. Not a junker.

CHAPTER FIVE

The three sat outside with Ananya and a young Native American girl she brought to introduce to them. "This is Sasha. She was best friends with my twins. She can talk to all the young Natives because she gets along with everyone."

"Glad to meet you, Sasha," Matthew said, turning to the group. "This heat is stifling. We need a big fan or a storm right about now. But that isn't what I want to talk about. We've gone through half your list, Ananya, and haven't learned a thing we didn't already know. Actually, I should say we've gone through all the people who live close to Bigg's Junction. What about other people? Are there any ranches? Do you think we'd have any luck with ranchers?"

"Yes," said Sasha. "I'm going to bring my boyfriend, Tiny. He knows everyone for miles."

Ananya smiled. "His last name is Hawks Tooth. I also know a few of the people who live towards the high desert. I know one old timer who will say he doesn't know anything, but just might if approached by you. I'll call him and tell him you're going to come out and visit him. There's also an Indian family out I-97 who grow apples and raise sheep, pigs, and horses. His name is Hiram Black Hawk, but everyone calls him Black Hawk. I think it would be good to talk to them just to see if their stories change or if they might know something. He sometimes does odd jobs for the Garritys."

Matthew said, "Can you give us addresses and tell us what direction to go?"

"Of course. I'd start with the Black Hawk family. The old guy is more likely to talk to you for two hours. He's always happy to have company and talk about most anything."

"What's his name?"

"Jasper. Jasper Hayes. You start up the hill on 97 going south out of town. You go about ten miles until you see a road to the right called Mesquite Creek Road. Take that road about three miles until you see the creek on your right. Follow it until you see a small house on the creek. It's not a shack. Just small. If I call, he'll be waiting. When should I tell him, you'll be out?"

"We'll start out with the Black Hawk family and go from there." Matthew said.

"Good. If you see Jasper first, you'll never get away until he's worn out. Black Hawk and Gagana have four children, so it's best to call ahead. I won't tell you the kids' names because you'll never remember them. They might be interested in your church."

"Will you call soon?"

"Right now." Ananya went into the house. Maggie could hear her talking but couldn't tell what she was saying. Five minutes later she came back out. "Jasper will see you whenever you get there tomorrow afternoon. If he isn't in the house, he'll be in the barn. Black Hawk and Gagana want you to come before the kids get home from school, so you won't meet the kids. They don't want them to hear any conversation about the dead girls, so you need to be there by one." Ananya smiled again. "Thank you again for talking to people. I just know eventually you'll talk to the right person who'll know something that we missed five years ago."

CHAPTER SIX

The next afternoon the three headed out into the desert, enjoying their first long drive together in the new car. "Do you notice mile after mile of barbed wire fencing?" Francesco asked.

"To keep the cattle from congregating on the highways. Much of it is free range land, but there are also huge cattle ranches," Maggie said. "You seldom see the ranch houses because they are often nestled near water and trees.

"What is that water ahead?" Francesco asked. "Maybe a lake way off in the distance?"

"It's an optical illusion, a mirage. Many a person has driven off the highway believing there was a lake in the distance. Even I've seen a mirage that I was sure was a lake. I took a picture so people would believe me."

"I believe you," Matthew said. "I bet sunsets here are gorgeous when there are clouds in the sky"

"They are. I think our turn's coming up. Left to the Whitefish place."

"Is this reservation land, Maggie?" Francesco asked

"Not sure. Could be Warm Springs Tribal land. We'll have to learn the boundaries."

They made the left turn onto an almost nonexistent road, just a rough strip of soil, bare of sagebrush and grass. "We should have brought the truck. This road is beating up the new car," Francesco noted. "I'd love to come up here at night, maybe in August during the Perseid Meteor shower. I'll bet the night skies are spectacular. What type of animals live here?"

"Wild horses, deer, antelope, porcupines, coyotes, fox, owls, hawks, eagles and all manner of rodents. And, yes, they survive well in the desert. Actually, where we are isn't considered high desert. That's further south. Look off to the right. A house. This must be the Whitefish home."

Gagana met them at the door. She smiled and held out her hand. "Welcome, I'm Gagana. Please come in. You remember Sasha?"

Sasha shook hands with everyone, then sat on the floor next to Gagana's chair. "I'm not sure how I can help, but I'll do whatever you ask."

Gagana said, "I understand you want to talk about the twins. I'll tell you what I know, which isn't much. One of you men should go out and talk to my husband, Black Hawk."

Francesco said he would go out. "I want to see the marvels of the desert on the ground."

"Turn right and you will see some stock loading pens. He's repairing the corral fence."

"When the twins disappeared the tribe literally combed every inch of the desert and the river. We didn't find even a trace of them. No hair, no clothing, nothing. It was like they vanished off the face of the earth," Gagana said.

"Do you think the sheriff and the state police did their jobs?" Maggie asked.

"Oh, yes. They spent weeks talking to everyone who lived in the area. Nothing. I know you drove out to learn something and absolutely nothing is what I know, and I'm sorry for that. May I get you an iced tea?" Gagana got up from her chair.

"That would be great. Thanks," Matthew said.

Gagana headed into the kitchen. A few minutes later she returned with the tea. They sat for twenty minutes, making small talk before Gagana said, "Would you like to see our pens? We graze sheep, a few head of cattle, and some pigs. Black Hawk also breaks colts for people."

Maggie's eyes opened wide. She blinked. "Sheep? I'll bet you're not popular with the ranchers."

Gagana laughed. "We don't have enough to cause much of a stir. We have about fifty head of sheep and about the same number of cattle. We have enough land that our neighbors don't complain. The biggest ranch near us mostly deals in horses and steers for rodeos. They're across the highway from us. Sasha, you take them out to the pens. I'm making dinner for the kids." They thanked Gagana and walked towards the barn where Black Hawk was working.

Black Hawk, a wiry man, didn't talk much. Francesco stood at the corral watching him work. There was no conversation. Black Hawk kept compacting soil around a new fence post with a heavy tamping bar, occasionally kicking more soil into the hole, without more than a head shake for a greeting to the newcomers. He said a few words to Francesco as they left but continued to pound.

On the way past the house, the three thanked Gagana and Sasha for their help and insights and hoped the family might come into town to see the new church.

"I would like that," Gagana said. "Please let us know when you're officially open for business."

"You're welcome any time," Matthew said.

The three walked back to the car, got in, and started back down the road. As soon as they were out of range of the house, Francesco said, "Black Hawk didn't talk much. The only thing he said that got my attention, was that we must find a way to go to the horse ranch across the road. He said they get horses and bulls ready for rodeos. He also said that very few men, if any, work there, which is odd. He takes care of the gardens and picks up trash. He also said, rodeo life is mainly a man's hobby. It's back breaking work getting animals ready to be ridden in competition. His question is who's taking care of the livestock? He's never seen any sign of animals."

"Does seem odd. Did you get a name?" Matthew asked.

"Leo Garrity at the Rodeo Stock Ranch. Black Hawk says he's a small man, has two sons who ride in competitions and who must also do work preparing the stock for rodeos. He also said that they are not friendly in the community. People rarely see them. It seems the older son comes into town once in a while to get drunk and disorderly. Black Hawk thinks something is going on at the ranch that the community doesn't know about. As a Native American, Black Hawk says he is not welcome to go there unless he's hired to work. He thinks that as priests, we might be able to go there and find out something. He suggests that Maggie not go with us."

"Strange. I'll call and see if we can make an official visit tomorrow," Matthew said. "Let's also call the sheriff and see what he knows about them."

"It sounds like that ranch is right near Jasper's place, Matthew. I have a hunch you might want to talk to him after you see the Garritys. You know, being neighbors and all, he might have interesting information that no one has thought to ask about," Francesco suggested.

"Good thinking, Francesco. Maggie, would you call—"

"I'm on it, Boss." Maggie said. "I'll call Ananya and ask her to let Jasper know plans have changed—the instant you get me to a telephone."

"Why don't you just use my . . ." Matthew ducked his head sheepishly.

"Right!" Maggie chuckled. "What good is a car phone if you forget to put it in the car?"

"Should've brought the truck," Matthew mumbled while Francesco turned his head to hide his grin.

Maggie turned her attention to the scenery on the road back. She pointed out large depressions in the desert that in the spring filled up with water. "They're man-made stock tanks. Notice there is still muddy water in some places and it's still green around the edges. Next spring we'll drive out and see them full of water with vegetation and flowers all around them. If there's been a lot of rain over the winter, the desert in spring is a gorgeous place to be."

CHAPTER SEVEN

The next afternoon, Matthew had permission to drive out and talk to Leo Garrity. He and Francesco drove out to the ranch. As they approached the house, they noticed five huge low-roofed barns, the sort you saw in racing country rather than large hay barns that housed feed and hay for horses and cattle. "Where are they storing feed?" Matthew wondered. "Let's split up. Father, you wander down to the barns and see what you can learn. I'll go in and talk to Garrity. If, for some reason, you are told to leave, apologize and get back to the truck. Hopefully, you will see something interesting."

"Aye, Aye, Captain." Francesco wore his usual smile. He headed for the barns, putting a limp in his walk.

Matthew headed for the house and said hello to a little boy who was playing with tiny cars on the porch steps. A small man met him on the porch. He extended his hand and introduced himself. "I'm Leo, what can I do for you?"

"I've been asked by Ananya to see if I can learn any new information about the disappearance of two Native American girls about five years ago." Matthew shook hands with Leo Garrity. "Beautiful place you have out here. Where does your water come from? I lived in the desert in the middle east for several years, so I'm familiar with water issues."

"We got lucky." Garrity smiled a half-smile. "We have an 800-foot well about a quarter of a mile from here. Cost a fortune to drill, but we get almost fifty gallons a minute, which is enough to keep this spread going."

"You are lucky," Matthew said, as he stared out towards the barns. "Rodeo stock must be a lucrative business."

"We get by. Now about the two girls. I don't know anything about them. Don't know anybody who does. They just up and disappeared."

"Are you aware that the bones of one of the girls were just found in the river when the dam lowered the water for a couple of days?"

Leo Garrity looked surprised and then recovered quickly, as if he didn't want the priest to notice. "I guess I didn't pay much attention to that. Sorry I can't help, but I've got work to get done today."

Matthew followed Garrity's look and saw Francesco limping from the barn.

"You okay, Francesco?" Matthew called. "You're limping again."

"I tried to twist my ankle again. I'd like to go home and put some ice on it. Sorry to cut it short."

"It's all right," Leo said. "I wasn't very helpful." He turned and walked back into the house. "Come on Toby, back in the house."

As Matthew turned the truck around, he could see Leo standing at the window watching them leave. "All right old man, what did you see?"

"Young girls. About six of them. I only stepped in the barn long enough to get a look down the aisle. The stalls have cots or beds in them. A young man stepped out of a room that either held horse feed or was an office. He asked me what the hell I was doing in there and told me to get out. That's when I put my limp in full gear."

"Who were these girls?" Matthew asked.

"I don't know. I never had a chance to talk to any of them."

"What did they look like?"

"All very young. Two were white, two were Mexican, a fourth, black and maybe one Native American. It all happened so fast I'm not really sure. They scurried back in their stall when the man came out and yelled at them to go back where they belonged."

"You said a Native girl?" Matthew asked.

"I think so."

"How old was the man?" Matthew asked.

"Twenty-five to thirty. He was tall. You could tell he did a lot of heavy lifting. Maybe weights, maybe bales of hay."

"Sounds like one of Garrity's sons," Matthew said.

"Maybe, but since I didn't see Garrity up close, I don't know. All I know for sure is that the man did not want me there." Francesco stared straight ahead, then turned back to Matthew. "Oh, and by the way. The little guy on the porch is the same little boy I saw throwing rocks at Dinty's."

"Oh? Let's file that away for future reference. They did not want us there, that's for sure. Two questions arise. One is, who are the girls? The second is, who is the little boy?"

"The third," Francesco stated, "is why does he look like a Native in the midst of all those white men?"

Once Matthew reached Highway 97, he turned right and sped back to the left turn to Jasper Hays's place.

They knew they were at the old man's place when they drove in. It was indeed small, but the outside was decorated with all manner of carved figures and bird houses, each painted the color that had inspired its creator on the day of its creation. One was a magnificent, ten-foot tall totem pole, its top sculpted into a flying eagle.

"I'm impressed," said Father Francesco.

"Me too. Perhaps we can get him to sculpt something for the church."

At that moment a bushy-bearded old man shuffled from the tiny house. He leaned on a cane and motioned for them to get out of the truck and walk towards three folding chairs set up near the house, then pointed with his cane for them to sit down. He did the same. "Well, what can I do for you two misfits?"

"Hi, I'm Matthew and this is Francesco."

"I don't get it. You're dressed like priests and you don't call yourselves 'Father'?"

"If you prefer, we can certainly do that. I'm Father Matthew and this is—"

"Aah, just joshin'. What can I do for the two of you? Ananya said you're helping hunt for her girls. I didn't know anything last time they looked. I doubt I know anything more now."

"Perhaps you do. What do you know about the Garritys?"

"Not much. They raise horses and bulls for rodeos, if raising them means they feed them and put bells on them to tickle their tums. I don't approve of how they treat their stock, but I can't do anything about it. They don't encroach on my land, so what can I say?"

"Do you know what they keep in those low buildings?" Father Francesco asked.

"I assume horses and stock. They've got a huge spread. Butts up against mine. I've got six hundred acres. They must have six thousand. I can't remember ever seeing anyone working their spread, though. Garrity's two sons check the fence line now and then, but that's about all."

Francesco continued. He wanted to ask about the girls but didn't know how to ask. Finally, he carefully said, "Have you ever seen any girls or women on the ranch? Are any of the Garritys married with children?"

"Have not, but there may be and I just don't know it. I don't get out much anymore. The older son used to raise hell in town, but I don't hear about them much anymore."

"I have a question," Matthew said. "What are the chances you've ever seen the rig they use that takes the stock in and out?"

"Sure. It's a big semi, actually two big semis. One for horses and one for the big bulls and maybe steers. Now that I think about it, they got three of those big rigs, but I've only ever seen two leave at a time. What you thinkin'?"

Matthew paced in front of the men. "I don't know what I'm thinking. There's nothing the matter with hauling animals in a big stock truck. No law against it. Do you know anyone who's worked out there?"

"Nah. Pa Garrity doesn't want anyone intruding on his privacy. He's a really difficult guy to talk to." He twisted his cane in the dirt. "I do know somebody who's worked out there. Black Hawk. He hauls trash sometimes. Does a little garden work. I'm sorry I'm not much help. You want to stay for dinner? I just caught a bunch of trout."

"Not now, but may we take a rain check? Maybe I could spend an afternoon with you fishing and trading stories." Francesco stood. "I fished as a child, but haven't picked up a pole since I joined the priesthood. I'd love it."

"You bet, Father. Any old time, you come on out. I'll be here."

CHAPTER EIGHT

Sheriff Rex Tyson was at the church talking to Maggie when they got back from Jasper's. Matthew walked around the truck to help Francesco climb down. His limp suddenly seemed real.

"How are you, Father?" Maggie asked, noting his limp.

"I'm fine. I just didn't want Leo Garrity to think I was snooping around, which, of course, was exactly what I was doing. I put a serious limp in my gait and now I'm stiff."

"Did you see any men? One man?" Rex asked.

"Matthew talked to Leo Garrity. He didn't say anything worth remembering, nor was he very friendly. We also talked to Jasper Hayes. What a character. About all we learned, though, is that there are three really huge stock rigs coming and going from the ranch.

"You didn't see any men other than Garrity?"

"Nope. Oh wait, I saw a man who came out of a tack room and yelled at some girls I saw and told me to leave. The girls stared at me and I stared at them. I'm really glad I had my collar on. I hope the girls understood that I was not a threat."

"Could you identify the girls? Native, Mexican, white?"

"All of the above, but no I couldn't identify them. It happened too fast. I just know these girls were very young, and of mixed races. I could hear sounds that leads me to believe there were many more girls in that barn than the six I saw. There was a din of young giggling. Girls. They may be working to keep the barns clean, although I couldn't tell where the animals were kept. Did you ever have a reason to go out there and talk to Leo?"

"No," Rex said. "They've never been a problem. Even the two boys never really caused criminal difficulties. They're obnoxious. The older boy, especially, likes to hell around sometimes. I've been called in on a few disturbances he's been involved in—petty stuff. Nobody likes them, but they don't vandalize. Never even had a speeding ticket. I won't call them good guys, but Garritys haven't been in trouble with the law, either."

Matthew walked over and sat by Maggie. "I got the feeling we weren't welcome out there. It's going to be difficult to figure out what's going on, unless we can see something. Maggie, could you ask Ananya what she knows? Since the original source was Black Hawk Whitefish, she may know something. The Native community seems pretty tight."

"I'll call and make an appointment to see her in the morning. Nice work, Francesco. I see you haven't lost your sleuthing skills." Maggie patted his shoulder as she went into the back room where the phone was kept. When she came back, she said, "By the way, I forgot to mention we have another Native source. Sasha, the Native American girl we met, told me her boyfriend thinks he might have seen one of the twins at a wild mustang sale."

"Is that Tiny?" Rex asked.

"Yes. How did you know?" Maggie asked

"Just a guess. Everybody knows Tiny. He works all the rodeos. He's too big to sit a horse, but he knows how to handle them. Tiny's always manning the gates at the bronc riding and the bull riding events. He's darn' near as big as the horses. Tiny's a really nice guy, but you wouldn't want to tangle with him in a dark alley."

"Sasha's going to bring him down on Saturday."

"Sasha's a good kid, too. And really reliable. Let Ben and me know if you find anything interesting. I know there was never a focus on Leo Garrity five years ago. Now that I think of it, he wouldn't cooperate with

Tom Marshall, the local detective, so they left him alone. I'll go back through my notes and see if anyone actually talked to him." Rex headed for his car and then turned back. "Oh, what I came to tell you—we have a positive identification on the remains. You found Lakota, Father Francesco. The twin we're looking for now is Dakota."

It was hot and humid the next morning, the sky full of short anvil clouds that predicted late afternoon thunderstorms with lightning and rain. The desert could always use a drink of water, but these clouds could travel hundreds of miles without actually developing into a storm.

On her way out the door to meet with Ananya, Maggie heard the phone ring. She raced back to answer. "Hello."

"I have a place for you to look at that I think you're going to love. It overlooks the river on ten acres of fenced pastureland. This is not the typical desert spot. It's an oasis." Real estate agent April Brown's voice rose with excitement. "Can you look at it sometime soon? The reason I'm pushing is that the owner wants a responsible renter who may be interested in buying if he decides to sell."

"Slow down, April. Where is it? How much?" Maggie's heart pumped faster. Oh, how she longed for a place to live that accommodated the three of them with some privacy. Could this be it?

"It's a palace, Maggie, with a 180-degree view of the river. You can sit on the veranda and sip mint julips. There's a barn and ten acres for your horse and an outbuilding apartment for Father Francesco. You take the next road after 97. It's where Eagle Creek dumps into the Columbia. It's maybe two miles east."

"This sounds too good to be true. Why is it available?"

"I told him about you three and he wants to meet you before he leaves town, which is in two days. He's going to the Middle East, I think to Iraq, to help set up an American university."

"Iraq? Matthew worked in Iraq for many years."

"Great, then they have something in common."

"How much?"

"He wants to meet and talk with you, and if he agrees to you as tenants, the rent will be very low. In return, you take care of the place and treat it as if it's your own, but you'll have to work that out with him. Could you come out today?"

"I'll talk to Matthew and the three of us will meet you as soon as we can get there." She called Ananya and told her she'd be a little late, and then she went to find Matthew and Franceso.

The three jammed into the truck and drove the two miles to a long driveway that wound up the hill. They crossed the creek on a well-constructed wooden bridge. April's car sat in the driveway.

The house was indeed a mansion, windows covering the entire front of the building. The view looked out over the bridge to the Washington side of the river. A man stepped out of the front door and walked across the veranda. He was ramrod straight as if he'd been in the army for most of his life. "Welcome. I'm Terry Bradcliff." They all shook hands.

April grabbed Maggie's hand. "You have to see this place and meet Martha. Let the men work out the fine points." The two women headed into the house.

Terry invited the men to sit. "I'll get straight to the point," he said. "April says you're building a church at the Junction and that the two of you would be perfect. I'm not sure how the lady fits in."

"She's my wife," Matthew said.

"Wife? Well I'll be damned. You trying to take on the church?"

"Already have," smiled Matthew.

"What I want is someone who understands people. Will know who to invite up here and who to leave alone. Someone who won't be bullied. I've had some problems with one family. My wife and I used to raise quarter horses. Her best mare was stolen by them. I've never been able to prove it, but I think Leo Garrity took her and sold her to a high-powered breeder. I just can't leave the place unattended for a couple of years while we go off and help to build a university in Iraq."

"What was it you think happened?" Father Francesco asked as Maggie returned to the veranda and seated herself on the wicker couch next to

Matthew.

"My wife used to ride Patches in parades and for the openings of rodeos. She also showed her in western classes. Patches was well known and sought after for breeding purposes. Martha, my wife, only bred her once and that was to a fine stud Leo Garrity owned. When Martha went to pick up the mare, Leo said she got loose and ran off. I never believed that fish tale for a minute. He sold her, but I can't prove it. I told him to never set foot on my property again. I want someone who knows their way around horses."

"Francesco and I don't really, but Maggie does." He put his arm around Maggie's shoulder. "She saved a boy and a horse from a forest fire last year. We have her horse boarded over at Grand Coulee until we can find a place to put her. This would be ideal. What are you asking for rent?"

"Not a damn cent. I want you to take care of the place. I'll probably sell it to you after a couple of years, if you're interested. I'll see how Martha and I get along in Iraq. You might keep an eye out for Patches. She's a paint, one big white spot on her left rear that extends down her leg. Another spot that covers the right side of her chest. White blaze and white stockings. She's big. Stands 16 ½ hands. She's a love. Martha's been heart-sick over that horse. We're leaving in two days, so I hope you can move in right away. There's a really nice cottage if you want your own privacy," he said, looking at Francesco.

"I will be happy to live there," Francesco said as he looked in the direction Terry pointed and saw a small building. Maggie cheered inwardly; a perfect arrangement for the three of them.

"By the way, if Garrity bred her, the foal would be about a year and a half old. You would make Martha so happy if you could figure out what happened to her horse."

Maggie said, "I'll keep an eye out. Is Patches friendly?"

At that moment April reappeared, followed by a tall woman bringing fresh coffee to them. "Hi," she said. "I'm Martha, and, yes, she's friendly. And I really wanted that foal."

"Honey, I told them about your mare. Maggie knows horses, and they promise to keep an eye out for her." Turning to Maggie, he said, "Hope you run across Martha's horse. If you do, call and we'll talk about what to do. And, be sure you know exactly where you found her."

Martha smiled, obviously approving of these prospective tenants. "You can move in the minute we leave, which will be at seven a.m. two days from now. Treat this place as your own. We'll talk maybe once a month to see how things are going. And thank you. We know our place will be in good hands."

Radiating a huge smile, Maggie said, "We'll go pack our meager belongings and move in on Saturday."

Ananya greeted them with a pitcher of lemonade. "It's lunchtime," she said. "I have some fresh Indian bread and I can make a salad for all of us."

Maggie was touched by Ananya's generosity but declined. "We need to get ready to move into our new house," she announced, barely able to keep from giggling in anticipation.

Beyond knowing about the one son's rowdy and often cruel behavior in the local watering hole, Ananya had little information to add about the Garritys. "They stay to themselves, and they don't much want to mix in, especially with us Natives. Black Hawk would know the most, I think. He works for 'em."

The three took their leave with promises to keep Ananya informed.

"Maybe Sasha and her boyfriend, Tiny, will be able to tell us more," Matthew said.

"Tiny thought he saw one of the girls once," Ananya said, her face turning wistful. "I wasn't supposed to know. Maybe he can tell you more about that."

CHAPTER NINE

On Saturday morning Maggie and Matthew sat talking about their new home while they waited for Sasha and Tiny. They were late and Maggie couldn't help wondering if this was a problem with Tiny.

A battered blue pickup missing most of its grill pulled up to the church, and Sasha and seven-foot Tiny emerged.

"Hi. I'm Tiny." He walked over, hand outstretched. "Sorry we're late. I had to change a tire. The right rear was flat and I had to call my cousin to bring me a tire the right size. Sasha says you want to talk to me."

"We do," said Matthew. "We're helping in the search for Ananya's girl. Tell us about the time you thought you saw Dakota."

"I always go to the mustang roundups and sales," Tiny explained. "It's my job to handle the wild ones, especially the babies who go berserk when they're separated from their mamas. This sale was about a year ago, down in Malheur. The buyers range from families looking to adopt a pet, to rodeo dealers looking for wild horses for their string. Horses that don't sell are usually turned over for slaughter. I hate that they do that, but they do it to try and control the wild horse population so there's more open range for cattle and sheep. Not fair."

"I agree. Who hires you?" Matthew asked.

"The rodeo association. I've been doing this since I was a sophomore in high school. There's always a lot of people milling around. I was back behind the pens working with a yearling that was intent on breaking down the fence. He was cryin' for his mama even though he'd been weaned months ago." Tiny shifted his tall body back and forth, hands on hips. "The wild ones stay together because they associate with their own band. When I was putting him back in his pen, a young woman walked by. I looked at her and I thought she looked like one of the twins, you know, grown up. She looked back at me. But instead of coming over to say hi, she turned and ran around the pens. I yelled after her, but she didn't turn around. After I got the yearling put away, I walked all over looking for her, but I never found her again. And you know, it'd been five years since I'd seen the twins, so I could've been wrong. I didn't see her for three sales. The next time I saw her was at the Pendleton sale. She was standing alone by a huge stock truck. I don't think she saw me, although I'm pretty hard to miss." Tiny ducked his head and blushed.

"You didn't go over to her?" asked Father Francesco.

"No. I had to pick up all the ropes scattered around the pens. And, again, five years is a long time. When I looked for her, she and the truck were gone. It was at the end of the sale."

"So, you didn't see who she was with?"

"No."

"Do you know who the truck belonged to?" Matthew asked. "Could she have gotten into that truck?"

"Yeah."

"Did you recognize the truck?"

"Not really. There are three rodeo guys driving that type and color of truck."

Sasha broke in. "I've seen at least five trucks that look the same. The trucks are mostly green and red, and none of them have any writing on the trailer. It would be hard to know exactly which truck she got in unless you got a license plate."

"The one I saw," said Father Francesco, "was red and had a huge front that hung over the cab."

"Yeah, they all do. Those are sleeper cabs that even a guy like me could fit into."

Maggie stood with her arms behind her back. "Did you ever notice who she was with?"

"No. She was alone both times."

"Did you tell anyone that you thought you'd seen her?" Maggie asked.

"Yeah, I told Sasha. She asked to go with me next time, just in case she showed up again. She thought maybe whichever twin it was wouldn't run from her. But she never showed. That made me think all the more that it was her and she didn't want anyone to recognize her."

Sasha interrupted. "A couple of weeks later I told one of the cops that Tiny thought he'd seen one of the missing twins, but the cop just treated me like I was a dumb local," Sasha grimaced. "The cop was the one who no longer works for The Dalles PD. His lack of interest really pissed me off. Can't remember his name. He tried to convince me that I was imagining things. So, I dropped it. I didn't tell Ananya because I didn't want her to get her hopes up. She found out, anyway. Hard to keep secrets in this place. Anyway, nothing came of it."

"What if the three of us went to the next sale?" Maggie asked. "Nobody knows us, so we should be able to blend in easily. Anyone asks what we're doing there, we say we just moved here and are looking for another horse."

"I'm known by the Garritys," Matthew said, "and so is Francesco. We could go with our collars on so no one would suspect us of checking things out, just in case the Garritys are there."

"The Garritys are there every time. They raise rodeo stock. This is a good way for them to pick out big, powerful yearlings on the cheap," Tiny said.

"Do we need a plan just in case she's there?" Father Francesco asked.

Sasha said, "The secret to the mustang sales is walking around and looking in all the pens, supposedly deciding on which horse you want to buy. If you do that, you'll fit in. When it's time to bid, in the afternoon, you go to one area where they bring out the horses. This is Tiny's job because he is able to handle the very skittish horses. The problem is, if we see this girl and now we know it would have to be Dakota, I think she'll run."

"You think if it really is Dakota and she recognizes you, she'll run?" asked Francesco

"I do. Tiny would know her, might tell someone he's seen her. If it's Dakota, she has some reason for not wanting to be found. I'm sure of it." Sasha fidgeted in her chair. "Come on Tiny. Let's finish up here, I have to dig some roots before we go back home."

"Roots? What kind of roots?" Maggie asked.

"They're called biscuitroot. They're all over the hills and prairies around here. They exist around Yakima all the way to Warm Springs and east to the Snake River. Along with salmon, this was the basic food staple of our ancestors. We still eat it when we can find it. It's our flour. You grind it up, mix it with water and either eat it as a porridge or cook it like bread. It has good flavor—not like the Camas bulb which is really nasty."

"You'll have to show me how to dig for this root." Maggie handed Sasha a bottle of water and a homemade chocolate chip cookie. "Please, everyone, help yourselves."

Tiny picked up a bottle of water, drained it and said, "If you want to go to a roundup, the best and biggest is down in Malheur county, which is directly south of us, but at the other end of Oregon."

"If we go to southern Oregon, we'll all go. Tiny, how do they round up the horses and get them to these auctions?" Maggie asked.

"They used to ride horses, but now they use helicopters to round them up. which I think isn't fair," Tiny said

"Which isn't fair to the horses, especially foals that might get lost from their mothers," Maggie sniped.

Sasha smiled. "I always thought I would like to have a horse, but my dad flipped out. 'We live in town. Where are you going to put a horse? Are you getting a job to house and feed it? Will you train it and ride it?' Somehow, I didn't plan on housing or feeding it. I got over my fantasy pretty fast."

Maggie laughed, "Like all the rest of us who have wild dreams about owning a horse. When we figure in the cost of feed and upkeep, we give up pretty fast. We have a horse back in Grand Coulee that we need to bring down here. I miss her. I saved her from a fire at Lake Chelan."

"What type of horse is she?" Sasha asked.

"Just horse. A mix. I don't know, but to keep her we need shelter, feed, and a place to ride. Up until now, I haven't had those things, but that's about to change," Maggie grinned. "Tiny, please find out when the next local auction is, and we'll all go."

CHAPTER TEN

"What did you think of Tiny?" Maggie asked as they packed their belongings into boxes to be hauled to their new home. "Besides being huge, I think he could be a big help."

"I like him and think he's probably a good ally. All muscle and bone. No fat on that kid. And, he knows the people and the culture," Matthew said, reaching for another empty box.

"Perhaps he knows more than he lets on. I hope we can meet with him again," Francesco said, lifting his glass and taking a large gulp.

"You won't have to wait long. He's coming back," Maggie said, spotting Tiny's head and body as he strode up the hill. He seemed different from when he was here with Sasha. More resolve. He carried a paper bag.

"Hi, Tiny." Maggie rose to meet him.

"Hi." He handed her a bag of biscuitroot. "I told Sasha I'd bring you these, but actually I wanted to talk about some things I didn't want to say in front of Sasha. I don't know what's true or not true, but I don't want her to get upset about something we can't prove."

"Prove? Like what?" asked Maggie.

"She mentioned the cop that treated her like dirt. It's true. He had no use for Indians. What is the word I want? He was always making up reasons why my friends and I should be arrested. Even though we weren't doing anything illegal."

"You mean profiling?" Matthew asked.

"Yeah, that's the word. When the twins disappeared, he went to every Native home and asked to see the men. Said he would find which Indian murdered the twins and he would kill him. Threatened them. He said nothing about arresting them and taking them to jail. He said nothing about a fair trial or anything like that. Besides saying this, he had no right to come to our houses. He had no jurisdiction on the reservation. When it was pointed out to him that he didn't have an Indian cop with him, he blew it off and said it didn't matter in a murder investigation. I always thought he knew something or he wouldn't have said it was a murder investigation." Tiny looked at the ground. "I guess since you found one twin, it could be a murder investigation, but five years ago nobody knew what happened."

Francesco glanced at Matthew. "The cop's name never came up before. I think we need to find out who he is and where he is. I know The Dalles police are not going to give us employee information, but perhaps there are other ways we can find out. Did you ever see him in a place that didn't seem right?" Francesco asked Tiny.

"Yeah, a couple of times. Believe it or not, I saw him at one of the horse auctions when he was still a cop. I didn't talk to him. In fact, I stayed far away from him. He never threatened me, but I'm sure that was because I'm twice his size."

"When was the second time?" Matthew asked.

"It was about a mare. Have you met the Bradcliffs? Great people."

"We have. We're moving into their house today!" Maggie said. "It's so beautiful and there is a place for our horse. So, what happened?"

"Well Martha took her mare to Leo Garrity to have her bred to this fine quarter horse stallion. She never got the mare back. Garrity said she'd run off. He refused to pay for the mare. A giant crock. At one of the auctions a few years ago, I overheard that same cop saying to some buyer that he had a really fine quarter horse mare that he'd be willing to sell. That had to be Martha's horse. Anyway, I've always wondered what happened to the cop.

Was he fired or did he quit? I think he's a big part of this puzzle. I hope you can find out what happened to him."

"I suspect you're right," Matthew said. "Do you know if they ever notified the police about the horse?"

"Not for sure. I used to help out with their horses and gardens. Martha had gorgeous gardens here in the desert. She would almost cry every time she talked about losing the mare. I looked on my own, but never found her."

"We'll put the cop and the Garritys at the top of our list of people to find out about."

"One other thing." Tiny stood to his full height and looked down at them. "Garritys have a Native American kid living with them. A kid that doesn't belong to any Natives between here and Warm Springs. I'd love to know that story as well."

"Are we talking a child or an adult?" Matthew asked.

"A kid, maybe four or five."

Francesco looked at Matthew, his right eyebrow lifting.

"I think we'd like to know that story too. Father Francesco saw a boy about four or five. The boy threw rocks at him in front of Dinty's, the same day he found the skeleton," Matthew said.

Tiny said, "I think I've seen that kid at Dinty's. Sorry, I have to go back and pick up Sasha. I just wanted you to know I'll help however I can."

"I'll call whenever we find something you can help us with. And we'll go to the Malheur County roundup. Thanks, Tiny. Someday this will all fit together," Matthew said as he reached out to shake Tiny's hand.

"You know my last name?"

"Yes. Ananya said it's Hawks Tooth."

"Yeah, when you need to talk to Indians, give me a call and I'll go with you. It's unlikely they'll be willingly talk to you, but they'll talk to Tiny Hawks Tooth." He smiled and walked to his truck."

With that Tiny was gone.

"Wow," Maggie said.

"Indeed. I think Tiny will help us put things together." Francesco said, watching Tiny drive away.

"For now, we have to get our own things together. Today is moving day," Maggie could hardly wait for mint juleps on the veranda. Well, a glass of the chilled Prosecco Matthew had brought back from The Dalles, on hold for a special occasion.

CHAPTER ELEVEN

S asha sat with Maggie as they compared Ananya's notes with the police notes.

"Do you mind if we talk about the twins?" Maggie asked.

"No. Go ahead," Sasha said.

"I assume you knew them well. Tell me what it was like when they disappeared. Ananya said the tribe hunted for them but felt the police did very little. What do you think?"

"I was the same age as the twins. They would now be eighteen. We were best friends. I listened to what other people said and what my mom and dad said, but nobody really knew anything. I don't know about the police except for the one cop who said an Indian did it." Sasha balled her fists until her knuckles turned white.

Noting her tenseness, Maggie decided she needed to probe more gently with her questions. "I don't understand why there wasn't at least one person who might have seen something."

"Nobody saw anything. All we heard was useless gossip."

Maggie took Sasha's hand. "Tell me about the gossip. Do you remember anything?"

"Not really."

"Did either of the girls have a boyfriend?"

"No. We were too young for boyfriends, at least that's what our parents said. My mom and Ananya said we should do things in groups and we should pay attention to school and get good grades and go to college. Both our moms wanted us to get an education. They went on and on about girls needing to be able to take care of themselves and any kids we might have." Sasha leaned her head against the back of the chair and closed her eyes.

Maggie laughed. "I heard that same lecture over and over, but I also paid attention."

"We listened too. I got good grades and applied to three colleges and was accepted by all three. Next fall I start college at Washington State in Pullman. I got a really good scholarship through the tribe."

"Congratulations, Sasha. What are your goals?"

"I want to be a vet. We, I mean the tribe, own a lot of animals, but when one is sick or hurt and needs a vet, we don't take the animal because we can't afford it. I have good math skills, and I love science, so I am hopeful that I'll be admitted to Washington State's veterinary program."

"Great. I have a mare that I plan to bring here soon. You can practice on her." Maggie thought about how to ask the next question. "Finally," she said, "Do you know of any other girls who disappeared?"

"No. Wish I could help."

"Did you ever see girls together that didn't go to your school? Like maybe at Dinty's? And then sometime later you saw them again?"

Sasha turned her head and stared at Maggie. She balled her fists again. Maggie could see that Sasha had a yes to that question. Sasha stared straight ahead, but didn't answer.

"What is it?" Maggie asked.

"I never saw the girls, but my friend Leena said she saw a bunch of girls out on the road by the Garrity place talking to that cop."

"Hmm. Did Leena know the girls?"

"No, and they've never been seen again."

"What do you know about that cop? You seem to really dislike him."

"He came to our community and threatened the men, young and old, said that he would kill whoever murdered the twins. The men were very concerned. The elders told the men not to get into any trouble, no driving tickets, no sassing any cop. They said it must be as if all of our young men disappeared."

Pretty much the same story Tiny told, Maggie thought. "What are the chances someone has a picture of this guy so we'd know what he looks like?"

"I doubt it."

"Are you afraid of him?"

"Oh, yeah. But he hasn't been seen in over a year."

"Are you going to be able to go with us down to the Malheur auction?"

"Yes. I'm going with Tiny. He thinks we should go separately so you'll be totally unfamiliar to anyone. If Dakota is there, I know I'll recognize her. I'll try to talk to her, but if that doesn't work and you are close by, at least you'll know what she looks like."

"Probably a good idea. I have to admit I'm anxious to go."

CHAPTER TWELVE

Tiny drove the road back from Warm Springs a bit too fast. He was in a hurry to get back to Biggs Junction to talk to Matthew, Maggie, and Francesco. As he approached the long hill down to Biggs Junction, he found himself behind a huge stock semi, the type he'd seen at the auctions. Red and white, with an overhead sleeper, exactly like the truck he thought he'd seen Dakota standing in front of at one of the auctions. He decided rather than stop at Biggs, he would follow the truck and see what happened. The truck rolled past Biggs and entered the freeway on the eastbound ramp.

They weren't more than two miles down the highway when the truck began to swerve. Some smoke appeared under the right side of the semi-trailer, and pieces of tire flew into his windshield. Flat tire. Tiny could see the driver struggling to control the big truck as the trailer started to swing into the freeway's left lane. Closely avoiding a major accident, the truck finally came to rest on the freeway shoulder without incident. Tiny could see that the left middle tire was shredded down to the rim. Tiny pulled over and jumped from the truck thinking to ask the driver whether he could use some help. As he approached the back of the truck, the right cargo door swung open.

A young girl stood at the edge of the bed, adjusting her eyes to the bright light. She jumped from the trailer and landed badly, falling to her hands and knees. Tiny saw a terrified, tear-stained face before the girl bolted away from the freeway and began frantically scrambling up the rocky bank. Tiny grabbed her before she could get far. She gasped for breath to scream, but Tiny covered her mouth with his hand as gently as he could, hoping she'd realize he was no danger to her. With a finger to his lips for silence, he tucked her under his arm, carried her to his truck, and put her on the passenger side. "It's okay. You're safe now but drop down out of sight and don't make a sound. I'll be back as soon as I close those doors and talk to the driver."

The girl, with petrified big brown eyes, looked up at him. Whether she trusted Tiny or was overwhelmed by him wasn't clear, but she did as she was told. Tiny walked to the big truck, looked into the bed and saw a half a dozen head of cattle. He carefully closed and latched the door and moved to the front of the semi. "You okay?" he asked the driver.

The driver sat frozen, eyes wide with shock, sweat running down his face. "Yeah, I'm okay. Just a little shook up. It's tough to stop one of these rigs when you're pushing sixty." The man got out of the truck and the two walked back to look at the tire.

"You want me to help you change the tire?" Tiny asked.

"Naw. I've got enough tires left that I can make it to the next big town that has a truck stop. I'll get it fixed then."

"You sure? I can help. Done this a lot of times."

"Looking at your size, I bet you can lift the whole truck. I'll be okay. I've got a guy up in the sleeper, but I'll bet he's awake now. If I need to change it, I'll get him up. Thanks for stopping and offering to help. My name is Jeff. Everybody knows me as Peanut." He held out his hand and the two men shook. "I'll be on my way."

Tiny dropped his hand and walked back to his pickup and got in. Tiny pulled out from behind the truck, telling the girl to stay down until they reached the overpass.

"What's your name?" Tiny asked. "And where are you from?"

From below the dash, the young girl answered, her voice quivering.

"My name is Gabriella. Gabriella Guadalupe. I'm from Mexico. Are you kidnapping me?" Gabriella barely whispered.

"No." Tiny answered as he pulled off onto an exit to return to Biggs Junction. "You can sit up in the seat now." She wiggled out from under the dash.

"How did you get in the back of a cattle truck?" he asked as she pulled herself into the passenger seat and fastened the seat belt.

She wouldn't look at Tiny. "I was kidnapped in Yuma, Arizona. That's where I go to school. I was walking with my mother and brother at a big farmer's market. I saw Fredricka, my friend from school. I ran over to talk to her. We talked and walked, and then all of a sudden, these two men grabbed us and pulled us behind the big tents. Fredricka kicked and bit one of the men and escaped. We both screamed, but I didn't react quickly enough because I was so scared. The two men forced me to walk between them, each one holding an arm." She shut her mouth and wouldn't look at him, but she held out her arm to show an angry bruise the shape of a man's hand.

Tiny leaned over to touch her arm. "It's okay. You're safe now. Tell me more."

"We headed towards a black pickup with a camper. They forced me into the back and I could hear them locking me in. I tried the door, but I couldn't get out." Gabriella began to cry. "I couldn't understand why nobody heard me scream or tried to help. Where am I?" she asked.

"You're at the north end of Oregon near the Columbia River. How did you get in the big cattle truck?"

"I don't know how far we drove when I was in the camper. It didn't feel like far. We stopped at a cattle yard. A big truck was waiting there. It was already loaded with cattle—calves, I think. They told me to get in and stay in the far back. I had no choice. They drove a long way, then finally they stopped and bought me a hamburger. I had to eat it in the truck along with the smelly cattle."

"Is that the only food you've had since Arizona?" Tiny asked.

"They stopped one more time. It was dark so I didn't know where we were or what time it was."

"Did they ever stop so you could use a bathroom?"

"No. Only once did I pee. Just couldn't hold it. It felt like we drove really fast the whole time." Gabriella gave him a sideways glance. "Who are you? Where are you taking me?"

"My name is Tiny. I'm taking you to good friends who will take care of you. Two priests and a lady friend of theirs will help you. You can stay with them until we figure out how to get hold of your parents. Do you have a phone?"

"No. We're too poor to have a phone."

Tiny didn't respond but it was obvious it was going to be tough getting hold of her parents. They drove silently until they hit the Biggs Junction exit.

He pulled up to the church and got out. Maggie and Francesco greeted him. They watched as Tiny walked around the truck and opened the door. Both were stunned when a young girl emerged, her clothes filthy and her hair matted with dirt. She smelled like a cow pen.

Maggie stepped forward. "Hi Tiny. Who's your friend?"

"Her name is Gabriella." The girl stood in front of the pickup, eyes downcast.

"Hi Gabriella. Where are you from?" Maggie asked as she pointed to the chairs that were always in front of the church. "Let's sit down."

Gabriella just stood there, unwilling to acknowledge these people. She looked at her feet, unmoving.

Tiny said, "It's okay, Gabriella. This is Father Francesco. He's a priest. There is another priest and Maggie's their friend."

"Priests? That seems so odd. I don't see a church." Gabriella lifted her lashes and peeked at them.

"We're transforming this old car garage into a church. Kinda like a mission." Maggie laughed. "Tell us where you're from."

Gabriella looked up and stared, shuffled her feet and then said, "I'm from Mexico, just across the border from Yuma. It's called Algodones. I go to school in Yuma. Everyday my mother brings my three brothers and me to school. After school, we go to the market. I'm sure my mother is freaking out. She doesn't know what happened to me."

Tiny offered, "She was taken from a market by two men and put in a truck. They tried to take another girl, but she was able to get away. I followed the truck onto the freeway because it is the exact type truck that I saw at the auction. Just past the Biggs exit, the truck had a flat tire. When I stopped to ask if I could help, Gabriella opened the cargo door, jumped down and tried to climb the hill. I grabbed her and stuck her in my truck before the two men saw her. I told her to keep her head down and not to make any noise. Needless to say, she was terrified. I'm pretty sure she thought she was being kidnapped again. I guess I figured you would know how to take care of her."

"We certainly do," Maggie said. "Let's get you home and into the shower. Then you can tell me what happened and how we get in touch with your parents." Ironic that Matthew is in The Dalles talking to Father Daniel and the police, she thought.

"Were there any other girls with you?" Francesco casually asked.

"No," Gabriella responded. "My friend got away."

"Do you know where they were taking you?" Maggie asked.

"Not really. I wasn't told very much. Mostly I was told to shut up and keep quiet. I was terrified they were going to hurt me." Tears formed in her eyes and slowly rolled down her face. "I don't know how to get hold of my parents."

"I bet the police in your town can help find them or we can call your school and ask them for help."

Gabriella's face lit up with a bright, hopeful smile. "We don't have police in my town, but you can talk to someone at my school in Arizona."

"I hate to interrupt this," Tiny said, "but Gabriella hasn't eaten in a long time. Do you have anything to eat or should I run down to Dinty's and get a hamburger?"

"Dinty's is a much better choice," Francesco said.

Gabriella's smile widened. "I'd love a hamburger, and French fries. And a vanilla shake, if that's okay."

Francesco got up and headed into the church. "I'll get some money. Anybody else want a hamburger?" They all said yes. When Francesco came back and handed Tiny money, he said, "Here's enough money for a feast."

Maggie asked, "Gabriella, back to where they might have been taking you, do you know where that might be?"

"Some town named Templeton or something like that. They said they were going to drop off the cattle and pick up another load."

"I think they meant Pendleton. Load of what? Cattle?" Maggie asked. "And how could you hear them talk in the back of a big truck?"

"Oh, that was when I was in the camper. I could hear everything they said. But I don't know what kind of a load they were to pick up. Just a load. They talked about the boss being pissed that they didn't have a big load. One guy said they'd make up for it when they got to Oregon."

When Tiny returned, food in hand, Gabriella waited patiently for her burger. "Thanks so much for this. I'm starving." She sat in a chair and juggled the food on her lap.

As she watched Gabriella eat, Maggie's mind swirled. Load. What could that mean? Gabriella inhaled her food in five minutes and waited quietly for what was to happen next. Maggie finished and held out her hand. "Come on Gabriella. We just moved into a new home. We're not settled yet, but there is a bed and the shower is great. We'll figure out where you sleep and how to reach your parents. Do you have brothers and sisters?"

Gabriella nodded her head. "Five," she said. "Three brothers and an older sister. My sister has always watched out for me at school." Maggie could see tears were behind the girl's words. She smiled, grabbed Gabriella's hand, and headed for her car.

"Francesco, why don't you call Tom Marshall and Father Daniel and tell them about Gabriella?" To Gabriella, she said, "Tom Marshall is a detective and Father Daniel is a priest. Maybe they can help."

"Done," Francesco said and headed inside.

CHAPTER THIRTEEN

"What a day," Maggie said, as they pulled up the driveway to the house. Gabriella inhaled, becoming more comfortable by the moment.

"I'm so happy to be rescued. Maybe tomorrow we can try and find my family?"

"I promise we will," Maggie said as she unlocked the front door. "I'll show you the bathroom. Take a shower, you'll feel so much better. Matthew should be back soon. Won't he be surprised to find he has a grown daughter?" Maggie laughed as Gabriella shut the door and turned on the water.

Forty-five minutes later, Gabriella appeared at the door, wrapped in a towel. "May I borrow a T-shirt? If you have a washing machine, I would like to wash my clothes."

"I should have thought of that," Maggie said. "I don't have many clothes, but you're welcome to any that I have." She moved from the kitchen down the hall. When she returned, she had two T-shirts and a pair of shorts. "I fear these shorts will be too big but try them anyway."

Gabriella scurried away. When she returned, she wore the shorts and a blue T-shirt. "I hope I won't be rude, but may I go to bed? I haven't slept for three days. I didn't sleep much riding with a bunch of smelly cows." She still kept her eyes on the floor.

They walked down the hall and Maggie pointed to the door on the right. "Pull the drapes shut and sleep as long as you like. Tomorrow we'll talk about your experiences. There's much more we want to know."

It was close to eight that night before Matthew arrived. She opened the door and handed him an ice-cold lemonade and kissed his cheek. He took it and they sat on the floor in front of the big window facing the Columbia River.

"How did your talk with Father Daniel go?" Maggie asked.

"I think the better question is how did your day go?"

"We have a young girl living with us?"

"What?" He looked quizzically at her.

Maggie laughed. "I wanted to tell you we have a new daughter but decided that was too much of a shock. So, yes. She was kidnapped. Tiny rescued her from a big a cattle truck. She is living with us until we can locate her parents in Mexico or Yuma where she goes to school. She's scared to death. I wanted her to meet you, but she asked to go to bed."

"What happened?" he asked.

"She was kidnapped by two men in Yuma along with another girl who managed to get away. Tiny rescued her from a cattle truck when it had a flat tire. He brought her to us, thinking we could take care of her. I'm hoping Tom can help us find her parents. She lives in Mexico without phone service but goes to school in Yuma. I'm hoping the school can contact her parents." They sat quietly, staring at the river. "Now, about your day," Maggie said as she cuddled next to him.

"Mine was interesting. Father Daniel wanted to know about our wedding. I told him how telephone calls brought everyone in the Grand Coulee valley to the wedding. Standing room only inside the church with people standing outside waiting to get a look at us. He laughed out loud when I told him about our kiss, that it went on and on, and that Father Francesco had stepped in and put a stop to it and then explained to the parishioners that we had never been intimate, that I had never broken my vows. I told him our honeymoon was two nights at an inn on the lake behind Grand Coulee Dam. I told him the men had threatened a shivaree, but fortunately it didn't happen."

Maggie laughed. "I hope they spent all night trying to find us."

"He was curious about why we decided to marry and why I asked to retain my collar."

"Did you tell him that we both knew this was love that would last a lifetime, that I was supportive of your choice to remain a priest?"

"I did. He admitted that he found it difficult to believe that I could walk away from church doctrine. I told him that I wanted to remain a priest, that a partnership built on love and respect should be allowed in the church, that we priests would be much better able to help parishioners if we had real experience in family life issues. I also mentioned the encyclical Francesco was writing, with our help, that defined the ideas around married priests and how it would help the church. I told him that Francesco also helped me write the letter to the pope asking to let me marry and remain a priest."

They sat quietly, holding hands, watching cars go back and forth across the bridge to Washington.

"After we talked awhile, Father Daniel told me that some people asked why a woman was living with two priests in Biggs Junction. They thought it was unseemly."

"Unseemly? I bet they had pointed noses and puckered lips," Maggie said.

Matthew laughed. "We've barely had a moment alone in the last two months. And when we're at the church, the three of us are too busy working to have time for behavior that might inflame those folks."

"Besides, not many people have been to the church to see what's going on." Maggie sniffed.

Matthew put his arm around her and pulled her close, her head resting on his shoulder. "So, is this Dinty's gossip or is there someone in the community who wants to save us or get rid of us? Shades of Grand Coulee back to haunt us? Did the bishop place a call to one of the locals?"

"I hadn't thought about the bishop having a say," Maggie said, sitting up straight and looking at him.

"Father's point was that we're probably going to have to tell people we're married and deal with the fallout from that. He doesn't seem to think most people will object so much as they will want to know 'why'? Why would a priest choose to marry? Why would he be allowed to marry? Has the church changed its position on married priests? He thinks we'll have to answer a lot of questions."

"We had better figure what we're going to say sooner rather than later. I'd hoped to put it off for a while longer," Maggie said. "You're the one the questions are directed at."

"True, but you're the one they're going to condemn for leading a priest astray." Matthew pulled her to him and kissed her neck. "Come on. Let's go practice."

CHAPTER FOURTEEN

The phone rang and rang. As soon as it stopped, it rang and rang again. As Matthew came in from scraping old flaky paint from the walls, he thought someone must be very anxious to get hold of them. He picked up the phone. "This is Father Matthew. How may I help you?"

"It's me," came a gravelly voice.

Matthew wanted to play with the old timer but controlled himself. "How may I help you, Jasper?"

"I hiked the berm across the neighbor's back yard and you won't believe what I saw. Can you and that old man come out? And bring your hiking shoes."

"What did you see?"

"Not telling. You gotta see it. And bring a camera."

"Okay. We'll be out as soon as possible."

"What does that mean?" asked Jasper.

"It means within an hour. I have to corral Maggie and Gabriella, the girl staying with us, and let them know we're going over to your place."

"Okay," said Jasper, "but hurry up. I don't want this to disappear. And bring something to see long distances."

"Do you mean a telescope, which I don't have?"

"No, the thing with two eyes."

"Binoculars?"

"Yeah, binoculars."

"I do have those."

As he hung up the phone, Mathew called to Francesco. "Father, grab the camera and put on your walking shoes. After I leave a note for Maggie, we're heading over to Jasper's." He scribbled a quick note, pulled the binoculars out of one of the storage bins and headed for the truck.

Jasper met them as they drove in the yard, wildly waving his arms. "What took you so darn long?"

"Jasper, it only took a half hour. What's so important that we have to hike and take pictures?"

"You ain't a-gonna believe this, but girls. Lots of girls."

"What?" asked Father Francesco. "How many girls and how old are they?"

"Younguns. Up to fifteen, sixteen, maybe. They're havin' a picnic out behind the barn. I mean over the hill from the barns. I didn't count the number, but I'd say thirty."

"Francesco," Matthew asked, "how many girls did you see in the barn the day we were there?"

"Maybe six or eight, but remember I heard a lot of voices without faces."

"Well come on. We gotta git going before they disappear," Jasper said.

After fifteen minutes, puffing his way along the rocky path, Francesco said, "I have to stop. Why don't you two go on ahead? I'll catch up in a minute."

"Are you okay?" Matthew asked.

"Yes, yes," he said. "Do I follow this path all the way?" Francesco asked as he handed the camera to Matthew. "I'll get there as fast as these old legs will move."

"Keep on the path," Jasper said and motioned for Matthew to hurry. "The fence is down so you can step over it."

Jasper was right. There must have been at least thirty young girls. From the men's prone position on a small rise, and looking between the sage brush, they could see a long table set in the middle of the field and covered with food. They could tell there were lots of salads and it appeared the girls pulled meat from a large pot. They watched as girls came to the table and chose what they wanted. "When I first seen them, the girls were sittin' around talking. They looked all kinda fresh. Some had on shorts, others long pants. Most wore T-shirts."

"Any adults?" Matthew asked.

"Nah, but now I see one of Garrity's sons out there. He wasn't there before."

"Which son is it?"

"Don't know. Probably the tall one. My eyes don't see so great anymore."

"How do you know it's him, if you can't see him?"

"The tall one always wears a big Stetson hat. Guess it makes him feel big."

The conversation stopped as Francesco picked his way to the hill where Jasper and Matthew lay in the grass, Matthew taking pictures. Francesco arrived and Matthew motioned him to get down out of sight.

"Take a look, Francesco," Matthew said as he handed the binoculars to him. "Is there anyone you recognize?"

Francesco dropped to his knees and took the binoculars. He didn't speak. Finally, he said, "Oh, my."

"What?" Matthew asked.

"They all look so young, not more than thirteen or fourteen."

"Is that little boy running around the same little boy you saw at Dinty's?"

"Yes. I believe he is. He's swatting everything with a stick, so it's a good guess."

"Do you recognize any of the girls?"

"No, but that doesn't mean much. I was in and out so fast. This number of girls suggests that I was right to be concerned. Did you take pictures, Matthew?" Francesco asked.

"I did. Now let's get out of here so they don't see us or hear us talking."

"Ain't likely they can hear us, but we get off this hill, we can all talk. Sorry to make you move when you just got here, Father. We'll let you rest when we're back on flat ground and behind my fence." Jasper led the way back down the hill.

"What made you take a look today?" Matthew asked.

"Just curious. I've lived here sixty-some years. In all that time these are the only neighbors that don't talk to me. I'm a nosy SOB, so I've been takin' a look ever now and then. Today I hit the mother lode."

Matthew stopped to let Francesco rest. "I think the first thing we do is call Tom Marshall. He needs to see these pictures. How long will it take to develop them? And who can develop them without letting the whole world know what we found?"

"I have a friend who works at the pharmacy. She'll do it and keep it to herself. Wish we could identify the girls and what they're doing there. I got a hunch," Jasper said.

"What's your hunch?" Francesco asked.

"Not sure yet, but let's think about who might know. You'll call Tom. I'd ask questions about whether they've heard anything about a bunch of young girls staying at the ranch."

"Good suggestion, Jasper," Matthew said. "I'll go back to The Dalles and talk to Father Daniel. Maggie, if she has time, can talk to Ananya and ask more direct questions of Gabriella, like when she was kidnapped and what she might have heard the men talk about. She might remember something she didn't remember earlier because she was terrified. And Father Francesco, would you write down exactly what you saw in the barn?"

CHAPTER FIFTEEN

Inside the Garrity home, Cody Garrity stood, fists clenched, defying his father and brother. "I will not help you abuse young girls. You've got a bunch of girls outside, feeding them and housing them, and you've got a different bunch coming tonight to add to the mix. When do you think this is all going to blow up in your faces?"

Buddy, was equally defiant. "Yes, you will help out, you little creep. You live here, eat our grub, screw an Indian in our house. You will help out."

"Dad," Cody pleaded with his father, "how can you condone this?"

Neither son was ready to give in.

"Stop your scrapping." Leo Garrity chewed on his cheek, something he did when tension crept in. Ignoring Cody's comments, he said, "Cody, you can manage the catering. The caterers can't stay this time. Food will just be delivered, so you can manage getting it on the tables and ready to be served."

"Dad, you know I don't like this. I've never been critical, but this can land us in prison for the rest of our lives."

Leo Garrity looked at his sons, sick of their constant bickering, turned around and walked away, saying, "Cody, you will handle the food tonight."

The food arrived at the ranch at ten. Disgruntled, Cody saw to the unloading into the barn closest to the road. The room was paneled with shiny mahogany halfway up the wall. The upper wall was stucco, painted a warm beige. Cody noted that the food was mostly finger foods. No preparation necessary. He refrigerated the food and then set up small tables, complete with dinner plates and crystal wine glasses. Candles were placed on each table. Intimacy was the goal.

Bottles of red were placed on each table, and the white wine cooled in the refrigerators.

At eleven, more girls arrived. Girls with eyes that feared the unknown, tears flowing. Cody noticed they all carried suitcases. He said to one group, "Here, let me help you with your suitcases."

They looked at him like he was nuts. "You new here?" one girl asked.

"Sort of," Cody responded. "I'm helping out."

"Well," said a tall blond girl, "these suitcases hold our fancy clothes. We take showers, try on our clothes to make sure they fit, exchange if they don't, put on makeup and brush our hair. Most of us know the drill."

"You've been here before?" Cody asked.

"Not here, but someplace exactly like it."

"Why do you do this?" Cody asked.

"Money, honey. I grew up poor. My mother is a drunk and my 'fathers,' you note more than one father, were gamblers and pimps. They all did coke and meth. I stayed away from drugs, but I'm too young to get a job, so this is how I make money. My mother's latest boyfriend, tried to sell me, but my mother had a fit, so I left."

"And you like this?"

"I didn't say that. It's how I survive.

Cody could only think about what his brother and father were doing. "What's your name?

"Roberta. But everybody calls me Bertie."

"How old are you, Bertie?" Cody asked.

"Fifteen, goin' on thirty. Hey, what's your name?"

"Cody."

"Cody, there's one girl who may need help, but the rest of us will be busy. She's pregnant. Nobody knows, or they'd kick her out and leave her on the side of the road. I don't know what she'll do when she starts showing. Could you make sure saltines are available. She's having really bad morning sickness, and the crackers help settle her stomach."

"I'll have some ready."

"Thanks. Are you going to be here all night?"

"Hadn't planned to be."

"Think about it. Where are the rest of the girls?" she asked as she walked away.

Cody didn't answer. He slipped into the back room. Maybe he should stay to see what really happens. Without a light, he could stand in the dark and see everything through the tiny window. Truthfully, he didn't want to know.

Cody decided to stay all night and watch from the shadows. What he saw made him sick.

Men arrived at midnight. Men of all ages. The quality of their tuxes told him something about the man. Some had more money than others. There seemed to be a pecking order of who got to choose a girl first. The older men chose first, then those who had asked for a certain girl, and finally, the younger men, who appeared to be doing this on a lark. Cody thought about what his brother charged. Each man met the price tag of $5,000. Twenty men. $100,000 in four hours. And Buddy is doing this twice a week, with special requests thrown in for $50,000 to $100,000 each.

The barns collectively held thirty stalls that had been converted into rooms with soft beds and minimal, but exquisite, décor, including a chair and a small table.

When the girls came out, they were impressively beautiful. Expensive dresses, adult make up. The woman named Ilsa had done a beautiful job of turning them into stunning fashion dolls. They mixed with the men, ate finger foods and drank small amounts of wine. Then each left with the man who had paid for her. Cody couldn't help wondering how the very young survived these nights. He wanted to throw up.

By the time they left, he'd heard girls screaming in fear and pain. One man had to be pulled from his room for beating a girl. The man threatened to kill Buddy. Buddy cuffed him alongside the head and locked him in an empty stall. "And shut the fuck up or I'll be back to permanently shut you up."

"I knew Buddy was doing illegal things. How naïve of me to think that the girls weren't being mistreated. And, Dad, how do you tolerate this on your ranch? Haven't you thought about the fact that you could go to jail and lose everything you own? What can I do?" Cody whispered to himself.

CHAPTER SIXTEEN

Francesco poured a glass of water from the canteen and sat down at the small card table that served as a desk and began to write. The police wanted to know exactly what happened and what he saw. He mumbled to himself. I better get this done. What do I remember? Nothing except that I'm sure there were more than six girls in the barn. What did I really see? An aisle, nicely swept. Don't know about the stalls, but I'll assume they had hay in the stalls. And then again, maybe not. It didn't really smell like hay or horses. No smell of rubbed tack or horse manure, or even a sign that horses lived there. No sign of flies. Fly paper hung near the first stall into which the girls disappeared. Did I see any sign of girl items hanging on feeding hooks inside the stalls? No, but they could be lower than feed hooks. Any sign of a window? No.

And what about that man? Where did the man come from? From behind me as I faced toward the stalls. So, he was already in the barn. He came out of a tack room or an office. Did I recognize him? No. Was he tall, short? He was tall with mean eyes that glared at me. He had a hat on, so I couldn't really see his hair. What did he say? 'What are you doing in the barn? You're not wanted, now get out.' What did the man yell at the girls? Told them to go back to their beds. Beds? I didn't see beds. Does that mean they're living in the barn?

Francesco got up from his chair, poured himself another glass of ice water and walked out into the sun. He gulped half the glass. He rethought what he had just written. Seemed okay. Suddenly he grabbed his throat, searching for his collar. I think I forgot to tell Matthew something very important.

The man had a gun.

CHAPTER SEVENTEEN

etective Tom Marshall and Rex Tyson walked through the door, followed by Maggie. "You're making some real progress here," the sheriff observed.

"It's slow," Maggie replied, looking around the big room that would become a sanctuary for worship. "Especially with these distractions. But one dead and one missing girl definitely take priority."

They saw Francesco bent over his notepad at the card table. Maggie found some well-worn folding chairs for them all to sit on, and they joined the priest. As soon as Francesco finished writing, Tom said, "I know you saw a man in the Garritys' barn. I don't suppose you recognized him?"

"No," was Francesco's response. "I didn't pay attention. Well yes, I do remember something. He was tall with mean, dark eyes. He wore a Stetson. I was told to get out. So, I did. I'm sorry." Matthew strode in, soaked with perspiration from his hard labor outside, and leaned against the wall behind Francesco. He gave the old man's shoulder an encouraging squeeze.

"That's okay," Tom Marshall said. "What are the chances you could tell us more about the gun?"

"Does Oregon have registration laws?" Matthew asked.

"Yes, but limited to guns purchased in a store. The first thing you need to know is that you're in eastern Oregon, and that's gun country. East of the mountains, pretty much everyone either owns firearms or has easy access to people who do. My biggest concern is, did he threaten you with the gun? Did he point it at you? If it was a pistol, was it holstered or in his hand?"

"No. He didn't point it at me. He held it down at his left side, so I guess that means he was left-handed and it was a pistol. I didn't see if he had a holster or not."

"Good," said Rex. "What did the gun look like? What color was it, black, silver, indigo blue? Was there a wood grip? Did it have a long barrel?"

"Short," said Francesco. He bowed his head in his hands. "I'm so sorry I can't tell you more. I just wanted to get out of there."

"Don't beat yourself up. We're just glad you remembered. We'll file it away. It may be something that will turn out to be important, but I'd like to get back to the girls you saw in the barn," Tom said. "Tell me about the girls."

"I wrote some notes about what I saw, so I wouldn't keep forgetting anything." Francesco pointed to his notepad. "The girls I saw were very young, perhaps twelve to sixteen or seventeen. Two of them were white, one black, and three might have been either Mexican or Native American." Francesco went on to describe the barn and how the stalls he saw contained cots and no sign or smells of horses. Finally, he described again how the man had told him to leave. Tom took notes, and from time to time asked Francesco for details.

Tom put down his notebook. "Thanks, Father, that information helps a lot. I'll be back to you, if I have more questions."

"Okay, now it's my turn," Maggie said. "We have more to report. Do you know Tiny?

The officers nodded their heads. "We know Tiny. He's a good kid," Rex said. "Why do you ask?"

Maggie explained, "Yesterday on the freeway, when he stopped to help a big rig with a flat tire, a young girl opened the back of the truck and in apparently great distress, jumped out. She tried to run up the hill, but Tiny grabbed her. He put her in his truck and told her to keep her head down and keep quiet. She did, though he says she looked terrified. Tiny then went and told the driver he would be happy to help him change the tire, trying to get more information about what he was up to. The guy refused assistance, so Tiny left and drove on up the freeway. The girl told Tiny she'd been kidnapped by the people in the truck."

"Where is the girl now?" Tom asked.

"She's at our house, sleeping. The poor kid was exhausted, so we thought we'd give her a chance to rest before we called you in. So far, she hasn't said much, but once she's awake and has eaten, hopefully she'll be more ready to talk."

"Good. She's in good hands. We can get her statement later. Have you asked her what she was doing in the back of a cattle truck? And were there cattle in the truck?" Rex opened his notebook and wrote notes as they continued talking.

"All we know is that she was kidnapped in Yuma, Arizona," Maggie said.

"Did she know where she was headed?" Tom asked.

"Some town that sounded like 'Pendleton,' so we think that's where they were headed. She said they were supposed to pick up a shipment. Of what, we don't know. And yes, there were six head of cattle in the truck."

"Did Tiny get a license plate number?" Rex asked.

"I asked him," Matthew said, "and he said no. The plate was badly mud-spattered. But he did note there is a pretty sizable dent over the left side back tire. He said that he would recognize it if he saw it again. It looks like somebody backed it into a tree. He's also sure it's the same type truck that he saw Dakota standing next to at one of the horse auctions."

"Is anyone scheduled to go to a roundup and auction? They just had one a month or so ago in Hermiston. The next one won't be for a couple of weeks."

"Yes," said Maggie, "all of us are going down to Malheur County. They have a big one coming up. Brings in people from Oregon, California, Nevada and Idaho. We figure the three of us aren't known so we can move freely. Tiny works there, so no one will ask questions about why he's there."

Maggie stood up and heaved a sigh. "Pardon me, but I need to leave. It's about time Gabriella woke up. I don't want her to think she's been abandoned." She turned to the detective. "So Tom, you'll meet her and help us find her parents?"

"Get her address and I'll call. If nothing else I can call the sheriff in Yuma who can contact the school. As to going down to Malheur, it's out of our jurisdiction. Besides we're known, but I'll ask my brother to go down. He manages farm labor for a couple of the pea and hay growers up in Hermiston. He's almost as big as Tiny and he'll be glad to help. His name is Harold, but we call him Coyote."

"That's an unusual name," Francesco said. "How did he come by it?"

Tom grinned. "When he was about nine, we were having problems with rats in the barn. He decided one day, when Mom went to town, that he could climb up on a chair and then to the counter to get the rifle down that lived above the refrigerator. He checked the gun to make sure it was ready, put a round in the chamber, loaded his pockets, and headed for the barn. He popped a few rats, but instead of getting rid of them as he shot them, he left them in a pile outside the barn door. When he opened the door to check his pile, a couple of coyotes were helping themselves to the bounty. One coyote, instead of running off, stood and challenged, Harold, so he shot it. We teased him about being a great coyote hunter. The name stuck."

Maggie laughed and then asked, "What did your mother think of the story?"

"She was not amused, but she let it go."

"Can't wait to meet him. Shall I call him Coyote, or will he be offended?"

"He will not."

Maggie smiled at each of the officers and thanked them for their help. "Tom, I'll bring Gabriella into town so you can talk to her and I can buy her some clothes. She was a dirty ragamuffin when she arrived."

"How old is she?" Tom asked.

"I haven't asked her, but I'd guess fifteen, maybe sixteen. She has bruises on both arms where the men grabbed her. She said she tried to fight, but they wouldn't let go."

"And one girl got away?" Tom asked.

"That's what she said. She said she twisted and tried to pull away, but the two men held her arms. She doesn't need a doctor, but she looks terrible."

Francesco pulled himself from the chair and handed his notes over to Tom Marshall. "Thank you, gentleman. If I remember anything else, I'll call." He wandered off towards the back of the church. "I have an altar to install."

"Thank you, Father," the officers said simultaneously.

CHAPTER EIGHTEEN

Ananya demanded, "Is it true you have a kidnapped girl staying with you? How did this happen? I learned this from Tiny." Ananya's voice was high-pitched, on the edge of shouting.

"Hi Ananya, I was just about to call you."

"What happened?" This time she yelled.

"I'm just going out the door of the church. I'll be over in a few minutes, but I can't stay long," Maggie said, moving her phone from one ear to the other.

"Fine," was Ananya's terse reply.

Maggie decided to walk to Ananya's so she had time to think about what had just occurred. She would give Ananya news about the young woman who had been kidnapped.

When she arrived, Ananya was sitting on the small porch, a cup of coffee in her hand, a second cup and the coffee pot beside her. Maggie sat down and slowly poured a cup of coffee.

"I'm sorry I snapped at you," Ananya said. "I'm concerned that this girl's kidnapping will signal a nightmare for someone else's family. I want you to keep me involved. I'll help any way I can."

"It's okay," Maggie said. "I understand. I'm hoping together we can talk to Gabriella, that's her name. You know more than I do about surviving this situation. The police are calling her school in Yuma in hopes of finding her parents who live in Mexico. So far, I really haven't learned very much because she hadn't slept in three days. Come home with me and we'll both talk to her."

"How did she come to be with you?"

"As you know, Tiny found her when she jumped out the back of a semi. That's pretty much all we know until we're able to talk to her and find her parents. She was kidnapped in Yuma, Arizona. Changing the subject Ananya, what more do you know about Leo Garrity and his ranch?"

"I'm not sure what you want to know. He has a huge ranch. He has several barns that house horses and bulls. He's been out there for years and he isn't very friendly. That's about all I know. He's well known in the rodeo community, but around town nobody really knows him or pays much attention to him. Why?"

"I'm not sure why. Matthew and Father Francesco went out there yesterday. Francesco said he saw some young girls in the first barn and that the barn didn't house livestock. Do you know anything about that?"

Ananya turned her head towards Maggie, her eyes widening. "No. Who told you to go out there?"

"Black Hawk and Jasper. Neither said what he thought, only that he thought Matthew should go talk to Leo Garrity."

"Black Hawk is a quiet, very honest man. If he said something, I'd be inclined to believe him. I assume he didn't know anything about the twins. Jasper, on the other hand, is quite a character. Again, I believe that anything he said would be true. Maybe embellished, but true. When we searched five years ago, both men helped out. Black Hawk spent hours covering reservation land every day for a month. He and most of the tribal community went into every canyon, pothole, and gully on the reservation. He'd call every day. It was always bad news, but he'd let us know where they'd been that day. His work is part of my notes. I'd do most anything for that family. Jasper checked all along the railroad tracks by the silos. As for Leo Garrity, he helped out for about two days. I'm not aware of anything he actually did."

"Show boating? Pretending he was concerned?"

"More like that. I don't know that he actually accomplished anything."

Maggie said, "Matthew and Francesco felt the same. Francesco actually went into the building nearest the house and saw six girls, but he was threatened before he could talk to them."

Ananya immediately sat up straight, eyes forward. "I wish I could ask him who was there, but of course he wouldn't know them anyway. What could that possibly mean?"

"I don't know, but he also saw the same little boy there that had been throwing rocks into the street at Dinty's. And, he says the boy looks very Native American."

"Oh my," was all Ananya could say, her hand flying to her throat.

Maggie held her hand out to Ananya. "Come on. Let's go see if Gabriella is awake."

CHAPTER NINETEEN

Gabriella heard the front door open. Terrified, she got up from the cushion in front of the window, ran down the hall to her room, and locked the door behind her.

"Gabriella? Are you up?" No answer. "Let me go down to her room and see if she's awake." Knocking on the door, Maggie whispered, "It's me, Maggie." She tried the handle and found the door locked. "Gabriella, it's Maggie. I'm hoping you would be willing to talk to me and Ananya. Ananya is a local woman whose twin daughters disappeared five years ago. She would very much like to hear what happened to you. It would help both you and her to talk and listen. Could you open the door?"

Maggie could hear the lock click open. Gabriella opened the door and peeked out. Still dressed in Maggie's T-shirt and shorts, she asked, "Are my clothes ready?"

"They are," Maggie said. "I'll get them." She walked to the dryer and pulled out Gabriella's clothes, walked back and gave them to her. Gabriella came out a few minutes later and sat on the window seat cushion. She stared at the floor. Maggie and Ananya were seated in occasional chairs which they turned to face the window. Slowly, calmly, not wanting to startle the girl, Maggie opened the conversation.

"Gabriella, this is my friend, Ananya. Five years ago, she lost her twin daughters. No one knows what happened to them. Please tell us what happened to you and how you reached us."

Gabriella did not look at the two women, but finally said, "My friend and I were at the market with my mother in Yuma. We go to school close by. My mother takes my brother, sister and me to school in Yuma and picks us up every day." She looked up at the two women, fearful, as if they might say something judgmental about how she should not have allowed herself to get caught. "We live in Mexico, just over the border. I saw my friend at the market so I told my mother that she and I would walk ahead and would meet her at the parking lot where our car was parked. Mom said to be there in twenty minutes. When we were back by the produce trucks, two men stepped out from between two trucks and grabbed us. My friend screamed and bit the man holding her. She was able to break away and run for help. But these men were fast. They each grabbed an arm and said that if I screamed or struggled, they would kill me and find my family and kill them. They hurt me putting me into the back of a camper truck." She pulled herself off the pillow, stood, and pulled up her shirt sleeves and showed them the now purple-colored bruises on her arms.

"After they put me in the camper, they drove really fast out of the park and onto the highway. In the camper there were a few bananas and oranges for me to eat. I could hear them talking about being late to meet the truck that would take us up to Oregon. They drove for maybe an hour and then I could tell they were pulling off the road. They placed me in the big cattle truck, but they didn't bring the bananas and oranges. They told me they would stop for food later. I was starving.

"It was dark and stinky in the truck. There were six head of young cattle tightly tied to the rail hooks. They couldn't get away, but I still had to be careful because they crashed back and forth into each other. There were a couple of bales of hay that I slept on until they were fed to the cattle. I was so scared. Then, hours later, when they stopped for a flat tire, that's when Tiny saw me getting out of the truck. It was my lucky day because one of the guys forgot to lock the door. I was terrified of Tiny. He's so big and I wanted to cry, but he didn't seem to want to hurt me, so I did as I was told."

"What a harrowing experience," Ananya said. "Did they feed you?"

"Twice in about two days. I was starving when Tiny brought me to Maggie and the two priests. They bought me a hamburger and a milkshake. Best food I've ever eaten." They all laughed. Maggie thought Gabriella seemed to be improving.

"Did the men say what they were going to do with you?" Ananya asked.

"No. They said we were going to a town called Templeton, but Maggie thinks they meant Pendleton. They were supposed to pick up a load, but I don't know what the load was. Maybe cattle. Have you tried to contact my parents?"

"The police are trying, but since they live in Mexico, it's more likely they will call your school," Maggie said, taking her hand. "I know this will take time, but you are safe with us."

"I'd like to ask a question that will be emotional for you. I don't mean to hurt you, but I'd like to know how you thought about getting away?" Ananya asked, her face full of understanding. "As Maggie probably told you, the old priest found the bones of one of my twins in the Columbia River. There is no way you can know about her, but just in case one twin is still alive, what might she be thinking?"

"I'll try to help you, but I'll probably cry."

"We understand," Maggie said. "Before we start does anyone want a cold lemonade?"

"I do," said Gabriella.

"I'll get it. I'll be back in a jiff." Maggie returned with three glasses of lemonade.

"First I was terrified that I would never see my parents and brothers and sisters again. I thought a lot about them, especially my mother. I wanted to let her know that I want to live so I can see her again. I spent a lot of time thinking about why two men would want to take me. I had no answers."

Ananya's eyes filled. She reached over and took the girl's hand but said nothing.

"Then I thought a lot about my friend who got away and how, if I ever got back to Yuma, what I would say, because I feel like I will never belong to my old group of friends. They're always going to want to know what happened and I won't want to talk about it."

"How old are you?" Maggie asked. Gabriella made no response. Maggie went ahead and talked. "This is very adult thinking, Gabriella. May I ask the two priests if they can come and listen? I'll ask them not to say a word, but they have experience with situations like this. Especially Father Matthew. He lived in Iraq for a time and knows about these things."

"I'd rather not," Gabriella said. "You can tell them what I said."

"Okay," Maggie said. "Go on . . ."

"I'd like to know why your mother is so important to you," Ananya asked.

"All the time I was in the back of the truck, afraid I'd never see her again, I thought about how sassy I'd been, thinking I had all the answers. Now I just want to see her and have her hold me tight. And my dad, too. I had wanted a job on the U.S. side of the border and my parents said no, not until I'm eighteen. I got really mad at them. They tried to convince me that it was for my own protection. I thought I knew everything. In the back of that truck I kept yelling, 'I'm so sorry' to those cows. My mother was always telling me to watch out for strangers. My dad tried to tell me to kick and scratch and bite, but I never thought it would happen to me, so I didn't listen." She began to cry, great sobbing gasps. Ananya got up to sit beside her on the window seat and put her arm around the girl's shoulders.

"Do you want to stop?" Ananya asked.

"No. I want to get it all out. Maybe I can cope with the fear better. Anyway, I stomped off to my bedroom, slammed the door, and refused to come out and talk to them."

"The next day I felt guilty and put on my best smile, especially when Mom said we would go to the market after school and get fruits and vegetables."

"Gabriella, I have a question that the priests and the police are going to want to ask you. Were you ever touched sexually by either of these men?" Maggie asked, looking straight into her eyes.

"Thank God, no. It was always a matter of hanging on to me so I wouldn't run. I tried to fight to get away. The whole long drive I wondered if I was going to be turned into some kind of prostitute. I've heard about that happening to girls who look like me. All I could think about was how to get away. I figured the first opportunity I got I would run. I couldn't believe my luck that the door of that truck was unlocked and that this very big, scary man was there when we stopped. I was terrified. He literally picked me up and put me in his truck and told me to stay down. I prayed hard that he was my savior, not another evil man." She began sobbing again. Ananya held her while she sobbed. Some minutes later, still in the comfort of Ananya's arms, she sat up, wiping her eyes. "I hope the police can find my parents so they know I'm alive. Their grief must be greater than mine."

Maggie heard the door open. "Here comes Matthew. I'll repeat your story to him." She got up and met him at the door. They hugged and kissed briefly. Gabriella stared at them in disbelief. A priest kissing a woman? That's against church law.

Maggie related Gabriella's story while the girl stayed in the window seat and nodded, tears sometimes brimming and falling down her cheeks.

Matthew walked over to the girl and knelt down beside her. "Quite a story, Gabriella. I suggest that you three ladies go to The Dalles tomorrow, talk to the police and find out if they've found your parents, and then visit Father Daniel to introduce Gabriella and say hello. He will be interested in your story, Gabriella."

CHAPTER TWENTY

Friday's sky was the color of aquamarine crystal, momentarily cool and clear. Maggie and Gabriella picked up Ananya and headed for The Dalles. Gabriella fidgeted in the back seat.

"What's the matter, Gabriella? You seem nervous." Maggie asked.

"I'm nervous about talking to the police."

"It will be fine," Maggie said. "Ananya and I will be with you all the time."

"Okay," she said. She sat silent in the back seat as if trying to figure out something important. Finally, she asked, "Maggie, I have a question that I'm afraid to ask. Why did you kiss Father Matthew? I know that's against priest's rules."

The time has come, Maggie thought. She hesitated a moment to figure out what to say, but then she got straight to the point.

"Matthew and I are married." Both Gabriella and Ananya inhaled loudly and deeply.

"What?" asked Ananya.

"How can that be?" asked Gabriella.

"It's a long story."

"Please tell us," Ananya said. "I had no idea you were even close. I thought maybe you were Matthew's sister."

"I'm glad you saw us that way. We planned to tell everyone after the mission was up and going, but maybe this is a better way to let people know. When we were in Grand Coulee, Matthew helped me with a family matter. We hung out together and I did a lot of volunteer work for the church. Matthew knew that we were falling in love. With Francesco's help, Matthew wrote a letter to the Vatican asking that he be allowed to marry, but that he also be allowed to remain a priest. Of course, he was denied."

"Oh, that is so romantic." Gabriella put her hands on her knees and dipped her head. "Then what happened?" Gabriella was obviously eager to hear the fine points.

"Well, the bishop in Spokane wrote a letter. It went something like this. 'It has come to my attention that you are having an affair with Miss Maggie Callahan. You are permanently banned from ever serving as a priest in the state of Washington. You are to report to my office immediately.'"

"Wow," said Gabriella. She said it like it was a statement of fact. "Then what happened?"

"We went to Father Francesco to discuss how to handle this. Ironically, Francesco had written a document—an encyclical—about priests being allowed to marry. This is when I learned that Francesco had helped Matthew compose the letter to the Pope."

"Oooh," Gabriella sighed.

"So, you are married now?" asked Ananya.

"We are."

Ananya asked, "Where and when did you get married?"

"It was Francesco who said we should marry immediately. He said he had heard rumors for some time that there was a group of women who believed we were having an affair, and they hadn't hesitated to tell anyone who would listen, probably using the telephone tree. He knew we had to squelch their efforts. Francesco said he would officiate. He told us to invite everyone in the valley, knowing full well that they couldn't all fit inside the tiny church. But he wanted the bishop to know how much Matthew was loved by the community."

"Did they all show up?" Gabriella asked, joy in her voice. She twisted her hands as if the story might disappear before she heard it all.

"They did," Maggie smiled. "Matthew said, on his way out the door to see the bishop, 'I wish we'd had an affair so we could have enjoyed ourselves as much as the gossips think we did.'"

Ananya said, "I'm sure they thought you were pregnant."

"Did you kiss at the wedding?" Gabriella quivered in anticipation.

Maggie smiled, "We did and it was the best kiss ever. We had never kissed before. Not a real kiss. It was such a long kiss that Francesco had to ask us to stop and told the group that we had always been celibate, that Matthew had honored his vows. The crowd cheered and one boy went out the back door to tell the others. When we walked down the aisle into the late afternoon sun, the tables were set with food and drink. Everyone cheered. It was such an odd, but incredibly beautiful experience. I'll always remember and cherish our wedding."

"It's sooo romantic." Gabriella lay on her back, her emotions seemed to be running high. She couldn't sit still and kept moving from one side of the back seat to the other, fearing she would miss parts of the conversation.

"It was very romantic. My mother came from Seattle and brought a beautiful lace dress for me. My brother came. My brother and Matthew knew each other from when I was surrounded by a forest fire. But that's a whole story in itself," she laughed.

"How did you come to Bigg's Junction?" Ananya asked.

"Matthew called many parishes until he found Father Daniel who was willing to have him as a married priest. We drove over for an interview. They talked for hours about his expectations, and he asked Matthew's philosophy on all manner of church issues. When they finished, Matthew was given the task of developing a mission here." Maggie laughed. "The goal was to get more of the ranchers and tribal members to participate. I didn't imagine we would be converting an old auto shop into a church, but I have to admit I love doing it."

Ananya said, "One thing is missing from this story. Why was the bishop so angry with Matthew? That was a terrible way to treat him."

"I'm afraid I was the culprit." Maggie grinned. "Actually, that's a story

I'll tell you sometime over a long cup of tea."

In a soft voice, Ananya said, "I'm so very glad you're here, Maggie. I feel in my heart that you and Matthew and Francesco will bring my other daughter home."

CHAPTER TWENTY-ONE

Detective Tom Marshall walked into the briefing room at the Wasco County Sheriff's Station, extending his hand to each of the women as Maggie introduced him to Ananya and Gabriella.

"Hi," he said, looking at Gabriella. "Are you the young lady who escaped the cattle truck?"

"I'm Gabriella. Yes, I was in the cattle truck that had a flat tire. Tiny rescued me when I tried to escape. Maggie and Matthew took me in until we can find my parents."

"Gabriella, were you kidnapped?" the detective asked.

"Yes."

"How and where were you taken? Describe how they did it."

"I was in Yuma, Arizona at a farmer's market. I was walking with a friend, but my mother and brothers were close by. Both of us were grabbed, but my friend got away, screaming and hollering. I didn't."

"What are the chances you knew who the men were who took you?"

"I didn't know them, but I know I would recognize them if I saw them. That's why I want to go to the mustang auction tomorrow. But Maggie and Ananya say I'm too young, that I could be kidnapped again, but I know I would recognize them."

"I have to agree with Maggie and Ananya. If they recognized you, I suspect they would try again to take you and if you refused, they'd resort to violence. They would take you so they could make sure you couldn't talk. You not going doesn't mean a lack of courage or unwillingness to help on your part, it's just not safe. My cousin Coyote will be there. He won't be recognized as helping law enforcement, but he'll know a lot of the people there. He and I will have direct communication if something happens."

Gabriella stood up and faced the group. This was her last chance to convince them. She pulled her black hair back and put her hands behind her back. "I know how I was captured. I think there were supposed to be other people, probably girls, in the truck. Something happened and the drivers didn't get the 'pick up' they were supposed to get." Gabriella began to pace. Maggie couldn't tell if she was trying to make a point or she was nervous. "Those two men were upset that something went wrong and that they had no idea what. Besides, the guys at the auction have never seen me."

"No, no, and no," Detective Marshall said. "You're too young to set yourself up for something that we don't know how to monitor. They may be killers. In fact, I'll bet they are. You will not be a sacrificial lamb."

Ananya broke in. "I would like to go. This may all be tied in with my twin girls and what became of them. I want to help."

Maggie knew Ananya was thinking about what Gabriella had said about her parents' grief and she marveled that the woman had kept her own emotions in check. She would want to comfort the girl, not add to her misery. Everything in Ananya's being was probably aching to go to this auction to find her missing daughter, but Maggie knew it wasn't going to happen.

"Ananya, you are very well known," Maggie said. "People would recognize you—possibly the very people who are responsible for what happened to Lakota and Dakota. If they're tipped off, it could ruin what we're trying to do, here."

"That's right," Tom Marshall confirmed. "You would be in danger, too."

"But what about Maggie?" Ananya asked, her eyes full of concern.

"Won't she be in danger, too?"

"There will be officers there, local to the area. They will be waiting in the background to help," Tom explained. "And Maggie and the fathers will have walkie-talkies so they can call for help at any time."

"Then wouldn't Ananya and I be safe?" Gabriella asked.

"No. We have no way of knowing whether the men who took you might actually be at the horse auction. There may be others looking for young children to take. I will not be responsible for telling your parents that you were kidnapped a second time."

Gabriella sat down without another word, her head down, playing with her fingers. Obviously she could not win the argument. Trying not to cry, she lifted her head and looked at a picture of President Clinton hanging on the wall. Ananya took her hand. "We can help most by staying home, Gabriella," she said, her voice thick with disappointment.

Tom sat down beside Gabriella. "Look, you can be of great help. Describe to me the men who took you. Tall, skinny, fat, what? Were they white, brown? Did they have accents, like a southern drawl, or like Mexican? Can you give me any information that might help me recognize them?"

Gabriella sat up. "Yes. One man was tall with dark hair. He did not look Mexican, but his hair did. He was big like a football player. Actually, he was the nicer man. He'd keep hold of my arm, but he wasn't bruising me. He wore a dark blue, red-plaid shirt. Instead of jeans, he wore blue fabric pants like Dockers."

"Wow. You're a great observer. Did you see any scars? Anything unusual?"

Gabriella scrunched up her nose, tipped her head to think about the question. "Not really, but the other guy was much shorter and he was mean. He'd pull me to make me go faster. He was the driver of the truck. He's the one Tiny saw. He had dirty blond hair, a scraggly beard, and the meanest eyes I've ever seen. He wore a cap backwards on his head. He jerked me if I didn't move as fast as he wanted. He was scary. He probably would have killed me, if I'd tried to run."

"Did either of them have a name? What did they call each other when they were talking?"

"The big guy was Stud. The little guy was Peanut. No real names. Oh, one other thing, I remember Peanut had a tattoo, a huge dragon."

"Which arm?" Tom asked.

"The left. I'm pretty sure the left. It had red fire coming out its mouth. He'd say to me things like, 'You get sassy and this dragon's going to eat you.' I think he was saying he'd kill me."

"Gabriella, that's the best clue yet," Tom Marshall said. "I'll keep an eye out for that dragon. Peanut can change his looks in many ways, but unless he has the dragon burned off, it's a huge clue. Even if it's burned off, it would leave a scar that would make anyone take a second look."

Gabriella no longer looked dejected. She had contributed and the detective said she'd done a good job. Instead she asked, "Have you found my parents yet?"

"I'm expecting a call from your school this afternoon. I'll let you know as soon as I've heard. Where will you stay when Matthew, Francesco, and Maggie are gone? I want you near someone who is aware of your situation."

"We are on our way to visit Father Daniel," Maggie said. "I hope Gabriella can stay in one of the guest rooms near the recreation hall. She will be right here if you get in touch with her parents while we're gone. And thank you, Tom, for your words of wisdom. Will we meet Coyote before we go?"

"Probably not. Coyote looks like me, only taller. He'll have direct communication with me. I'll keep my phone clear." He shook hands with Maggie and Ananya and to Gabriella, putting a hand on her shoulder, said, "Don't feel like you're not helping out, that we're not listening to you. Our first priority is your safety. And Ananya, Maggie's right. Your presence could blow the whole plan."

Gabriella nodded in understanding, but her expression clearly showed she still wished she could go. Ananya's clenched jaw showed she was holding back tears.

To Maggie, he said, "Remember, stay close to Coyote in Malheur make sure you're in sight of Matthew or Father Francesco. I don't want you in any kind of danger. Also, keep in contact with Tiny and let him know Coyote is on the job. Oh, give Tiny the description of the tattooed man and remind him to get to Coyote immediately if he sees him or the truck driver."

"Thanks, Tom. I'll pass this on." She smiled. "Now how about those walkie-talkies?"

CHAPTER TWENTY-TWO

The three women found Father Daniel at the altar with two young boys, teaching them the process of becoming an altar boy. They waited patiently while the boys practiced lighting and snuffing out the candles. When finished, Father Daniel turned to Maggie and Ananya. "To what do I owe the pleasure of a visit?"

"Father, I would like to introduce you to Gabriella. She's the girl I told you about," Maggie said. "Tiny saved her from the cattle truck."

Father Daniel's warm smile drew Gabriella to him.

"Father, tomorrow we head down to Malheur County to a mustang auction. We don't want to take Gabriella for fear the men who kidnapped her might be there and recognize her. Tom Marshall's cousin will be there, but he might not be in the right place at the right time if Gabriella were attacked. We're wondering if she could stay here for a few days where she will be safe."

"Of course, she can stay. I'll have sheets put on one of the guest beds. You think you will be gone two or three days?" he asked Maggie.

"Yes," Maggie responded.

"Would you have anything I can do, Father?" Gabriella asked. "I don't like sitting around."

"Of course. We can cut and arrange flowers for Sunday's mass. Two big baskets. I'm sure there is something else you can help with in the meantime."

"I'm pretty bummed that I can't go. I would like to see wild mustangs."

"I'm sure you are," Father Daniel said. "But you should feel grateful to everyone who's helped keep you safe. What happened to you was awful, but how you handle it now will keep you strong. Gabriella. Has anyone you know ever been assaulted?" Father Daniel asked as he came down from the altar and sat in a pew.

Gabriella eyed the priest, then looked down. When she finally looked up, tears slid down her face. "Yes, my cousin, Isabella, was raped by a boy from her school. I always wondered if she was picked out because she always smiled and said hi even if she didn't know the person. The boy took her behind the high school under the bleachers that bordered the woods. Isabella wanted to go to the police, but my aunt said her name would be tarnished if anyone knew. Isabella told her that everyone already knew." Gabriella looked straight at the priest. He seemed to welcome her ideas, even though she twisted the hanky Maggie had given her into a tight string.

"What got her the most was that no one believed her. They believed the boy, said he was a very nice young man, because he went to church. Those were the exact words people used as if she didn't go to church. She went to mass every Sunday. It wasn't fair to her, yet she was viewed as the girl who took the boy out behind the barn."

"How old were you when that happened?" Maggie asked.

"I was almost eleven. She was fifteen." Gabriella took a deep breath and then said. "I don't understand why people don't believe a girl when she says she's been attacked. They could at least show sympathy or ask if she wants to talk about it or is there anything they can do."

Maggie nodded her head in agreement. "Gabriella, girls must be taught not to be afraid to tell an adult, a parent, a minister, the police. And if they won't believe her, we need to find a place where someone WILL listen and show sympathy."

"Later, another girl from school was told by a friend that a man might be interested in talking to her, that he was a photographer, and a pretty girl like her might get modeling jobs. Her name was Tia and she said no. Tia later found out what the guy really did. He trafficked young, beautiful girls. If Tia had said yes, she would have been pulled into a sex ring.

"I'd like to believe that story isn't true, but it is. My sister took care of herself and me and guided me away from doing anything stupid." A smile crossed Gabriella's face, and through her tears, she said, "And here I am, kidnapped. Very ironic. I owe Tiny, Maggie, Francesco and Matthew a lot because they believed me."

Maggie and Ananya sat quietly, listening to Gabriella's story. Maggie shook her head as if to remove cobwebs. There is work to be done here, she thought.

"Gabriella," Maggie asked. "How do girls your age think about prostitution or sex trafficking?"

"We talk about prostitution. Girls who are prostitutes, and I only know of two, do it for the money, but they don't really talk about it."

"They don't talk about it because they fear getting caught?" Ananya asked.

"Yes. And they don't think anyone will believe them anyway," Gabriella said, wringing her hands again. "I think once they get pulled into it, they don't see any way out. So they keep on doing it. Then if they want to get out, they think no one will believe them, about the way they were tricked in the first place. Or worse, the people who could help get pissed because they think that's just an excuse. And then," Gabriella's breath caught in a sob, "they can get kidnapped and who knows what can happen?"

Maggie broke the silence that followed Gabriella's revelations. "I think part of it is because our culture allows boys to get away with what boils down to sexual assault by saying, boys will be boys. And then as they get older they learn they can get away with just about anything because nobody talks. Then there are those who turn the fear and vulnerability into a business. Young girls, and even grown women are not trained in how to handle themselves in such a crisis, especially in a society that tends not to believe them.

"We three will have to think about a way to change how the world treats women," Maggie said, half to herself.

"In the big cities," Father Daniel pointed out, "there are organizations that help women work through the trauma brought on by assaults. Perhaps you could get help in how to organize such a service."

"This will be my new mission," Maggie declared.

"Good. I'll assist, especially if we can do this for young Native girls. They are particularly vulnerable," said Ananya. "It will be my mission, too."

"Good." Maggie got up to brush the tears from Gabriella's face and kiss her cheek. "You'll be fine here. Father Daniel will look after you. We'll tell you everything when we get back."

"I know. Thank you." Gabriella put her arms around Maggie and held on tight, then turned to Ananya and offered a hug.

"Gabriella, you are very brave to tell us this story," Ananya said as she accepted the hug. To Maggie, she whispered, "Please, please, be careful."

CHAPTER TWENTY-THREE

Saturday morning dawned a beautiful day for a road trip. Tiny and Sasha drove up as Francesco and Matthew pitched sleeping bags into the back of the truck. Tiny got out and loaded a large cooler into the truck. "This ought to keep you from having to stop at too many restaurants along the way."

Matthew opened the lid. "Wow. Do I assume you smoked all this salmon?"

"Well, actually my mom and sister did. I fish, they preserve. The apples are from our orchard."

"This is so kind of you, Tiny," Maggie said as she walked out of the mission. "I'm ready. All the doors are locked. Tiny, Tom Marshall wants you to know that if you recognize the man you saw in the truck, find his cousin, Coyote, and let him know. Tom won't be there."

"Okay," Tiny responded.

Maggie handed out the walkie-talkies and explained the basic procedures for their use, as Tom had explained them to her. "We're all tuned in to the same channel," Maggie said, "so all we have to do when we get there is turn them on and push the right buttons."

"Over and out," Tiny grinned. "I love these things!"

"We'll see you there," Francesco said, holding the truck door for

Maggie.

"Buckle up, everybody. It's 400 miles to Malheur. Enjoy the scenery. It's a long drive, but a beautiful drive," Matthew said, as he turned the key in the truck. He leaned over and kissed Maggie.

Francesco smiled, turned his head to the window and said in an overly-dramatic voice, "At this rate it's going to take us more than six or seven hours to get there."

"Yup," said Matthew, smiling at Maggie. "But if we behave ourselves we'll be there by two o'clock, or thereabouts. i

In time for a good look-see before auctioning starts. Everybody ready?"

"Nope," Francisco said, copying Matthew's tone. They all laughed.

"This will be a better trip than the one from Grand Coulee," Francesco said, once they were on Interstate 82, southbound. "Maggie, what new things can you tell us about how to adopt a wild horse? And, what about a little history to help the miles pass by."

"Well, let's see what I can pull out of my history hat. Wild mustangs have a lot of history. They came to Central America via Spain. In fact, horse heritage goes way back to early man living in what's now Mongolia. The nomads that tamed and trained them used them to migrate, but not for war. Later, horses gave Ghengis Kahn the idea that he could conquer the world."

Francesco laughed. "Imagine that! 'Horsepower' takes on a new twist. But how about more recent history?"

"In modern times horses were allowed to run free until ranchers and farmers killed as many horses as they could, right along with grizzlies, wolves, coyotes, and mountain lions. In the 1970s, the feds, the Bureau of Land Management, who had previously sided with ranchers and given permission for them to kill anything that bothered cattle, changed their laws because environmentalists put on pressure to save the wild animals because some were headed for extinction."

"As well as glue factories. Didn't somebody named Wild Horse Annie save the mustangs?" Francesco asked.

"Yes." Maggie smiled. "History called her Wild Horse Annie, but her real name was Velma Johnston. She worked tirelessly to save the wild horses."

"I remember something about her," Matthew said. "She lived in Texas but worked out of Nevada."

Maggie said, "True. She stopped the practice of planes rounding up the horses to be corralled and taken to slaughter. It took a lot of years for her to win the fight. Today, I look at the land the horses graze and there isn't much food for horses or cattle."

"I'm glad the horses now have a chance at survival," Francesco said. "Changing the subject, do you think we'll learn anything about what happened to Gabriella? In a way I wish she could have come along. We're searching for a needle in a haystack without knowing what the needle looks like."

"Tiny knows a bit. He saw one of the men," Matthew said. "We'll just have to rely on him and the detective."

CHAPTER TWENTY-FOUR

They pulled into the auction parking lot and parked close to the pens. They could see horses milling anxiously in two holding pens. Maybe twenty in each. As they got out of the truck, they could hear yearlings and babies neighing, frantic to join their mothers. They ran in circles, constantly screaming for their mothers. All the horses were in constant motion indicating their uneasiness at being confined and their fear of the unknown. Several rubbed against the side poles, trying to knock the fence over. Constant neighing and pawing of the hard ground greeted potential buyers.

Francesco noted, "They're so beautiful. Maybe when we bring your horse from Chelan, we should get her some company."

Maggie smiled. "I'd love that. Our new home would house another horse. Matthew, let's get her down here as soon as we are able."

"Done. We'll go get her ASAP."

Francesco remarked, "I've never been around horses, but I think I'd like to care for them and learn about what qualifies as a good horse. Like the lady you talked about earlier, Mrs. Johnston, I think I could support programs that were against killing these beautiful creatures."

As they walked towards the horses, Matthew said, "There's Tiny. He's heading straight for us with a very determined walk."

"You two talk to Tiny. I'm going to look at the babies and yearlings. I want to see how they're being treated."

"Whoa, lady, we're supposed to stay close," Matthew reminded her.

"I have my walkie-talkie." She patted her shoulder bag. "And I'll keep you in sight." She walked off towards the foal pens, immediately forgetting her promise to stay within sight of the others. She wandered through the trucks, casually looking for a red one, thinking it was silly of her to do this, since she'd never seen the truck Gabriella had been in.

Tiny approached Matthew and Francesco, no smile on his face. He did not reach out his hand to shake, but said, "She's here. I spoke to her, maybe five sentences before she ran. It's Dakota. I asked her if Sasha and I could help in any way. I asked what happened to her, why she disappeared, and did she know what happened to Lakota? She told me not to speak to her. I asked why. I said I could help her leave right now, that she would be safe. She turned back, with tears running down her face, and said. 'You can't help me, Tiny. Leave me alone or they will take my son.' I was shocked. Couldn't think of anything to say."

Matthew and Francesco looked at each other, then back to Tiny.

"I finally asked her, you have a son? How old is he? 'Four,' she said, between gulping sobs. I told her, Dakota, please let me help you. There are two priests and a young woman here to help you. Please. We'll sort out what happened to you. Where do you live?"

"She said, 'I live in Bigg's Junction, same as you.' Another shock. I asked her where. Dakota was scared and said, 'I can't tell you. I'm afraid they'll kill me and my son, too.' With that she turned and ran back between the trucks. She didn't look back."

Tiny stopped to draw a deep breath. Obviously, he had more to report.

"I followed her at a distance hoping to see who she met or what truck she got into. A big red and white cattle truck similar to the one I found Gabriella in was part of the line. I looked at it, but it wasn't quite right. Looking around to make sure no one was watching, I pulled the back door open. Nothing but halter clips. I moved on to another semi that I could open without being seen. Again, nothing. I did the same with a third truck. I kept thinking, I'm running out of luck. That truck was also empty except for empty coke bottles. I took a chance on a fourth truck. My gut told me to carefully open the door. I looked around for a camera, then slid the door opener. It didn't move. I checked the roll bar system, saw that it needed to be lifted and I did it. Then I opened the door. Mattresses were strewn everywhere on the bed of the truck. There was also a slew of tennis shoes and snuff cans. The place smelled like human feces. I shut the door immediately, wrote down the license plate and noted that the truck was green with white trim, not the red and white truck I'd followed when I found Gabriella. Dakota just vanished."

"Did you see Coyote?" Matthew asked.

"I walked the full perimeter of the auction grounds looking for either Dakota or Coyote. I moved between dirty semis and then on to the three car parking lots, hoping to see one of them. Nothing. I wondered how Dakota could just disappear. I finally saw Coyote who was watching the auction.

"I walked over and stood a few feet from him. There was no appearance that we knew each other. We discussed the horses and then I passed him the truck license plate number and briefly described what I'd seen. I also told him that I'd seen Dakota and what she had told me.

"Coyote listened, holding one hand with a radio phone to his ear, the other hand motioning to me. He said to me, 'Walk around a bit and then head to my truck. I'm in the far-back parking lot on the north end, maybe five rows from the back. I want more information. I'll get this to Tom right now.'

"When I got to Coyote's truck, he had Tom on the radio and he was telling Tom everything I'd told him. Coyote asked me if I thought I could go back and pick up one of the cans without leaving my fingerprints on the can? I said I could, I had gloves, as long as no one was watching. Then he asked if any of those red and white trucks looked similar to the one Gabriella was in.

"I told him not really. The truck she was in was all red, with white trim around the windows. I didn't get a good look, but the trailer looked like it had been painted by an amateur. I never saw the cab up close. The green truck was also hand painted.

"Coyote asked Tom's questions, 'Could you recognize Gabriella's truck, if you saw it again? Also, would you recognize the driver?'"

"Absolutely, on both counts. I told them, remember, there were two men in the truck. I didn't see the passenger. The driver told me that guy was asleep, something I thought was odd when the truck had just had a flat tire. Made me wonder if I might have known the other guy.

"Tom told Coyote that this was good information and he was calling this into the sheriff's office, asking them to notify all the local police as well as the state police. He said he'd send requests to out-of-state police and ask them to check their records for any red and white trucks that might have been involved in an accident. Since we know Gabriella was taken in Arizona, he'll include all southwestern states. I left Coyote on his radio," Tiny said.

Matthew watched Tiny take a deep breath and thought how alert he was to everything going on around him.

At that moment a piercing scream came from the direction of the corrals.

CHAPTER TWENTY-FIVE

Two men grabbed Maggie's bag and then dragged her between the cattle trucks toward a white van parked near the road. The shorter man, his left arm covered with a red, fire-breathing dragon tattoo, pulled her to him and covered her mouth with a gloved hand. She tried to bite him, but her teeth merely slid down his leather gloves. She struggled and tried to kick. To hold her in place and stop her from fighting, the small man bent her wrist backward until she felt it crack. The taller man let go of her arm and grabbed her hair. "Stop fighting, bitch. You won't win this one. I'd just as soon not kill you, but I will if I have to. Hurry up before somebody shows up and sees what we're doing." The tall man opened the van door, and pushed her inside, then shut and locked the door. The two then casually walked towards the front of the van, got in, and drove away.

Maggie landed on her knees, her arms outstretched. Pain pulsed through her arm. She wasn't sure if the tattooed man had broken it before he pushed her into the van. Didn't matter. It was broken now. She held it against her stomach as she groped around in the pitch-black. With her left hand she felt around a rubber mat, looking for something familiar. Finding nothing, she sat for a few moments considering her pain and then began to scoot away from the door. Unless she could find something to wrap around her wrist, she was just going to have to hold it close. When she reached the side wall, she found it was covered with a soft blanket. She cuddled against it, holding her wrist.

How could she contact Matthew? Where was she going? Why hadn't she activated her walkie-talkie, or at least stayed within view of Matthew? She closed her eyes.

Odd, she thought. I don't think I'm alone in this van. Is there another person in here? She was scared.

"Who's here?" Maggie asked.

A trembling female voice came from somewhere in the far back of the van. Fear radiated from her voice. "Who, who are you?"

"I'm Maggie, who are you?"

The voice did not answer.

Maggie asked, "Do you have a name?"

Again silence. Maggie scooted towards the voice. "I'm looking for a girl named Dakota. There are several of us who came to the mustang auction in hopes that we would find her. Her friends, Tiny and Sasha, are here. Tiny is sure he saw her at the adoption center near Pendleton. If you're not Dakota, then we can talk about who you are and how you ended up in this van. Please tell me your name."

The voice did not answer.

Maggie said, "I think my wrist is broken. Do you know if there is anything in this van that I could wrap around it? It's really beginning to throb."

"No. I don't think there are any bandages or any type of medical supplies. How did you break your wrist?" the voice asked.

Maggie, encouraged that the person wanted to talk, said, "I tried to break away from the man with the tattoo. He jerked my wrist back so I wouldn't struggle. I think I felt it crack. Or it may have broken when he threw me in." No response.

"The other man grabbed me by my hair. It felt like he pulled the top of my head off. Like I'd been scalped. I have curly red hair. Can you imagine me with a bald spot on the top of my head?"

No laughter. The voice, a little louder now, said, "The man with the tattoo is Harry, but they call him Peanut, He's as mean as they get. He was in the Marines. That's where he met the other guy. The other guy's name is Jake, but they call him Stud. They were both pitched out of the Marines for disobeying orders."

Maggie wasn't sure what to ask next. She wanted to know how the voice knew the two men, but was afraid she might clam up. Instead Maggie asked, "Do you think they can hear us talking?"

"Not in this old pile of junk. Can't you hear the rattles? Besides there's a panel between us and them."

"If you know this van and the drivers, why are you back here in the dark? And why is it so dark?"

"No windows. They might want to pick up somebody. Somebody like you. They don't want them to be able to see where they're going or where they've gone."

Maggie didn't respond immediately. "Where are they taking us?" Maggie asked.

"I'm not sure. Probably northern Oregon."

Maggie's head spun. Northern Oregon might confirm this person is Dakota. "What do you know about Northern Oregon?"

No response. Maggie let that question sit. She'd try it again later. Instead she asked, "When are we allowed to pee or eat?"

"I don't know. We usually stop every two hundred miles or so, but I've never had anyone back here with me that I didn't already know."

"What do you mean, didn't already know?" Maggie shifted a little closer to the voice, being careful of her throbbing wrist. "Who was brought to these mustang adoptions?"

"I don't know. Just girls I live with. We try to take care of each other."

"Could you tell me about these girls? Where do you live? Are you working at some job?"

"Not exactly."

"Then what?"

Another silence. Maggie thought about how the girl might answer the question, if, in fact, she answered it at all. Silence. Maggie could feel the girl squirm. Then the girl began to cry, softly.

Maggie reached her hand into the black space, hoping to touch Dakota's arm or hand. "Let me help you," she whispered.

"How can you possibly help me? You will be sold, just like me and all the others."

There. It was out. Maggie shifted again. The girl was silent. "What do you mean by sold?"

After a long silence, the girl said, "You will be sold to men for sex." Finally, the girl asked, "What's your name, again?" Silence. "Please, what's your name?"

"My name is Maggie Callahan. I'm married to a guy named Matthew. I'm sure he's going nuts trying to find me. I don't suppose you have a radio phone of any kind?"

"No. They'd never allow us to have anything like that."

"One question, do you know someone named Lakota?"

At the sound of the name, a gasp escaped the girl. She whispered, "How do you know Lakota?"

"I don't. I just thought you might know her." The silence was so extended that Maggie surmised that a major decision was being made. Would she tell me what she knows?

"I recognize the name," the girl said.

"Lakota died five years ago. My friend, Father Francesco, found her skeleton in the Columbia River."

The girl cried, "No, no, no!"

From the front of the van, someone pounded. "What's going on back there? Shut up or I'll come back there and shut you up."

"So, they can hear us?" Maggie asked. "Do you know which man is yelling?"

"It's Peanut, the guy with the tattoo. They can't really understand what we're saying, just that we're talking. Who are you and how did you get in the van?"

Maggie whispered, "It's an accident that I'm here. I was looking at the foals. They were very upset and I was trying to calm them. Unsuccessfully,

I might add. Suddenly the tattooed man grabbed me from behind. The other man took my bag and grabbed my hair. The truth is we were here to find a missing girl. My friend, Tiny, said he thought he'd seen her at a mustang adoption sale near Pendleton. He thought maybe she would be at this sale. Can you tell me who you are?"

"Maybe. You must be very beautiful or they wouldn't have bothered with you. How old are you?"

"I'm thirty."

"That's really strange. Usually they only take girls between ten and fifteen, up to eighteen. Young girls are so frightened they won't fight back."

Unlike Gabriella, Maggie thought. "I may not have much time to figure out what is going on here, so I'm going to ask some very pointed questions. I hope you answer honestly. We'll do our best to find a way out of this mess, Dakota."

"Why do you think I'm Dakota?" the girl asked, after a long pause.

"A guess. A friend or relative would react to Lakota's death with emotion. You reacted like a sister."

There was only silence.

CHAPTER TWENTY-SIX

The moment he heard the scream, Matthew started running. "Maggie," he shouted. He knew by the sound it was Maggie. Had she fallen in a horse pen or had one of the foals kicked her? Oh, God, Maggie. He plowed through the trucks. She was nowhere to be seen.

He started back toward the sale site to find Coyote. As he approached, he saw him talking to two officers, the local authorities. Coyote was on a radio phone, Matthew assumed to Tom.

To the officers, Coyote said, "Scour the area. See if you can figure out who screamed and what happened to the person, then hit the road. I'll bet the white van we saw leaving a few minutes ago held the screamer. One of you head north and the other, south."

Coyote waved to Matthew. "Did you see what happened?"

"No," Matthew said, "but I'm sure it was Maggie."

"Maggie?" Coyote asked in a disbelieving voice. "Maggie?"

"I'm sure it was her screaming. There was no one back by the foal pen, but that's where she was going."

As the men sorted out directions, a young boy ran up to a crowd standing by the bleachers. "Dad. Dad. Listen to me. Want to tell you what I just saw, Dad." The boy tugged at his father's shirt sleeve. "I think we need to find a cop. Do you know where a cop might be?"

Bill Kensey turned from the man he was talking to and said, "Why do you think we need to find a cop, Charlie?"

"Cause, I saw two men put a lady inside a van and then drive off. It looked like she didn't want to go into the van. She was kicking at the man who had his hand over her mouth."

"When did you see this?"

"Just now. I ran as fast as I could."

Speaking to the other man, Bill asked, "Do you know where those cops are?"

"Yes, one's over there talking to a big guy and a priest. They should hear what Charlie has to say."

"Come on, son. You can tell them what you saw."

Coyote noticed them walking towards him just as the police officer broke away and began to jog toward the parking lot. "How can I help you?" Coyote asked.

"My son says he saw a woman thrown into the back of a van."

"Maggie," Matthew said. "What did she look like?"

The boy answered quickly, "She had curly red hair and another guy looked like he was pulling out her hair."

"Tell me exactly what you saw, young man. Everything. How old are you and what's your name?" Coyote said, as he kneeled down to talk to the boy.

"My name is Charlie and I'm nine. I was standing beside one of the trucks near the horse pens. I was looking for a horse for me. My dad said we'd adopt one, if it was a decent horse."

Matthew wanted to grab the boy and run back to where he'd seen her. He wanted to know exactly what happened, but Coyote was asking the questions, so he listened to what the boy said.

"She had on jeans and a long-sleeved green shirt. I heard her scream. That's why I turned and looked."

"Shit. That's Maggie," Coyote said. He looked at Matthew and could see he was about to explode. "Did you notice which way the van went? Did you by any chance catch the license plate number?" Coyote asked.

"Nah. Sorry." The boy looked downcast that he'd forgotten to do something important. Suddenly, he smiled and said, with a burst of energy, "I think it had Oregon plates. I can tell you it didn't have windows and it drove out on the gravel road that leads to the main road. I don't know which way it turned."

Coyote held out his hand to the boy and his father. Charlie grinned and shook his hand. "Good job, Charlie, and thanks for telling me. Will you be here for a while? I may need to ask you more questions."

"We'll stay as long as you like. We'll be over at the auction," Bill said.

"Guess your hunch is correct, Matthew. Maggie's been taken." He didn't wait for a reply, but radioed into Tom's office. "Tom, you aren't going to believe this, but it sounds like Maggie was taken."

"What do you mean, taken?" Tom shouted. Coyote pulled the radio away from his ear. "Do you mean kidnapped?"

"Yeah, I mean, kidnapped. Don't have much information. A nine-year-old saw her put into a van. Look for a white van. It may have an Oregon plate, and the van is windowless. They have maybe a fifteen-minute start." Coyote listened and then disconnected the call. "I'll keep in touch," he said to the dead phone.

"What's going on?" Tiny asked Matthew as he and Francesco, puffing and short of breath, arrived.

"Maggie's been kidnapped. Put in a white van, no windows."

"Does Tom know?" asked Francesco.

"Yes. Coyote's already called Tom, asking him to be on the lookout for a white van. The two officers working the auction are already dispatched to find the van. Unfortunately, the kid who saw it happen, didn't think to look for a license plate."

"How long have they been gone?" Tiny asked.

"I don't know. Maybe twenty minutes," Matthew responded.

"Me and Sasha, we'll head north. Do we have a description?"

"Only white van, no windows. Maybe Oregon plates."

Coyote interrupted, "Tiny, if you find the van, follow at a distance. I'd like to know where they're going." He wrote something on a card and handed it to Tiny. "If you spot them, I want you to call either me or Tom as soon as you can find a telephone. You have both numbers on this card. Be careful at food stops that they don't figure out that you're following them. And don't try to talk to them, just in case they might know you. Oh, and do not try to apprehend them. These are very bad men. Call."

"Yeah, I can do that. Here comes Sasha. We'll be gone in five minutes."

Tiny explained to Sasha what had happened. She grabbed Matthew's hand in both of hers. "Think positive thoughts. Maggie's strong and smart. She'll figure a way out of this."

Matthew muttered, tears welling in his eyes, "Only if she has a chance."

Coyote, seeing how close Matthew was to breaking and running, said, "You and Father go home, Matthew. You're better off there than here. Tom will call if we get news. You might follow Tiny. Every time you come to a gas station, drive around behind the building and take a look. They have to get gas. This is how they'll take care of Maggie so she doesn't get away. One is going to take Maggie to use the bathroom and buy some food. The other will hide the van. They'll stay out of sight as much as possible." He pulled another card out of his pocket and gave it to Matthew. "If you find them, call this number and I'll get men to you. You have your car phone with you, right? Now go."

"Thanks, Coyote. We appreciate you being here and helping us." Both priests made the sign of the cross and left.

CHAPTER TWENTY-SEVEN

The van stopped at a grungy gas station. "It's Oregon, so an attendant will fill the tank. Go on in. I'll pull around the building and then come in," Peanut commanded, his surly attitude on display. Stud opened the side door and let the two out. He shoved Maggie's bag at her, lighter by one walkie-talkie. Not that it would have done any good here, wherever they were, thought Maggie.

Coyote was right. Stud and Peanut tailed Maggie and the girl everywhere they went. No chance to alert someone or search for a phone. They picked up a lot of junk food in addition to cold hamburgers, and shakes. Maggie also picked up several bottles of water, adhesive tape for her wrist, and apples.

When they got back in the van, Maggie could see the van's interior. There was a panel behind the front seats. In the panel was a sliding glass window that could be opened only from the driver's side. The walls, except for the sliding door, were covered in heavy quilted blankets, the type used to protect fine furniture, for storage, or to keep noise down.

Maggie leaned against the van's side wall, hoping the girl would sit beside her so they could talk without being heard. She did. Maggie handed her a bag of chips and a bottle of water.

Maggie had looked at the girl when they were in the store. Native, definitely, long black hair. She'd bet anything this young lady had Ananya's eyes. She would wait until the girl felt comfortable enough to tell her who she was and where she came from.

The girl said, "Thanks for getting extra food."

"You're welcome," Maggie said. Trying to figure out a first easy question, she asked, "Where do you live?"

"I live on a big ranch. There are lots of barns and some horses and rodeo stock."

"What do you do on the ranch? Does your family own it?"

After a minutes-long pause, the girl inhaled a deep breath, sighed, and whispered, "I'm held there."

Oh my God, this has to be Dakota. "What do you mean, you're held there?"

Another extended pause. "I'm never allowed to leave alone."

"But you were at the adoption center. How is it that you're not allowed to leave the ranch, but you're allowed to go to the horse auction?" Maggie knew she was applying pressure, but she had to try and get the girl to talk.

"Okay, I'll tell you. We're prostitutes. We're trafficked prostitutes. None of us by choice. The girls are raped over and over. All of us were taken from someplace else and brought here. I'm lucky, I only sleep with the owner's youngest son. I usually sleep in the big house, but I spend my days with the girls. I'm their moral support." The girl's head drooped forward. "I've never been able to figure out how I could escape. Now I won't leave. Unless someone saves all of us, I'll never leave."

Maggie couldn't believe what she was hearing. "But, why?" Maggie asked.

"I've had lots of chances to run away, but they know I won't, so I'm given freedom that does not include calling home. I saw the old guy that lives next door watching us one day. He's been out there several times. Once he brought two others with him. That time we were having a picnic-barbecue. The food was so good. Usually we only get good food just before the customers arrive."

Matthew and Jasper. "First," said Maggie, "Tell me about your home with your parents. What's the real reason you don't you run off?"

The girl's voice trembled, "I have a son. The father is the youngest son of the rancher. He's been very good to me, but my son is the reason I don't leave."

"So, you have privileges the others don't?"

"Yes. Cody's brother threatens me with the notion that they will kill my son if I try to escape. I know that won't happen because the owner loves his grandson. I also know that if something happens to Leo, Buddy will kill me and my son."

"What your boy's name?"

"Toby. He's the best kid. He's fun and energetic. I'd like to leave the ranch, but I won't unless I can take Toby. His father once told me he wanted to marry me, then suddenly there was no more talk. I'm sure his father and brother said that was a bad idea. We don't marry Indians."

"I'm so sorry, but I do understand why you won't leave." Maggie reached for the girl's hand and squeezed it. "Now where did you live before? Tell me about your family."

"I lived close by. My parents are both Native, my dad a Celilo and my mother a Sioux. They met at a powwow in Teton. My mother agreed to move here. Native culture was our life, although I went to public schools."

"So, you would love to go back?"

"If I could, yes. But, not without Toby."

Maggie thought she knew what the girl would tell her, so she asked. "How many girls live at this ranch, and what's going on"

"The number of girls changes fairly often, like every six weeks or so. Girls are picked up and put in big cattle trucks. They can come from all over the country. Sometimes they're brought in via big buses. Usually there are between twenty and thirty girls. The girls are all young, maybe between the ages of ten and eighteen. All are beautiful. They come from lots of different foreign countries and they're all different races."

"Who brings the girls to the ranch?" Maggie asked.

"They've got hired men. They are paid by the head. I don't know how much they get paid, but it's enough that they keep at it until they voluntarily quit or are caught."

"How many men bring girls?"

"I don't know for sure. I've seen five guys who are regulars and then there are others."

"What happens when the girls arrive?" Maggie, asked.

"They're taken to a big shower room in one of the barns, ordered to shower and wash their hair, and this woman helps them put on makeup and style their hair. Then they put on the new clothes they brought in the suitcases. Sometimes that's funny. The clothes are either way too big or way too small so they end up exchanging clothes until they have a better fit. There are cocktail dresses, some formals. They have to wear that when the men come."

"I guess I don't understand how so many men can come and go and no one who lives around here notices them."

"They come at night, usually in a few limos. Each man has bought an evening with the girl of his choice. They choose the girls when they get there. The new girls are terrified. Many of them get sexually injured and have to have medical care. I take care of them until the doctor comes."

"Ugh. Is there a doctor who lives at the ranch?"

"No, the doctor comes when called. He lives far away, so he's not known to the community. I suspect he's actually a veterinarian because he always goes to see the cattle and horses. A cop comes either when called or when things get too rowdy or a girl gets beaten up. He's usually here when the girls leave. I'm guessing he collects the money."

"A real cop?"

"Yes. Well, no. I think he's a retired cop, but he may be a cop who lost his job. I'm pretty sure he helped put this whole ring together. And, I'm pretty sure I saw his face when we were kidnapped."

"Do you know his name?"

"Art Camden."

Maggie inhaled. "Let's change the subject. Where do these men have their party?"

"There are five barns at the ranch. They all look like they hold horses, but the three furthest away from the house are beautifully decorated on the inside. In the first barn, there is a big room where the men choose a girl. They drink and eat while the girls wait to be chosen. The food is catered. The caterers are gone before the girls and men arrive. If a girl is chosen early, she can eat and drink with the man. In the other two barns there are well decorated rooms. The men take the chosen girl to a room and have four hours to be with her. They have to be in the limos and out by 4:30 a.m."

"And do you wonder if any of these men have daughters? Do they think that this could be their daughter? No. They would say their daughters would never do this, never mind that these girls are essentially kidnapped. This is sex trafficking." Maggie's tone was sharp.

"If a man really likes a girl, he asks that he has her next time he comes. He's usually allowed to do that. Most men, however, like to have new girls each time."

"How often do men come?"

"Two times a week in limos. Usually not the same men as last time. They can also sign up to come by themselves. That man may ask to have several girls with him. That's a ten-thousand-dollar night."

"OH! Do many do that?"

"Yes."

Maggie shook her head. This was a world she knew nothing about. "Why do you suppose they took me? I don't exactly fit the mold."

"You were easy to take. Nobody watching. You're very beautiful. You fit the bill."

Maggie couldn't help but think about Gabriella. She was so lucky that Tiny saved her before something like this happened to her. Now, how the hell do we get out of here? And how do I get her to admit she's Dakota? And, how do I get a message to Matthew? Maggie threw her head back against the blanket, put her taped-up wrist to her chest, and stared into black space.

CHAPTER TWENTY-EIGHT

"What the hell just happened?" Matthew challenged himself for a reply as he started the truck. "Maggie kidnapped?"

Francesco laid a hand on Matthew's shoulder. "I don't know. It seems that Maggie was in the wrong place at the wrong time. Remember, Matthew, your years in Iraq. You were a natural detective. You'll figure this out. Let's try to catch up with Tiny. We'll check every road stop and gas station along the way. If Tiny finds the van, he's going to stop whenever the van stops. And he'll let Tom know where he is. He'll let us know if he sees Maggie. He has your car phone number. We'll get her back, Matthew."

"Thanks, Francesco. I needed that. I know you're right. I just feel like Maggie's in danger and there's nothing we or I can do."

"Remember when you used to say to me, 'stay strong,' when I wanted to do the unpriestly thing of whacking the bishop? Well, I say that to you now."

Head down, Matthew said, "I know. Thanks."

"And now," said Francesco, "it's time to speak directly to St. Jude. I think this is exactly the sort of impossible situation that he responds to. Let us pray.

"Pray for me, who am so miserable. Make use, I implore thee, of that

particular privilege accorded to thee, to bring visible and speedy help where help is almost despaired of."

Matthew listened to the purring of the truck, then spoke to Francesco. "Thanks for that prayer. I needed that. Thank God you're here. You are truly my best friend, well aside from Maggie.

Again, the old priest reached out a hand and put it on Matthew's shoulder as the truck rolled across the gravel toward the highway where it would turn north.

CHAPTER TWENTY-NINE

atthew, I wish there was some way to contact you. Sitting on the floor of a pitch-black van, hour after hour is not helping me concentrate. I'm terrified that I don't know what's going on. I believe the young lady in the van with me may be Dakota. I saw her in daylight. She is very beautiful and she has a son. Now I may be reading into it more than there is, but remember when Francesco found the skeleton, he talked about meeting a little boy about four that looked Native?

The girl scooted close to Maggie and extended her hand. Maggie held it, a mixture of terror and anger went through her. How was she going to save this girl and bring these monsters to justice? After a few minutes, Maggie asked. "Do you know any reason these men would take me? I can't believe it's just because of the way I look."

"I don't know. We don't have anyone to help guide the girls. They may want you as a den mother to keep the girls under control."

"Are these girls scared when they arrive?" Maggie asked.

"Maggie, they're terrified and that's how Buddy and Art want to keep them. Scared."

Maggie asked the question she was sure she already knew the answer to, "Just so I know, are these girls being forced to do this?"

Maggie knew by the girl's silence that she had asked the right question.

Then the girl said, "Yes, you're right. They do scare them into submission, but they've found there's far less trouble with the girls trying to run away if someone is watching over them who is nice to them. That's not an entirely true statement because the turnover in girls is about three weeks at most. Some stay longer, but only if they're not a problem."

"So, the constant not knowing what will happen next, is what causes fear and encourages them to be cooperative?"

"Yes."

"Tell me about how some of the girls came to the ranch. What stories do they have to tell?"

"Every girl has her own story. Like I said, they come from all over the world and different cultures. The ones who don't speak English have a really rough time. Two sisters came from Romania. After arriving on a ship, they were standing on the dock waiting for their aunt to pick them up. When most people had left the ship, they were still there. A man walked up to them and volunteered to help. Neither could understand the man, but he was able to communicate that he would help them find where the aunt lived. He took their suitcases and walked towards the parking area. The girls were scared but didn't know what to do."

Maggie sighed. "So, he put them in his car and that was the end of any chance to find the aunt. He drove around and pretended to look for the address, but soon gave up. He took them to his home and gave them each their own room."

"How did you know, Maggie?"

"Just a wild guess." Maggie kept her real thoughts to herself.

"Anyway, their rooms were beautifully furnished, canopy beds, new clothes and jewelry. They thought the man would help them. Over time, he asked them to massage his back. His back was sore all the time, he said. As a reward, he would take them out to eat and then to a movie. In about two months it turned to sex. Three-way sex."

"How did they find their way to you?" Maggie asked.

"Apparently the man was feeling heat from the police. He didn't realize it was a cop asking about his beautiful granddaughters. When the cop asked too many questions and wanted to meet his granddaughters, he panicked and called a friend to come and get them. They were jerked out of his home, put in a truck, and driven away. They had no chance to escape. They were told nothing about why this was happening or where they were going. It took several weeks and a long-distance truck ride before they were brought to the ranch."

"How are they doing now?" asked Maggie

"They aren't here anymore. They were taken away maybe three months ago. They were told they would go to a big city where they would be taken care of in style. Translated, they were going into a high-end prostitution ring. They would be available to very rich men. The two said that no matter what happened, they would always try to escape. They said they would stay together."

Maggie knew the answer to this question, but she wanted it said. "How do the girls react when they get to the ranch?"

"Oh Maggie, it's awful. The first time I saw what was going on, I thought about running away, but I feared I couldn't even make it to my mother's house before they caught and killed me. The girls who knew why they were there, just stood around, talking. The new, very young girls, didn't understand what was about to happen. When they found out they screamed and cried and tried to get out, but the door was always locked. Buddy always made sure no one could escape. Everyone was really scared."

The van started slowing. Maggie grabbed the girl's hand. Her voice stern, she said. "Listen to me, if we are stopping for gas and we're allowed to get out of the van, you must be aware there are people looking for me. If you see anyone you know, you must not acknowledge them except to blink your eyes, so they know you are aware. If I see Matthew or Francesco, I will do the same. These guys have guns and we don't want anyone to get hurt. But if the police are there, then be prepared to be rescued, but there may be gunfire, so try to get behind something and lie down on the ground. If no one is there, then we get back in the van. And wait for the next opportunity."

"Okay," the girl said in a voice that communicated that she didn't think anything like that would work.

To keep their minds on other things, Maggie said, "I suspect I'd be good at mothering girls. My husband, Matthew, is a priest. I've learned a great deal from him and our friend, Father Francesco about the human need for closeness. Francesco is the one who found Lakota's bones."

The girl was silent for a long pause. Maggie wondered if she was going to talk about about Lakota and what might have happened on the river bank. Instead, she said, "Priests don't marry."

"It's true. We are married. And I can tell you about it sometime, but now let's talk about you and how we're going to get you and the other girls to safety."

CHAPTER THIRTY

Motes of dust danced in the atmosphere as the sun descended, a warm glow covering the desert floor.

"Where are we?" Sasha smiled at Tiny and squeezed his hand.

"We're north of Burns, but barely. Still a long way to go." Tiny rolled down the window to let fresh air in. Sasha did the same and let her arm feel the breeze.

"Why do you think they didn't stop for gas in Burns?" Sasha wondered out loud.

"Probably didn't want a lot of people watching when he let Maggie out to pee and get something to eat. In a big town, too many people might know about Maggie being kidnapped. Out in the middle of nowhere, it's more unlikely anyone would pay attention. The driver can park behind a building and merely follow her in."

"Is this what happened to Gabriella?" Sasha asked.

"Probably. Yes."

"She was so lucky you were there."

A roadside café and gas station loomed. Tiny pulled up behind the station. Sasha brought out a twenty-dollar bill and wandered towards the food shack while Tiny got out and looked in the back door of the shop. No one there. He got back in the truck, drove to the pumps, and the attendant filled the tank with gas. Tiny followed after Sasha into the store. She was paying for water, cookies, and two sandwiches.

"No one in here," she said.

Tiny moved in behind her and asked the cashier, "Have you seen a white van or a red-headed woman in here in the last hour or so?"

"Well sir, yes I have. There was a dark-haired girl with her. Two men stayed very close to them the whole time. One guy waited outside the restroom door while each girl peed. I thought it was really odd."

"How long ago were they here?"

"Oh, half an hour, maybe forty minutes. One guy almost pushed the redhead out the door. I could tell she didn't want to go."

"Did you call the sheriff?"

"Sorry, no. I just thought the guy was a jerk."

"I'm calling Tom and letting him know she was here," Tiny said to Sasha. "Thanks for your help." Tiny reached across the counter and shook the man's hand.

As Sasha opened the door, the man called out, "Wait. I forgot. The big guy asked the small guy if Biggs was their last destination. I hope that's helpful."

"You bet it is, and thanks." Tiny looked at Sasha. "They're going to Biggs Junction. They're going home. Now all we have to do is figure out which home is theirs." Looking out the door and spotting two phone booths, he slapped down a twenty-dollar bill. "You got a roll of quarters, mister?" he asked.

Tiny pulled Coyote's card out of his shirt pocket while Sasha broke the seal on the roll of quarters, gave a few to Tiny, and dumped the rest into her purse.

"Coyote, Tiny here," he said as soon as he heard Coyote's voice. "I'm at a road stop a few miles out of Burns. We just found out we're maybe half an hour or forty minutes behind the white van, and Maggie and a dark-haired girl are definitely in that van. The gas station attendant said he heard the guys say they're headed for Biggs Junction."

Coyote said he and Tom would coordinate roadblocks in an effort to intercept the van. "I need to get on this," he said. "Can you get Father Matthew on his car phone and let him know?"

"Sure," Tiny said and hung up the phone. He fished around his wallet and came up with Father Matthew's car phone number. Sasha supplied him with another handful of quarters.

Francesco answered the mobile phone with a booming "hello."

"Hi Father, it's Tiny. A guy at a Shell station you'll soon see, saw Maggie and a girl, probably Native, come into the little store to buy food. He said there were two men with them."

"What? Maggie? Are you sure?" Francesco was nodding his head towards Matthew.

"Yes, we're sure. The guy in the gas station store described her."

Matthew yelled, "That's great news. I'll pick up my speed now and try to catch up with you."

"Tom says to tell you they're setting up roadblocks to try to catch the van."

It took over an hour for Matthew and Francesco to arrive at the first roadblock. They could see a white van on the side of the road. Matthew yelled, "There's the van. Do you see Maggie?"

"No," said Francesco. They parked behind the van and walked over to the officer who seemed to be in charge, standing at the edge of the highway.

Introducing themselves, Matthew asked, "Was a red- headed woman and a young Native woman riding in this van? If so, where are they?"

The officer shook his head. "Another man, big guy, asked the same question thirty minutes or so ago. There was no one in this van and I understand the driver was not at any mustang auction and doesn't know what we're talking about."

"Do you believe him? Where could they have gone?" Francesco asked, his voice sounding far away and deflated.

The officer extended his hand and said, "My name's Mark Peters. We got the message to set up roadblocks about an hour and a half ago. Unfortunately, the white van had probably already passed through. There's no major highway exit, except this turn-off to Idaho, but we have another block set up down the road. Under the circumstances, we can't hold this guy."

"Thanks." Matthew, frowned and grumbled, "I knew this was too easy." He thanked the officer and headed back to the truck mumbling, "Damn, damn, damn."

CHAPTER THIRTY-ONE

A t another gas stop farther north, the white van pulled over. The two passengers were allowed to use the restroom and pick up something to eat. They were followed closely the entire time by Stud or Peanut. When Maggie left the restroom, Stud grabbed her wrist and didn't let go. "Stop, you're hurting my other wrist," she yelled, hoping someone would pay attention. No one did, but Stud released her wrist. She picked up water, chocolate covered almonds and two packages of doughnuts. Maggie smiled when the girl chose two cheeseburgers and two chocolate shakes. This girl must be perpetually hungry, she thought.

When she paid for the food, Maggie tried to leave a message with the cashier with her eyes. She couldn't tell if she'd been successful. Why would the cashier know she was trying to talk to her? Stud grabbed her wrist again, but not so tightly. Maggie wondered if the cashier noticed.

Heading back to the van, Peanut opened the door and helped the girl inside. "It's still a long ride so settle in," he said. Maggie noticed his uncharacteristic courtesy and thought, this girl must have some kind of power over these thugs. Not enough to keep her out of the pitch-black back of a not-to-clean panel van, though.

Stud, still holding Maggie's wrist so she couldn't bolt, helped her in. As she stepped up, Peanut pushed her. "Get in, bitch." Maggie was ready for something like that to happen, so she caught herself and only stumbled, saving her wrist.

"Asshole," Maggie spat through clenched teeth.

Peanut laughed and slammed the door. They were once again enveloped in darkness.

Maggie fumed through her pain. She couldn't think of a way to help them escape. The guy named Peanut wasn't going to let her go. He'd protect the girl, but kill me, she thought.

Maggie asked, "What is the possibility there is something back here that we could use as a weapon."

"Probably nothing," the girl responded. "Wait, there might be a tire wrench. I saw one a while back. I'll scoot over to where I saw it and feel around."

"Thanks," Maggie said. "I'll check the door side."

On their knees they ran their hands sideways, back and forth, across the floor and down the sides of the van.

"I found something," the girl said. "I think it's a jack handle. Not as good as a big metal wrench, but it's heavy."

"Good." Maggie replied, scooting to the rear of the van. "Let's keep it between us, and if anyone tries to hurt one of us, we whack them as hard as we can, always keeping in mind that there is another man."

"It's mostly Peanut we have to fear," the girl said. "I think Peanut has some mental problems. He's mean, just for the sake of being mean. And, he enjoys beating up on women."

CHAPTER THIRTY-TWO

"Why don't you call Tom and Jasper and see if there's anything going on at home and let them know about the roadblocks and that we are on our way home? Maybe something's happened that we don't know about."

"Good idea, Matthew." Francesco pulled out the mobile phone only to discover there was no reception. "We're going to have to call from a high place. Can't get a connection here." Matthew picked up speed. "It's about 250 miles from here to home. I'll stop at the first gas station we come to. A phone booth will probably be a better place to call from. Hold on. I'll try not to get a ticket."

Francesco laughed. "I put my collar on. We'll be okay."

The first gas station was thirty miles down the road. Matthew pulled over to a phone booth on the side of the road and called Tom who answered on the second ring. "What did you learn?"

"Nothing we don't already know," Matthew replied.

"Go home, Matthew. You're better off close to a phone." The empty silence told Tom that Matthew wasn't buying his suggestion. "It's better to wait at home for information. Then you can act—maybe check out the ranch where Francesco said he saw young girls. Maybe you can ask the Garritys for a donation for paint for the church or some other plausible reason. Better to stay busy with things that might actually help."

Matthew half-listened to the instructions. "Thanks, Tom. Good advice. We'll be home in a few hours." He disconnected and called Jasper.

Jasper answered the phone immediately. "Jasper, what're you doing? Sitting on the phone hoping it will hatch?"

"Smart ass priest," Jasper shot back, laughing. "What's up?"

Matthew didn't want to scare Jasper, but he also didn't want him to take this as a casual situation. "Jasper, Maggie was kidnapped at the horse adoption site."

"What?" Jasper shouted. "Maggie's been kidnapped?"

"We have no idea where she is or where she's going. Tom Marshall has roadblocks up. In fact, we hit one north of Burns. No Maggie. Jasper, she's with a young girl."

"Now that's odd." Jasper's voice was calmer. "What can I do?"

"Maybe take a look at the ranch. See what's going on."

"You think the family got hold of her for their little business?"

"I don't know. Just a thought."

Jasper yelled into the phone. "Wouldn't surprise me that creepy family got hold of her. You bet I'll take a look. And, if I see a red-headed woman, I'll call the cops."

Matthew said, "Call Tom, please. He's in charge of trying to find her."

"Okay. Think I'll call Black Hawk and see if he wants to help."

"Black Hawk?" Matthew asked, remembering the quiet man he'd met.

"Yeah. He was the main search leader when the twins disappeared. He was best friends with Jaden, and it always bothered him that neither twin was found. I know he'll want to help. See you when you get back. I mean, I'll see you tomorrow." He hung up.

When Jasper arrived, Black Hawk was working with a young colt in a small, round paddock by the barn. "Hey, Indian." Jasper smiled and waved at Black Hawk.

Black Hawk waved back and said, "Let me finish up and put this youngster back with his mama."

"Hope you can spare a little time. I need your help."

"What's going on?"

"Well Maggie was abducted at the horse adoption site. I want you to come with me out the back way to look over the berm at Garrity's." Jasper said.

"I am so sorry. What do you think happened?" Black Hawk asked, concern on his face.

"Don't think anybody knows, but I volunteered us to help find her."

Black Hawk wrapped the lunge line into a tight circle and led the colt to a back paddock. Jasper followed and watched while Black Hawk turned the baby in with its mother.

Black Hawk said, "You know it's getting dark. Won't be able to see much."

"That's the whole idea," Jasper said. "We can see without being seen. If my hunch is right, they'll have yard lights on like it's Christmas. We need to see what goes on over there at nighttime."

"Let me tell Gagana."

"Tell 'er we'll be there for awhile. I brought apples."

"She'll fix us a couple of sandwiches."

As they walked towards the house, Black Hawk picked up an axe that was leaning against a fence that held ten pigs.

"Are you getting ready to slaughter?" Jasper asked. "Let me know and I'll come help."

"Will do. I have five pigs already sold," Black Hawk said. "Come on in while I explain to Gagana what's happened."

Gagana met them at the door. "Hi Jasper, come on in."

"I need to go with Jasper for a while tonight," Black Hawk said. "He wants to check Garrity's ranch. Maggie's disappeared, probably kidnapped."

how?" she asked. "Why would the Garritys be involved?"

"Don't know for sure they are," Jasper said.

"Wait, then why do you want to check Garrity's ranch?" Gagana asked.

"Because I've seen a lot of strange things goin' on over there, but can't figure out what it means. Maybe lookin' late at night, we'll get more information."

Gagana shook her head, then turned and went to the kitchen. In a few minutes she was back with sandwiches and two slices of apple pie. "Here's a midnight snack. Better grab your rifle, Black Hawk." To Jasper she said, "You heard this from Matthew?"

"He called around dinnertime. He and Father Francesco are on their way back. Matthew's pretty shook up, mainly because neither he nor the police know what happened to her."

Gagana told them that Gabriella had come out to pick flowers for Sunday's service. "I sure hope something good happens before somebody has to tell her that Maggie is missing. It will be like being separated from her own mother again. She hadn't wanted Maggie and the two priests to take off without her. She'd figured she could help, maybe recognize somebody."

"Yeah, we know, but think what would have happened had she been there. She would've been kidnapped again. Gagana, will you call Father Daniel and tell him what's going on? He should be prepared to handle any questions that might come up with Gabriella or anyone else." Jasper put on his hat and moved towards the door.

Gagana nodded her head and shooed them out the door. She called to the children to get out of the pool. "Dry off before you come inside," she yelled.

Jasper stood on the porch and smiled as he watched the kids slapping water at each other, appearing not to have heard a word their mother said. He thought they looked like a bunch of chickens flapping their arms in the warm evening air. Sometimes he wished he had grandchildren, but Gagana and Black Hawk always allowed him to hang out with their kids. Jasper thanked Gagana, waved at the kids, and walked to his truck.

The two men walked back through Jasper's land, following the trail that led to the big field behind Garrity's barns. In half an hour they were up against the berm looking out towards the five barns. As the rosy sunset bathed the desert, there was nothing to see, only lights slowly coming on around the house. Nothing out at the barns.

Jasper said, "Are you up to moving a little closer? Let's get behind the barns."

The two belly-crawled around the berm, then lay there for an hour eating the sandwiches Gagana had made, watching for any activity. As Jasper predicted, yard lights came on, illuminating the house and the barns. Black Hawk poked Jasper's arm and pointed towards the driveway. Jasper rolled onto his belly to get a better look.

A light blue paneled van drove around the house to the farthest barn. A man came out of the barn and met the driver who opened the sliding door of the van. They started hauling something into the barn.

"Who is that, anyway?" whispered Jasper. "And what the heck does it say on that van? My dadgum eyes aren't as good as they used to be."

"Well, I don't recognize the driver, but the other man is Cody Garrity. And it says 'Party Time Catering' on the van. It looks like they're carrying trays into the barn—probably food."

They watched until the barn door closed and the catering van drove away. It was nearly pitch dark, and the two men whispered their guesses as to what they had just seen. More accurately, Jasper whispered his guesses while Black Hawk characteristically listened.

Nearly an hour later, both men became alert as a huge bus, followed by a black car, entered the circular drive, angled slowly around, stopping in front of the house. A man got out of the car. Then a woman wearing stiletto heels and a blue dress that shimmered in the lights, swung long legs from the car. The man held out his hand to help her out of the car, and they walked up the steps of the wide-porched home, opened the door with familiarity, and went in.

"Listen, Jasper, I know that guy, the one who just went into the house."

"What? You do? How do you know him?" Jasper asked.

"He's the cop who up and disappeared about a year ago. He's the cop who talked to everyone when the twins went missing. He's the one who constantly accused the tribe of murdering the twins and keeping that information from the police. Nobody believed him, but he kept saying it. Tiny had a run-in with him. He egged Tiny on, daring him to threaten him so he could take Tiny to jail. Sasha kept Tiny from totally losing his temper. Tiny can tell you all about him. He's a mean, mean cop—name's Art Camden."

The two men watched the bus drive on around the house to the barns and unload twenty to thirty young girls. Lights came on inside the second barn, and Cody Garrity opened the door. The girls all had suitcases and they filed past him into the barn.

Jasper whispered to Black Hawk, "What the hell is going on?"

"Dunno," Black Hawk responded.

"Are you sure? You said you saw young girls in the first barns one day when you were working."

"I did, but not recently."

CHAPTER THIRTY-THREE

The girls put down their suitcases and stood like lost sheep, huddled together in the middle of the floor. Heads turned towards the door when the woman in the blue shimmering dress walked in. She lay her purse on the table and looked coolly at the girls.

One girl giggled, speaking of Ilsa's blue spiked heels, whispered, "How does she stand up in those heels?"

"I don't know," giggled another. "My mother has shoes like that, but she never wears them unless she's going out to a bar or on a date. She said the shoes make her calves burn. She figured she was ruining her feet wearing those spikes. I asked why she wore them. She said, 'Beauty. Men expect beauty.'"

"My name is Ilsa. I am your guide." The girls huddled even closer to each other. "You will listen and do as I tell you. Just so you know, when the evening is over, some of you will be moved to an area where each of you will have your own room and bed, just as you were promised. Some of you will leave."

"Who will leave?" one girl asked.

"It will depend on how well you do tonight. However, I don't have time to discuss it. There are three showers at the back of this building. Each shower holds five girls. After you shower, take the dresses you were given and dress yourselves. Fluff them up so they are presentable. Blow-dry your hair. Make it pretty. I can help you if you need it, and I can show you how to use the makeup you'll find on the counters in the big dressing room. When you're finished, go over to the first building. I will be waiting for you." Ilsa smiled at the girls and pointed them toward the showers.

"What do you think is going to happen to us?" asked one young girl, a blonde whose hair reached down her back.

"You've never been here before?" another girl asked. The girl shook her head.

"Then you're screwed. For sure, you're screwed." The voice came from an older girl in the back of the room. "Take your shower, put on your dress, and then come out here and I'll tell you." Several girls turned, staring at the speaker, waiting for her to say something helpful. Then, like cattle heading for the slaughter, they formed a line to get into the showers.

It was fun for a few minutes. They tried on dresses until every girl wore a dress that made her look beautiful and innocent. Hair brushed to a shine and makeup applied. Black liner applied to eyelids to make the eyes stand out, just as Ilsa had shown them.

Once ready, they reassembled and one girl asked, "Tell me what she means?"

No one was willing to tell her.

"I will tell you," said the oldest of the group. She was tall with long, naturally blonde hair.

"You will go into the dining room. You will eat and drink champagne. A man will choose you, take you to a room and then kiss you. He will give you an expensive gift. React as if you're surprised. If you cry or try to resist, the bottom line is you won't get paid. Remember each of you will make about two-hundred dollars, maybe more. Some will make much more. That's a lot of money for those of us whose families are dirt poor. Over the years I've made thousands of dollars. At least half of it, I'm allowed to send to my family."

A very young Latina girl said, "That doesn't seem too hard."

The voice of an older, sarcastic girl, said, "Ask her if she knows about sex."

"How many of you have never had sex?" the older girl asked.

The youngest girls slowly raised their hands. "I'm afraid," one girl said. "I know nothing about sex other than what I learned in health class."

"If the man who chooses you takes it slow and easy, talks to you and slowly takes your clothes off, it will be easier. If the man who selects you is rough, then he's likely to hurt, you'll probably cry or scream and be very difficult. Remember, you don't get paid if you scream or make trouble."

"What do we do if that happens?" another girl asked.

Ilsa came back into the room and called the girls over to her. She looked them over, pulled down a few skirts, and said, "If you resist there will be consequences. Remember the money. You don't get money if you're a problem. Do not fight," Ilsa said, her voice harsh, not comforting the younger girls.

Several girls began to cry. They clung to each other, sobbing that they wanted to leave. One girl ran to the door only to find it locked.

Older girls stepped in and tried to comfort them, whispering that it's not so bad after the first time.

Ilsa brought the girls back to order. "Look at you. Your mascara has run down your cheeks. Help each other fix your makeup. Later, after we come back together, I want you to come and tell me if any man was abusive. He will never be allowed to come back."

"Why do you have the power to make the man go away," another girl asked.

"I don't have any power," Ilsa said. "I tell the men in charge that a certain man should not be allowed to return." In a softer voice, she said, "I'm leaving the group, so I don't know what will happen next."

"Why are you leaving?" one girl asked.

"Because I'm marrying a man I met a few years back. I've been dating him for about a year. He's a fine man." Ilsa unlocked the door and walked out.

The same sarcastic girl said, "She thinks she'll have a better life. And she probably will. Beats the heck out of waiting to be chosen."

"Does she love him?" a young girl asked.

The girl looked at the group, "It's a way out, it's not a fairy tale. It's time to go back to the main room," she said. "Remember, you may eat the food, but don't become a glutton."

CHAPTER THIRTY-FOUR

"Maggie, are you awake?"

Maggie sat up straight. "Yes. Just a little drowsy." She shook her head to blow away the cobwebs so she could pay attention.

The girl did not respond immediately, then in a whisper she said. "I'll tell you everything. I'll also tell you how to behave when we get wherever we're going."

"You are Dakota?" Maggie asked, shaking her head so she would be alert.

"I am." The girl whispered so softly Maggie could barely hear her.

"What happened that day?"

"Lakota and I were walking towards the river, something we did almost every day after school. We loved to watch the water move. On that day we climbed down through the boulders. We had our backs to the road, when suddenly two men were behind us. To this day I can't figure out why we didn't hear them. One grabbed me and the other man tried to grab Lakota. She had time to try and fight, but the rocks were too big and slippery. When he grabbed her, he cussed her out and pushed her in the river, holding her head under water. I tried to scream, but the guy holding me put a gloved hand over my mouth. I watched Lakota struggle, but I couldn't help her.

The two then dragged me back up through the rocks. This was in broad daylight. One pickup drove by, but I couldn't signal it to stop. They put me in the back seat of a car and told me not to scream. I've carried the guilt of Lakota's death all these years, but I don't know what I could have done to save her, and I've always hoped she might have survived."

Maggie whispered, "You can't hold guilt over something that was not your fault. Give me your hand." She caressed Dakota's hand and said, "I am so sorry for the loss of your sister and all the terrible things that have happened to you, but I want you to try and release these thoughts. I want to hear it all so maybe we can figure out how to fight this."

Maggie could feel Dakota shudder. She wasn't sure Dakota would respond. Maggie said, "We'll use this time in the dark to settle back, hold hands, and you can tell me everything. I'll just listen, but if you need me to discuss something, please say so."

"First," Dakota asked, "please tell me how my mother and father are. I've wanted to call them, but knew that if I did, I'd lose Toby. That's how they keep me in line."

Maggie squeezed her hand. How could she tell Dakota about her father? Maggie took a deep breath and said, "Your father is no longer alive. About a year after your disappearance, he was killed. Your mother thinks he couldn't cope with you two vanishing and him not being able to find out what happened to you or rescue you. He was a broken man."

A sob broke from Dakota's throat. Her head went down between her knees. Maggie grabbed her and held her while she cried.

After a while, Dakota pulled away. Maggie said, "Talk whenever you're ready."

"I want you to ask questions. It will help me remember. My circumstances were different from the girls who were brought in. The owner's youngest son, Cody, liked me, so I only had sex with him. I was raped in the beginning, but now he's actually very kind. Kind, but not good. If he were good, I would have been released years ago. Then we had Toby. His grandfather loves Toby. He and Cody take Toby everywhere. I like Leo, but I don't trust him. Cody's brother, Buddy, his real name is Homer, scares me. I don't like him around Toby, but there's not much I can do about it. The best thing is that Buddy pays little attention to Toby. I suspect there have been words between the brothers and the dad about Toby. I'm sure Buddy calls him an Indian brat." Maggie couldn't see her, but the tone of voice told her Dakota had nothing good to say about Buddy.

"A while back, a couple of priests came to the ranch. One priest was really old. He came out to the barns to look at the horses. Only there weren't any horses, just a bunch of girls. I saw him and he saw us. There were maybe six of us. I didn't say anything, but I know the old man knew we were there. I wished I'd said something, but I didn't. Buddy came out of the tack room and told the old priest to get out and never come back. I was scared Buddy was going to shoot him. The other girls and I talked about it later. I'm always scared that Buddy's going to fly off the handle and injure or kill somebody."

"Buddy told the old priest to leave and never come back. We girls just stood there and gawked. After they left, Buddy, called us to come out in the aisle. He told us to forget we'd ever seen a priest. 'If the priest gets nosy, we'll be forced to take you away,' he said. What he really meant is that we would disappear, be killed."

Maggie inhaled. "The priests are setting up a mission in Bigg's Junction."

"You mean a church?"

"Yes. A small church. They are working with Father Daniel in The Dalles. They're just about ready for parishioners."

"Wow. I didn't know that."

"Probably because they didn't want any girls to ask to go to church. Tell me more about these girls." Maggie said.

"They bring them in to have sex with men who pay a lot to have sex with young girls. Some live here for a couple of months, others are moved out the same day. Badly behaved girls are removed, girls who try to get away disappear. They don't want any girls escaping."

"How are the girls found?" Maggie asked.

"Men like Stud and Peanut find them. They drive all over the country to find beautiful young girls. Some come from around the world. There is constant turn-over, here. They don't want any girl to get away and tell someone at Dinty's what's going on. After they've spent a month or so in one place, they're moved. Most girls are really young. I was thirteen and most of the girls are that age or younger. A few are older, but they usually have the job of keeping the young ones from running away."

"How did you end up with the brother. Wasn't he part of the set-up?"

"No. He never participated or took money and constantly told Buddy and his father that someday they'd get caught."

"Are the girls paid? There must be a motive that keeps them in line."

"Yes. They're paid pretty well. One or two hundred dollars for each time they have sex. Most of the girls are from extreme poverty and want the money. If they don't cause trouble, they're allowed to send money home. But, being allowed to do that takes a long time. They have to show they are not rebellious."

"So, are you saying the girls never try to escape?" Maggie asked.

"Yes, they do, but the rumor gets around pretty fast that's a dumb idea. They know Peanut and Stud will come and get them. I remember a year or so ago, a girl tried to run. She was fast and made it to the river. When they finally caught her, they brought her back and then beat her to death in front of us. She was an example of what happens when you disobey orders. Girls are always making plans to escape, but they seldom get a chance to escape and the thought of being killed helps them stay put."

Maggie felt nauseous. She was glad Dakota couldn't see her face.

Dakota continued. "The really beautiful girls are shown how to dress, eat at a fancy table, and mind their manners. These girls are paid more and eventually some of them are allowed to date a man if he's interested. They get used to the fancy clothes and don't want to give up the lifestyle, even though they're essentially raped at least twice a week. The tragedies mostly occur among the European or South American girls. They have nothing and they don't speak the language. I've held a lot of girls who cry and want to know how to get away."

Maggie leaned her head on Dakota's. "I've listened and there's one question I don't think you've addressed. How did they choose you and Lakota or do you think this was strictly coincidence or do you think you were targeted?"

"In the beginning I thought we were in the wrong place at the wrong time. Now, I think we were targeted without knowing it. A man and woman came through The Dalles, maybe six months, before this happened. They said they were looking for young girls who would be interested in the fashion industry and earning a living as a model. They made it sound very exciting. Big money, lots of beautiful clothes. We talked to our parents, but they weren't very excited. Finally, they said Lakota could go if I or a friend went with her. I didn't care about a modeling career, so I didn't want to go. Lakota said her friend Julia, who was a junior, had been the one who told us about it. My father was dead-set against her going, but finally said Lakota could go with Julia."

"Did anyone else in your group of friends go?" Maggie asked.

"Funny you should ask. No. Julia said no one else was interested. I don't think she talked to anyone else. Julia said she had talked to this group when she lived in San Antonio, Texas. She said she was recruited there, but never did anything because her parents wanted to move out of Texas. She seemed to know quite a bit about the organization. She told Lakota she was going to try out. She said Lakota could go with her. I've often wondered if Julia's parents moved out of Texas to get away from that group. And then they show up here. Julia said her parents never gave permission, but she went anyway."

"Things happened that weren't right?" Maggie gently pried.

"Yes. How did you know?"

"Just a guess. What happened?"

"Lakota told me that each girl would be photographed. I should say this took place in an old theatre that was used for community gatherings. The girls went in one at a time. When they went in the lights were on and then, suddenly, it was pitch black. The photographer kept talking trying to make Lakota feel comfortable, but she was scared and didn't know what to do. Then another man came in and pulled her blouse down to expose her breasts. She wanted to run, but this new guy, was blocking the aisle. When she was finally let go, she ran out and she and Julia left. I asked Lakota if Julia had been photographed. She said yes, but now she was afraid."

"And did Julia or Lakota tell your parents?"

Dakota began sobbing. "When she told me about what happened, I told her to tell our parents, but she wouldn't do it. She was afraid to tell Dad because she thought he would kill the guy and she was embarrassed that she had been so stupid."

"How did the two of you handle this?"

"I went to Julia again and told her that what had happened was illegal. Her eyes got big. I asked if she knew this would happen. She said no, but I didn't believe her. I said that she had better call those people and tell them to leave town or our dad would find them and beat them to death. She said she didn't know their phone number and I said you better find it. I learned later that the next day the two photographers left The Dalles without explanation, so I knew she knew how to get hold of them and warn them. I'm not sure if the Garritys were involved in that, but I've always wondered if that's how we got targeted."

"That must have been tough for you. Did you and Lakota find someone to talk to since you didn't talk to your parents?"

"Father Daniel. I did it during confession so no one could hear. I was so scared, but he put me at ease. After I told him everything, he said he would contact the police and that he would never use my name, only that a group of girls had been drawn into a bad situation that the police needed to know about. I never heard another word, so I assume Father Daniel did as he said he would."

Maggie was quiet for a long time and then she said, "Your parents and Lakota never knew that you had talked to Father Daniel?"

"No. I never told."

Maggie was silent and then changed the subject. "Did you know Stud and Peanut before they took me?"

"Yes and no. Stud works at the ranch. I've only seen Peanut a few times. He usually works with a guy named Jeff."

That information did not surprise Maggie. If they traveled all over the country bringing girls to certain towns, they were never in one place long enough to get to know the locals. "Dakota, do you know where we're going?"

"I think the ranch in Bigg's Junction where I live."

Maggie was surprised. Maybe there's a chance then that she could contact Matthew. "Dakota, tell me again why you think they took me?"

"We just lost the woman who is like the resident babysitter whose job it is to try and keep the girls happy and teach them how to behave. Ilsa was cold as a rock, but she knew her stuff."

Maggie spit out her words. "Keep young girls who are literally chained to a situation happy that they are there? Ridiculous. Somehow, I have to try and reach the three priests in my life, Father Daniel, Father Francesco, and Father Matthews plus Detective Tom Marshall. You and I are going to figure out how to end this living tragedy."

"I will do anything you say. Oh, Maggie, do you think we can find a way out? Remember, I won't leave without Toby."

"We are sure going to try. And we'll find a way to contact your mother. Not sure how we'll do this, so please don't push me, but know she's at the top of the list." Maggie squeezed her hand. "Thanks, Dakota, for being strong. We'll do this together." Maggie pulled Dakota to her and gave her a big hug. "Remember, you need to keep me informed whenever you see something. Also, know, that I am capable of logger language."

"What's logger language?" Dakota asked.

"Swearing, when it's needed," Maggie laughed.

Dakota giggled. "I know lots of logger language. My dad and Tiny are grand champion logger language users. Tiny's mom was always getting after him. She'd say to us, 'You remind him that swearing in front of girls is not appropriate.' We'd laugh and shake our heads and tell her he never swore around Sasha or us, but we knew she didn't believe us."

"One more question," Maggie said. "Why are you in the van? Why weren't you home with Toby? I haven't put that together."

"I'm in the van to make any girls they pick up less afraid and more comfortable. But you were different. You didn't seem to be afraid, so I decided to keep quiet until I could figure you out. I've gone to a lot of auctions and other events like rodeos, with big crowds. No one sees me."

"This gets more awful by the minute."

"I know, and I'm scared, Maggie."

Maggie grabbed Dakota and held her close. "So am I. So am I."

CHAPTER THIRTY-FIVE

The two men waited and watched as the minutes passed without incident. Finally, Black Hawk turned to Jasper and whispered, "Much as I would like to see what happens next, it's getting along towards midnight and I have to leave. I work here tomorrow."

"That oughtta be interesting! What are you doin'?"

"Tomorrow I clean the flower beds and mow the pasture, and there'll be trash to haul. I'll keep my eyes and ears open but won't talk to anyone unless spoken to."

"I'm stayin'," Jasper said. "You be careful walking back."

"It's you who needs to be careful. Don't get so close they can smell you." He chuckled and began to inch backwards, around the berm.

The words had no more slipped off Black Hawk's tongue than a ten-seat limo pulled up to the last barn. The driver got out, walked around the car, and opened doors while the riders disembarked. All the passengers were men wearing black tuxedos. They were ushered into the building. Then the doors shut.

Black Hawk crawled back over to Jasper. "Put your head down, you can be seen," Jasper hissed. "Anybody looking our way can see you."

"What's going on now?" Black Hawk whispered.

"Beats me," Jasper replied.

They continued watching. A few minutes later two more limousines pulled up. At least twenty more tuxedoed men entered the barn.

"Shit," said Jasper. "You better go home. I'll stay here and see if I can figure out what's happening. You and I both know what's happening; we just have to provide enough information so Tom Marshall can prove it."

Black Hawk began to inch backward, off the berm. "Hell, I'd better get a little blood circulating here," Jasper said as he inched back down the berm himself. Out of sight from the barns, he walked around and did a few calisthenics to limber up his old bones. That's why he didn't see a white van drive into the driveway and around to the far side of the house, park, and disembark a young Native woman.

In pre-dawn hours, Jasper, who had scrambled back to the top of the berm to catch a nap, was suddenly awakened by a car in the drive. He sat up, looked at his watch to note the time as 4:00 a.m. He pulled the borrowed binoculars from his pack and looked at the car. A black limo. He couldn't tell if it was the same driver as before. The driver entered the last building. Within minutes Jasper saw the lady in blue exit the building. Several men followed her. At first, she and the men seemed to be talking, then each man handed her an envelope. She smiled and moved away. In minutes, another limo drove up. Several men exited and did the same as those before. Each handed her a white envelope and then got into the car and left. The process was repeated a third time.

While Jasper waited, two men came out from the ranch house and walked towards the big barn. He watched Buddy Garrity and the man Black Hawk identified as a mean cop talking in what seemed to be friendly manner. He watched Buddy Garrity extend a manila folder towards the woman in blue. She took the envelope, then stuffed all the white envelopes inside and handed the envelope back. They hugged, and she got into the limo and drove away.

The two men remained outside, talking. Soon the bus pulled in. The cop pulled out a clip board.

Jasper watched as a number of the younger girls walked out and boarded the bus. Each girl spoke to the men, probably giving her name.

Then the bus drove off and the lights started turning off.

"What the hell is going on?" Jasper whispered to the air. Then he shook his head back and forth and whispered, "You know what's going on, old man. What we got here is a cat house using underage girls." After the bus left and the two men walked back to the ranch house, Jasper scooted down the berm and noiselessly walked back home. He really needed to talk to Matthew.

"Are you home yet?" Jasper spat into the phone. Matthew did not answer, so he left a message. "We got to talk." He dialed Black Hawk's number. "Sorry to call so early. I just got home. It was pretty quiet after you left. The limos came back for the men about 4:30 and a little later a bus came for some of the girls. A lot of the girls are still there. Pay really close attention when you're over there tomorrow, especially to the garbage. I suspect the garbage will tell us a lot about what's going on."

"Have you talked to Matthew?" Black Hawk asked.

"I called, but he didn't answer. I left a message."

"Did you call his mobile phone?"

"Consarned new contraptions," Jasper spat. "I never got his number and you can't get 'em out of the phone book. You have it?"

"Nope. Never thought I'd need it."

Jasper sighed. "He'll call when he gets home or gets up."

CHAPTER THIRTY-SIX

Jasper's mind was in full speed motion as he paced back and forth in front of his cottage. He knew he had to talk to someone besides Black Hawk about what he had seen. The phone sat silent. Matthew hadn't returned his call. Matthew had told him to call Detective Tom. But crap. Detective Tom wouldn't be in the office before eight.

He went back in his cottage and grabbed the phone, talking to himself while shoveling papers off his table. Then he sat in his armchair, talking to himself to stay awake, waiting for 8:00. At 7:30, he could wait no longer. "Where's the blasted phone book?" Finding it, he called the The Dalles police.

A woman answered and he shouted into the phone. "I want to talk to Detective Marshall. Is he there?"

"He is, may I ask whose calling?"

Still shouting, he said, "This here's Jasper and I got news. Get him on the phone."

"I am transferring your call, sir," she stiffly said.

"This is Tom Marshall, Jasper. What's going on?"

"Well, Black Hawk and me spent last night out behind Garrity's barn. We seen a bus full of young girls drive in, followed a little later by three big limos full of men all duded up in tuxedoes. Now what do you think that means? I think it means illegal sex."

Avoiding the direct question, Tom asked, "Did you see Maggie?"

"I did not. But me and Black Hawk think there's no coincidence between a bus full of young girls showing up, and then a bunch of men."

"How were the girls dressed?" Tom asked

"Jeans and shirts. But they all carried suitcases. One woman showed up in a shiny dress. When she left, maybe five hours later, she collected an envelope from each man. Then she gave those envelopes to Buddy Garrity. When the girls left in the bus, there weren't as many girls leaving as came. And, you know what else?"

"No. I don't know," replied Tom.

"A cop—Black Hawk says his name's Art Camden—was there. He showed up with the lady in the blue dress, and he was there when she left."

"And, when was that, Jasper?"

"Around nine last evening is when we got there. Twern't dark yet. The bus and the limos started arriving after eleven and they left after four in the morning."

"Did you recognize anyone besides Buddy Garrity and Art Camden?"

"Nah, just those two. Oh yeah, Cody Garrity took a lot of food into one of the barns earlier. 'Party Time Catering' delivered it. Then he opened the barn door for the girls when they got there."

"Thanks, Jasper, I don't want you over there again. I don't want you involved. You've given me information that the police need to follow up."

The look on Jasper's face clearly stated, *If he thinks I'm just waitin' around for him to do something, he's mistaken. I'll still go over at night. I just won't get caught.*

"Jasper. Did you hear me?"

"Yeah, yeah. I heard you."

CHAPTER THIRTY-SEVEN

Maggie and Dakota had felt the van slow down and make a slow left-hand turn. The quarter-mile drive was only slightly bumpy. Maggie said, "If anything happens to me, because I will refuse to allow anyone to rape me, try and get word to Matthew at the old auto repair shop, now turned into a mission."

The van stopped and sat for several minutes, no one opened the door. Maggie held the tire iron close by her side. When the door slid open, Maggie could see it was dark. Dakota's name was called. She crawled to the door where she was helped out. No attempt was made to bring Maggie out. The door closed leaving Maggie alone in the dark. Please don't let me die now. I love you Matthew. What a life we have planned.

Maggie could hear the sound of male voices retreating, but she couldn't understand what was being said. The voices faded. She sat for another hour, cold and hungry. With no sign of activity outside the van, she tried to open the sliding door, to no avail. The mechanism had been altered to allow no one to escape. By the time she gave up, the pain in her wrist was bringing on waves of nausea and she knew she had to rest. She lay on the floor beside the tire iron and concentrated on easing the pain. She finally dozed off, wondering if her fate would be to die in this van in the dark, without food or water.

A sound woke her. In a daze of pain and awareness, she sat up and felt for the tire iron. Then the door slowly opened, letting in morning light which momentarily blinded her, but not before she saw Peanut unhurriedly step up and into the van. Then it was dark again, except for a little slit of light coming through the not-quite-closed door. She could hear him unzip his pants.

"What do you want with me?" she asked.

"Well, sweetheart, I'm here to test the merchandise, make sure you're ready for the boys."

"I'm warning you, Peanut, don't touch me."

"Now how you plan to stop me?" He coughed a laugh. On his knees, he scooted across the van. He reached out his hand and touched her leg.

"I'm warning you, do not put a hand on me." With her good arm, Maggie swung the tire iron in a vicious circle, striking Peanut just below his shoulder. He bellowed and lunged towards her.

"You fuckin' bitch. You ain't going to see tomorrow." He dropped on top of her, trying to hold her down and squeeze her throat, but his injured shoulder wouldn't cooperate.

Maggie swung again, this time hitting him hard on the side of the head. She heard the crack and felt him collapse onto her body. She struggled to push him away, desperately trying to get her feet under him so she could push him off her body. *God, what have I done?* She scrambled towards the door and stumbled out, the tire iron still in her hand. Her feet on the ground, she looked around and then started running down the driveway towards the highway. *Matthew, please hear me.*

She heard feet running behind her. Two sets of hands grabbed her. She tried to swing the tire iron, but both men stepped aside, still holding her arms. She saw that one was Stud, but she didn't recognize the other. Maggie fought them with all the energy she had. She knew she couldn't keep swinging. She was getting tired, knew she was overpowered, and was consumed by the pain coming from her injured wrist, but she didn't want to give in. They dragged her between them back to the house. Her toes burned from the dry earth and gravel. They stood her at the bottom of the porch steps and waited for the door to open. It was then she noticed the sun was high. She had slept a long time in the dark van.

Leo Garrity pushed the door open and stepped out, followed by a young man she recognized as Toby's father, Cody. Leo stood at the top of the stairs and gazed down at Maggie.

"What's going on?" he asked the two men.

"She killed him boss. He couldn't keep his pants zipped and she had a tire iron and whacked him."

A shadow of regret crossed Leo Garrity's face that caused Maggie to feel she may have nothing to fear from him. "You certainly have caused us a lot of trouble, young lady. Why did you kill Peanut? You have left us with a mess to clean up."

"The bastard tried to rape me." She spat the words out. "And, you'll clean it up because you don't want the sheriff out here looking around."

Leo Garrity looked hard at her, obviously trying to decide her fate. In all his years, he'd only known one other woman to defy him using that same language. She was the mother of his two boys. He had married her.

Maggie, attempting to pull away from the two men holding her, yelled, "What do you want with me?" She wanted him to admit what Dakota had told her, that he wanted her to oversee trafficked girls. "Answer that. How will you answer in a manner that doesn't give away what I know you do?" Still, Leo Garrity did not respond.

"What do you want us to do about Peanut's body, Dad? And what do you want us to do with this bitch?" He punched her shoulder with his free hand. "I think she should be buried with Peanut." Buddy Garrity laughed, amused by his own depraved sense of humor.

So this was the elder son, Maggie thought, and every bit as vile as Dakota had described him. She willed herself not to react, to show fear.

"You take care of Peanut, Stud. Out back, in the field. Buddy, you can take care of the woman," Leo Garrity said. "But she is not to be harmed. For now, anyway."

"What, no coroner?" Maggie sneered. She knew she was pushing too hard, but she didn't want to give an inch. She wasn't shocked when the elder son dropped her arm and slapped her hard across her face, but her rage grew as she held her face. The pain was agonizing. Another time, she thought. She remembered what Dakota had said: the older brother was as mean and crazy as Peanut.

"Now you listen, bitch," Buddy said. "You do as you're told or you'll end up in the same hole screwing Peanut."

"That's enough, Buddy. Take her out to the barn. We'll let her cool off before we put her to work." Leo Garrity turned and went back in the house. "Make sure she knows what will happen if she doesn't cooperate," he said as he disappeared through the door. Maggie almost felt he was sending her a message.

Cody, walking to Maggie and taking her arm, said, "I'll take her, Buddy. Give me a chance to talk to Dakota and see how she is and what she knows."

"Don't let this one get away with anything, brother. I don't want to have to clean up after you, too."

Cody glared at him.

"No, brother. On second thought, me and Stud will take her. I don't trust you, Indian lover."

CHAPTER THIRTY-EIGHT

A fter he talked to Tom Marshall, Jasper dialed Matthew's land line again. "Pick up," he mumbled. "Guess I'll have to drive down to the church."

Ten minutes later Jasper was at the church. No pickup. No people. "Where are you guys?" he asked aloud. He started to turn around in the lot when an SUV drove up, stopped, and a red-headed man got out.

"Who are you?" Jasper asked as he jumped out of his truck. "You her brother?"

"I am."

"Thought so. All that curly red hair gave you away."

"Who are you?"

"I'm Jasper, Matthew and Maggie's friend."

"Do you know what's going on? Matthew called to tell me to come ASAP because my sister is in trouble."

"All I really know is that Maggie was kidnapped at a mustang auction down in southern Oregon. I've been spying on my neighbor's ranch. I don't know that what I saw is related to Maggie, but I 'spect it might be."

"What did you see?" Lucas asked. Jasper told him about what he'd seen at the ranch. Lucas listened without interruption. "Thanks, Jasper. Do you know what we should be doing?"

"I don't know. Matthew and Francesco should be home by now. I already called the detective in The Dalles."

"Is there a phone in here? Let's give them a call and find out where they are." It didn't take long to find a window with a loose screen and the window creaked open on newly-cleaned runners. Lucas gave Jasper a leg up, and within seconds Jasper was opening the main door.

Lucas found the phone and dialed Matthew's number. "Where are you, brother?"

"About fifteen miles out. We've spent the night driving the back roads looking for Maggie."

"I'm here with Jasper who's filled me in on last night's events, but no sight of Maggie."

"We'll talk as soon as we get there. We're both starving, so let's plan to meet at Dinty's. Bring Jasper and tell him to call Tiny."

CHAPTER THIRTY-NINE

When Matthew and Francesco climbed down from the truck, Lucas met them with hugs.

"My God, you look like a doctor," Francesco said.

"Is there a way doctors are supposed to look?" Lucas asked, trying to downplay his pleasure with his status as a first-year resident. "What's going on?"

"Let's go in and order. We're starved. Haven't eaten anything but fast food for two days," Francesco said, opening the door to Dinty's Café.

Once seated, Matthew related the full story as best he knew it, Jasper adding what he'd seen at the Garrity ranch.

"The truth is, Lucas, we don't have any idea where Maggie is. We know she's with a young woman, probably a Native American girl, but that's the sum total of what we factually know." He looked at Jasper. "Can you add anything to what you already told us?"

Jasper said, "No, except I saw a cop go in and out of the house. It's the same cop that gave Tiny and the Native guys a bad time when the twins disappeared."

"What twins?" Lucas asked.

At that moment Tiny came through the door and sat down. He rested his bare arms on the table. Lucas looked at his biceps and instantly decided he wanted to be on the same team as this guy.

"Tiny, this is Lucas, Maggie's brother," Matthew said, nodding his head towards Lucas. Lucas nodded, acknowledging the introduction. "Why don't you explain to Lucas about the twins and what you think happened."

"About five years ago," Tiny said, "thirteen-year-old twin girls disappeared. Native girls. Father Francesco found the bones of one twin. I believe I've seen the other twin alive. I also think the girl traveling with Maggie may be that girl."

"Jasper, tell us more about what you and Black Hawk saw," Matthew said.

Jasper sat up and looked from one to the other and related the story of what he saw. "And guess what else? Art Camden was there."

"Art Camden? Are you sure?" Tiny asked.

"Yup," Jasper said.

"I have an idea," Lucas said, standing up and beginning to pace. "Would it be out of order for all of us to drive by this guy's house? I'd like to see all the places that apply to this situation."

"Good idea," Matthew said. "Let's eat and get going."

"By the way, who's Art Camden?" Francesco asked Tiny.

"He's the cop who us such a bad time when the twins disappeared. He threatened me and other Native guys with arrest. He said we killed the girls. I admit, I don't like or trust the man." Tiny shifted in his seat, his jaw set. Everyone could see that he was ready to explode. "I don't know what happened to him, but suddenly he was no longer on the police force."

"Do you think we can talk to the detective about him?" Lucas asked

"Sure," said Tiny, "but I don't know if they'll tell us anything. I'll get some of my friends to keep an eye out for him. We can drive by his house and see if he's still there. If it looks like he still lives there, I'll get some friends to keep track of his comings and goings. These guys know how to be careful."

"Eat up, gents. We have work to do," Jasper said, as a stack of buttermilks and bacon was set in front of him.

"Indeed we do," Francesco agreed. "But I'm afraid you will have to do it without me. I won't be able to keep my eyes open. Could you take me home after we eat?"

"Of course, Father," said Matthew softly. The old man hadn't closed his eyes for over twenty-four hours and Matthew could see he was spent.

Everyone piled in Lucas's SUV. A tight squeeze, but no one complained. They dropped Francesco off at his bungalow and then drove west along the freeway until they arrived at The Dalles. Tiny told Lucas to pull off at the first exit. "Camden lives up above the water tank on about ten acres." They could see the water tank in the distance. "I think his street is Sprague. Turn left when you get there."

The house was old and small. The yard was well maintained. No flowers, but the lawn was mowed and it looked neat. Someone obviously lived there.

"I don't see his car," Tiny said. "Should someone go to the door?"

"No. Not a good idea," Matthew said. "If he's there, we don't want him to see the car or us."

"I agree," Tiny said. "I'll get some guys on it."

Back in Biggs Junction, Tiny picked up his truck at the café and drove to the converted garage to join the others. "Can I use the phone?" he asked.

Tiny dialed a friend. "I'll talk to you in an hour or so. Get all our buddies together. We have work to do. These are your instructions." Tiny related instructions. "Don't let Camden see you. Thanks." He hung up, and said, "There will be four or five guys on it."

CHAPTER FORTY

D akota tried to scream as she watched Stud and Buddy drag Maggie to the second barn, but Cody got to her in time to stop her. Neither spoke, as they watched Buddy push Maggie through the door. "Where will he put her?" Dakota hissed through her fury as Cody kept her from running to Maggie.

"He'll lock her up in the back room," Cody said.

"The room with the triple bolt system?" Dakota asked. "It will be impossible to break her out of that room without a ramming bar and a chain saw. You can't let this happen."

Cody didn't respond. It was obvious he wanted to hold her and comfort her, but if he did, Buddy would shoot them both.

Once Maggie was securely locked in, Buddy left to join his father and go to meet with Art Camden. He sneered as he passed his brother standing with Dakota outside the barn.

Maggie rubbed her broken wrist and thought about what had happened. *What have I done? Murder? It was self-defense, but the Garritys would say it was deliberate. How did I get myself into this mess? What about Dakota? What will happen to her? She'll probably be okay, but who knows? Buddy is a sociopath. Was there any sign of girls? No. What does Cody really know?* Rubbing her bruised arm and wrist didn't help a bit. It hurt worse than ever.

Cody took Dakota inside the barn.

"Dakota," he said, "I know this isn't very romantic, but these are not romantic times. I love you. Marry me."

Dakota, stunned, reached out her hand and touched his arm. She'd waited years for him to say this to her. Why now? would be the obvious question. "Where's Toby?" she asked.

"He's in the house. I told him I'd be right back. I wouldn't let him go to The Dalles with Dad and Buddy."

"Can you bring him out?" she asked.

"I can't right now. Dakota, no time. Believe me, he's okay."

Dakota looked straight at Cody. "You saw how Buddy treated Maggie, and there is no way we can open that door and get her out. One more thing. I don't know what's going on, but Maggie was kidnapped and I was with her. And you want to marry? It seems out of place. What's going on, Cody? Can you give me any idea about why Maggie was kidnapped and why you suddenly want to marry me?"

Cody grabbed her hands and held them to his cheek. "Dakota, I have a gut feeling that the bottom of Buddy's big money-maker is about to collapse. They don't share much with me, because they're about half afraid I'll go to the police. Toby is the reason you and I are still here and alive. Dad would kill Buddy with his bare hands if anything happened to Toby. I want you and Toby off this ranch. I'm sorry about Maggie. I'll feel guilty about leaving her. I don't have a key to let her out, so we have to marry fast and figure out an escape."

"Can we talk to her through the door?" Dakota asked. "Or is it too thick?"

They walked to the locked door. Cody said, "Can you hear me, Maggie?"

Maggie said, "Yes."

Cody explained what he intended to do. "I will help you," Maggie said, though she didn't know why. Right now, she didn't trust anybody, but Dakota was part of the plan and she wanted the best for her. "There are two priests down at the junction working on a mission church. They're probably gone now, but our house is the first exit off the freeway, heading east. Then it's the first right off the exit road, a long driveway. If you can smuggle the old priest up here, he'll marry you. I can't act as a witness, so you will have to ask Francesco to take care of the paperwork and get somebody else to witness."

Cody turned to Dakota, "I have always loved you, Dakota. I could never get dad to allow us to marry. I will go talk to the priest and explain what needs to happen."

"How do we get around the fourteen-day waiting period to marry?" Dakota asked.

"Francesco will know how to handle it," Maggie said.

"Dakota, how much does Maggie know about what goes on here?" Cody asked. "And, please tell the truth."

"Everything."

"Does she know why she was abducted?"

"No. I didn't know for sure why she was taken. She doesn't fit the type of girls usually brought here."

Cody said, through the door, "My brother wishes you no harm which, I'm sure, you don't believe. He wants you to teach the girls proper etiquette."

Maggie snapped, "Don't kid yourself, Cody. He'll kill all of us, if given half a chance. Please take care of Francesco. You must tell him I'm here, so he can notify Matthew and the police. Can you do this before Buddy and your dad get back?"

Cody left without answering. "Wait for me in the party barn," he said to Dakota. *What am I doing?* he said under his breath. He went to the house and asked Toby if he'd like to go to the store with him. Toby jumped up and down. "Let's go, Dad." He bounded through the door, still jumping.

"We have to be fast," Cody said to Toby, "before Grandpa gets get back."

Climbing into the truck, Toby asked, "Where we going, Dad?"

"To Dinty's."

"To Dinty's? Can I get an ice cream cone?"

"You bet, but we're going to get a gallon of your mom's favorite ice cream. We're going to have a party."

"A party. Wow. I like parties. Let's do it." He said, pounding his fists on the truck seat.

In minutes Cody went into Dinty's, leaving Toby in the truck. "I'll be back in a minute." Toby didn't argue. He could see his Dad ordering a big bucket of ice cream. When Cody got back in the truck, he handed the bag to Toby, then drove down to the freeway, turning right and covering two miles in less than two minutes. He turned up the hill onto the long driveway and into the small circular drive. The house appeared empty, he saw a cottage behind the house. Cody hoped Francesco lived there. He got out of the truck and walked to the door. He knocked and waited. When it opened, he saw an elderly man who looked like he had just wakened. "Are you Father Francesco?" he asked.

"I am. How may I help you?"

"I'd like you to come and perform a marriage."

"For whom?"

"For me and my girlfriend. I know there is a three-day waiting period, but it's very important to us that we are married now. Maggie said you would help."

"Maggie? Let me get my vestment and book and I'll be right out."

When Francesco got into the truck, he saw Toby and knew exactly where they were going. "I believe your name is Toby. Am I right? You threw rocks at me one day when I was passing by."

"Toby, did you throw rock at this man?"

Toby wiggled down into his seat. "Yeah, Dad. I was showing him that someday I would be a famous baseball player."

"That's true," Francesco said, smiling down at Toby.

Toby beamed.

When they arrived back at the ranch, Cody pulled up to the first barn, got out and helped Toby out of the truck. Francesco got out and waited for instructions.

"This way, Father."

They walked into the barn which was strangely and ornately decorated. There stood a beautiful young Native American woman. "Where's Maggie?" Francesco asked.

Cody answered. "Unfortunately, she's locked in a room that we can't get into. This is Dakota, Toby's mother. I feel like she's waited long enough for me to ask her to marry me." He turned to Dakota. "By the way, you look stunning. Peach is definitely your color. Pretty fast change."

Dakota smiled. "As soon as we're married," she said to Francesco, "We'll take you to her so you can speak to her. I want you to know for yourself she's okay so you can tell Matthew and the sheriff. They need to rescue her."

Toby jumped up and down. "Hurry up. I want ice cream. It's your favorite, Mom. Deluxe Rocky Road."

"And, Father, could you hurry up?" Cody asked. "Please. It's important. Is there such a thing as a short version?"

Francesco did a modified version of the marriage rites. Dakota and Cody stood hand in hand. When Francesco pronounced them man and wife, Toby jumped up and down. "Ice cream. Ice cream."

Francesco pulled some papers from his bag and asked the newlyweds to sign them. "I will find witnesses."

Bowls for ice cream came out and were filled. Cody ate a few bites and then said, "I will take you to Maggie, but we must hurry." To Dakota, he said, "I'll take Francesco home, and I'll be right back." He and Francesco left the new bride with her son who was happily shoveling down Deluxe Rocky Road ice cream.

Cody said to Francesco, "Thanks for understanding. This was a very private wedding. Please don't talk about this to anyone."

"As you wish. I will wait a few days before I find two witnesses and register the marriage."

"Thanks, Father." They entered the second barn and walked the length to the door of the back room. "Maggie's here." Cody explained about how only Buddy Garrity could unlock the triple door locks.

"Maggie?"

"Francesco. Is that you?"

"It is. I can't open the door, but I want you to know I'll call the police as soon as I get back home and talk to Matthew. He is scared he will never see you again."

"Francesco, please tell him I love him and will figure a way to get out of here."

Francesco said, "I will," as Cody pulled his sleeve to get him to leave.

They hurried to the pickup. Cody drove away, with Toby waving at Francesco from the party barn door.

Francesco walked to the big house and knocked on the door. Matthew, having just returned from The Dalles and hoping to get a few minutes of sleep, answered.

"I just performed a marriage at the Garrity ranch. The youngest son married Dakota. Maggie is there, but she is locked up in a room. Like a prison. Triple locks, and Buddy Garrity is the only one with the keys. I never saw her, but I told her you'd be calling the police. Let's call Tiny and ask him to meet us at your house. I'll tell all. I promised not to tell a soul about what I just did, but you I trust," he said with a smile on his face.

Matthew dialed Tiny. "Tiny, can you come to my house ASAP? There's news." Matthew called out to Lucas and they went outside to wait. Lucas could see Matthew mulling over something in his mind.

"Oh, we may as well have the whole team," Matthew said, and he went inside to call Jasper.

CHAPTER FORTY-ONE

Tiny arrived at the house fifteen minutes later, with Jasper close behind. "What's up?" Tiny asked as they all trooped inside the house. Then turning to Matthew, he said, "What's going on?"

Francesco started to answer, but Tiny said, "How does Francesco know what's going on? He's supposed to be asleep."

Francesco spoke up in his preacher's voice. "Because I just married the younger Garrity son to Dakota. Maggie is locked up in one of the barns."

"Huh?" Tiny's eyes flew open. "Is Maggie all right?" he asked.

"Maggie and Dakota both say she's fine, but there's no way to know. I talked to Maggie long enough to know she's all right for now," Francesco responded. "We have to believe Dakota."

"I believe you, but how do we get her out of there?" Matthew asked.

"I know you probably want a military style assault," Francesco said, "but that might get her killed and we don't have trained fighters. We need to listen to Tom Marshall. He can bring together an assault plan that has been thought through. No mistakes. Call him now."

Matthew growled, his arms pushing on the table. The others looked at him, feeling his pain, but not knowing how to help him. "That'll take days." He picked up the phone and called Tom Marshall. No answer, so he left a message. Matthew said, "So Maggie's locked up in the second building from the road. Locked, as in triple locks, and the only keys are Buddy's."

Trying to make Matthew feel better, Jasper said, "Matthew, you and me can take another look from the berm. Maybe tonight. Whenever you're ready."

"Thanks, Jasper. We'll do that." Matthew sank back into silence, then said, "Listen, Francesco has been in the barns. He knows where she is. We can go get her."

"Come on, Matthew. You know we'd be cut down before we got two steps up the driveway. We have to go talk to Tom Marshall," Jasper said. "He'll bring in the FBI."

They got to The Dalles before noon. Five rag-tag men asked for Detective Marshall.

"May I ask the nature of your business?" the receptionist asked.

"We have information about someone the police are searching for. Her name is Maggie Callahan," Matthew said, remaining calm.

"Thank you. I'll tell him you're here."

Moments later Tom came out. "I just picked up your message," he said. "What's the news?" he asked as he herded them back to his office. He pulled out folding chairs and motioned for them to sit.

"Maggie's at the Garrity ranch and the girl who was with her in the van is Dakota. Father Francesco was asked to go out to the ranch to marry Dakota and the youngest son, Cody. They said Maggie is locked up," Matthew explained.

Tom sat up straight, his gaze intense. "Francesco, tell me everything that happened. Where are they? Can you tell me anything that could help a recovery? Do you know where she's locked up?"

Francesco leaned forward in his chair. "I spoke to her, but all I can tell you is she's in the second building from the road. She's in a room so tightly locked, that only Buddy has the keys. It's like a prison. I heard her voice, but never saw her. Dakota said she's all right."

Changing the subject, Tom asked. "No other family members other than their son, Toby, in attendance for the marriage?"

"No. Cody said the rest were due back at any moment. He wanted this wedding to happen before they got back. He emphasized 'now' many times. Toby waited for ice cream while I conducted a very short wedding. Cody was antsy the entire time. He kept shifting feet. He was nervous, but not about getting married. I think he's worried about the safety of Dakota and the little boy. He and Dakota said their vows. That's about it."

"They didn't meet the fourteen-day requirement?"

"No, I'll take care of it later." Francesco looked directly at the officer when he said it. "Tiny and Sasha will be witnesses."

"What happens now?" Matthew asked. "How do we go in and get her out?"

"Matthew, there is no we," Tom Marshall said. "I'll call the FBI. There's a kidnapping involved and who knows what other crimes have been committed. I will be in charge of gathering a team to go after her."

"Remember," Jasper said. "Me and Black Hawk watched the ranch last night. About eleven, a big bus rolls in and unloads a bunch of very young girls. Then at midnight, there were limos with guys in tuxes comin' in. And, guess who else was there? No guess? Art Camden. I never got close enough to listen to what was said, but it was him acting like he was in charge."

Detective Marshall sat very still. Five sets of eyes stared at him, waiting for an answer. "Art Camden? That is news." He'd told Jasper to stay away from the ranch, but he didn't say a word because this was information he would not otherwise have.

Tom got up and put his hand out to shake each man's hand. "Thanks. I'll get back to you as soon as I put things together. I'll do it as quickly as I can."

They all felt like they had been dismissed. Matthew left first. His head swirling. "Why can't I just go get her?" he asked of no one in general.

Everyone trailed behind him. "I know what yer a-thinkin," Jasper said, "but you can't go get her by yerself. Let Tom Marshall do his job."

"When will he get around to it? Next week? Next year?"

Reading Matthew's mind, Francesco said, "It's going to be tough keeping you busy and out of trouble." Francesco didn't smile.

Back in his office, Tom Marshall was calling the FBI field commander in Portland.

CHAPTER FORTY-TWO

Father Daniel and Gabriella were outside the church working in the gardens. Gabriella lifted her head when the SUV drove in. She fairly flew to the two priests but stopped short when two more men got out and Maggie didn't. "Where's Maggie?" she asked.

Matthew, struggling with what to say, answered, "We have some terrible news that we hoped not to share until we had more information."

Father Daniel lay down his hand hoe, got up from the ground, and walked over to the four men. "What's happened?" he asked.

"Maggie was kidnapped at the mustang auction," Francesco said.

Gabriella screamed and fell to the ground, sobbing "How?" she wailed. "Why Maggie?"

"She was out by the baby horses. Two men put her in a white van and took her away. A little boy saw it happen and told his father. The young boy described Maggie perfectly." Francesco said. "We know where she is now, and she's okay, but we can't get to her."

"Father Daniel, may Gabriella stay with you a few more days?" asked Matthew.

"No. please. I want to help. Maggie's my other mother," she pleaded between sobs.

Matthew helped her up and held her. "Gabriella, we have to find out more before we can figure out how to help her."

"How about the police? Can't they go get her?" she asked.

"They're already involved," Matthew explained. "We have to be careful not to put her in more danger. I promise you we'll do everything we can to rescue her. Now, let me introduce you to Maggie's brother, Lucas. He's here to help."

Gabriella stood up, and through tear-stained eyes, held out her hand to Lucas who gently shook it, even as she clung to Matthew. "Hi," she whispered. "You have hair just like hers."

"Now, will you please stay with Father Daniel? I'll keep in touch so you and Father Daniel know what's happening," Father Francesco promised. "I want you safe."

"All right, but I don't like it."

CHAPTER FORTY-THREE

"Why the hurry to get married?" Maggie could tell Cody didn't want to answer the question. He and Dakota had come to the locked room, knocked softly, and asked how she was doing. Maggie responded, "How do you think I'm doing? I don't want to be here, and I don't understand why you can't do something about it."

"I'm so sorry, but I need to tell you something. Tonight they're bringing six new girls in and two nights from now, another busload of girls comes in. Buddy believes there may be cops snooping around. Not necessarily here, but around town. He and Art Camden talked about it. They think that you might be known in the community. Buddy doesn't want his lucrative business to end, but he's afraid someone out there knows about it."

"That doesn't really answer my question. Why the hurry to marry?"

"I love Dakota. I've tried for years to get my dad to agree to letting us get married."

"You have?" Dakota asked, "Why didn't you tell me?"

"I was afraid Buddy would have you murdered. He probably would have if it weren't for Dad. If this whole dirty business is about to turn ugly, I want to be able to take you and Toby away from here. I know Dad will understand. He loves Toby and wants you two to be safe."

"What about Maggie?" Dakota asked, her voice harsh.

"Maggie, I'll try to save you, too," Cody said. "But Dakota and my son are first priority right now."

"Tell me about the girls who arrive tonight. How do they fit into this picture?" Maggie asked. "And what about men? And what about a busload of girls coming in two days? Is there a way to contact them and tell them the evening has been canceled?"

"First of all, no men tonight. This is a test to see how you do with the girls. Buddy and Art know how they want this handled, but they aren't about to tell me. I'm the black sheep. I've refused to take any money, but I also know that if I rat them out, they'll kill all four of us."

"Oh," said Dakota. Fear in her eyes.

"Not good choices," Maggie agreed.

"Yeah, I know. I don't have many choices. I could keep Toby with me and risk Buddy shooting him if something went sideways, or I could leave him in the barn with Dakota and she could hide him. Neither choice looks easy. What I want to do is get my family out of here. Something is going to happen, and when it does, they need to be someplace safe."

"Let me think about this," Maggie said. "But in the meantime we have to find a way to get word to the outside world. Cody, can you call my husband?"

"Not a good idea," Cody answered. "The house has ears, and I'm pretty sure Buddy has a wiretap on the landline. Probably listening in on my radio phone, too."

"How about going into town?"

"I'm not leaving Dakota and Toby, and they never let us leave the ranch together. We wouldn't make it out of the driveway."

"We'll have to think of something else," Maggie said.

Just then, Dakota shouted, "I see Black Hawk's truck! Cody, we can trust Black Hawk, I know it. I'll go—he'll know me, and I can talk to him. Maggie, what do I need to tell him?"

Black Hawk saw a young woman in the shadow of the barn nearest the compost pile where he was dumping grass clippings. She appeared to be motioning him to him, so he walked towards her. He couldn't believe his eyes. "Dakota? Is that really you?" He stepped forward to hug her but backed off, in case he was seeing things.

Dakota smiled. "Hi, Black Hawk. Yes, I'm Dakota. I'm sorry, but I have to make this quick."

"What's going on?" he asked, recognizing the urgency in her voice.

"Listen, Black Hawk, when you're away from this place, find Maggie's husband, Matthew, and tell him to call the police and tell them there will be a bus load of girls arriving in two days around eleven p.m. The men will show up around midnight. There are also six girls coming in tonight. Tell him Maggie is here and she's okay, but she's locked up and Buddy Garrity checks up on her often. And don't tell anyone but Matthew. He'll know what to do. Now go." Dakota turned away, ran to the barn door, and disappeared inside.

Black Hawk got the message. It took him twenty minutes to finish his work. The drive to the mission took five.

Matthew's truck was parked out front. Black Hawk parked beside the truck, got out and knocked on the door. When no one answered, he opened the door and went in. He saw Matthew, Francesco, and another man deep in conversation.

"Uh. Could I talk to you?" Black Hawk asked.

"Of course. Sorry we weren't paying attention." Matthew rose and the other two followed.

"I have news," Black Hawk said. "Maggie is being held at Leo Garrity's ranch." Matthew's eyes widened as he drew close to Black Hawk. "We know she's there. Did you see her?"

"No, I didn't see her, but I did see Dakota. Dakota! I couldn't believe it was her. And she gave me a message from Maggie." He told them what he had heard from Dakota.

Matthew said, "Is Maggie all right?"

"I'm sure she is. She's locked up and Buddy constantly goes to the barn to check on her."

Lucas chimed it, "Let's call the guy named Tiny and the other old guy. What's his name?"

"Jasper," Francesco said. "I'll call him."

"Uh, Dakota said not to tell anyone but the police," Black Hawk cautioned, but no one was listening.

Francesco used the mission phone to dial Tiny. He then called Jasper and told him the same story. Then he called Tom Marshall.

"You sure about this?" Tom asked.

"Yeah we're sure. Girls only tonight. In two nights, more girls. And men.

"Good. I have the FBI in the loop."

Matthew heard it all as if in a daze. "That would be Maggie," he murmured, "working out a way to feed us information even when she's locked up."

CHAPTER FORTY-FOUR

The door swung open and Special Agent Bea Sanders stood with both hands on her hips waiting for Tom Marshall to look up. When he did, he smiled. "Well, look who the cat drug in."

"Careful, you ol' tomcat. I'll lock you up just to watch you fume." They shook hands and Bea sat in a facing chair.

"Fill me in, Tom. What's going on that you call the FBI in to help out?"

"Remember the Celilo twins who were taken five years or so ago? We found the bones of one twin in the Columbia up at Biggs Junction. DNA tests confirm it's one of the twins. The other twin is alive."

"So, what's that got to do with the FBI?"

"A woman we know, Maggie Callahan, was kidnapped at a mustang auction down in Malheur County. We believe a girl was already in the van that took her away, and now we believe that girl is Dakota, the missing twin. Kidnapping being a federal offense, I called you."

"I remember the twins." Bea said. "This happened just after I took command in Portland. I get why you called the feds."

Tom smiled. "You know very well that most of our crimes are small city stuff, petty theft, bar fights, couples having a shouting match, otherwise known as domestic disturbance, and long-term grudges. I work closely with the sheriff as well as with The Dalles police. We can use all our trained men, but it probably doesn't add up to more than twenty officers. Your people are trained for major conflicts."

"Why do I get the feeling there's more than kidnapping to this story?"

"Because there is. There's a ranch outside Biggs Junction that I've been told is trafficking young girls and women."

Tom could see he now had Bea's full attention. "The old guy who lives next to the ranch has seen enough to confirm the suspicion," he added.

Bea leaned back and shook her head. "This sounds like a big city mess. You bet we'll help out. How many men do you have available? Or the better question is, how many men do I need to call in? And how soon?"

"It's your call, but maybe fifty, along with the twenty or so trained officers we have available. I have a lot of civilians who, with proper direction, will help. The tribal community, guided by a guy named Tiny, can do a lot to help out. He knows how to not interfere with the police or overstep his bounds. He and his friends have the best eyes in the valley."

"Tiny? I assume that's his nickname."

"Tiny's about twenty-four, twenty-five. He's just shy of seven feet tall and weighs about 250 pounds, no fat. They called him Tiny in grade school to tease him about his height and it stuck. You refer to Tiny and everybody knows who you're talking about."

"He's a natural born leader?"

"Yes. Inside the Nation as well as out. I'd really like to recruit him to go to the police academy, but I don't think he'll go. Too much bad blood. I hope, later on, you'll talk to him."

Bea sat waiting. "And? They all want to help?"

"You bet, they do, along with other locals. Also, there are three priests. One of them is married to Maggie, the kidnapped woman." He waited for the shock to cross her face.

"Wife? Priest? You sure are full of surprises, Tom Marshall. Any of them know how to handle themselves in a tense situation?"

"Yeah, Matthew, Maggie's husband, served in Iraq before becoming a priest. Now here's a big piece of the picture. Maggie, from what we've been told, is being held, locked up, at the ranch. So first priority is to get her out safely. Father Matthew's a great guy, but I feel sorry for whoever took his wife. I keep telling him he can't go vigilante, that he can't go in after her by himself, that I'll bring in the FBI. But I know if he had a chance to go after Maggie, he would." Tom could see her getting ready to protest. "Don't jump to conclusions. Matthew knows his way around a battle." Bea sat back to continue listening.

"Another set of eyes belongs to the old guy who lives next door to the ranch. He saw a bunch of girls in the meadow behind the barns. That was a couple of weeks or so ago. They were having a picnic and he said the average age was probably fifteen. Then a couple of days ago he and his neighbor, Black Hawk, stayed up all night to spy. They saw very young girls arrive at the ranch followed a little later by limos full of men dressed in tuxes. He told Matthew, who told me."

"This talk is making me hungry," Bea said. "My brain needs nutrition if we're going to set up a plan." She smiled, picked up her coat, and headed for the door.

"There's a restaurant a few blocks away." Tom followed Bea out the door, eager to lay down plans. He stopped at his car to pull out his mobile phone and carry it with him. "Handy thing to pack along," he said, and Bea nodded.

They walked, not talking. Tom knew Bea was thinking about the logistics of how to make a raid happen on a ranch they knew nothing about. They chose a table in the back of the restaurant, away from the other diners.

"Bea, there's a short time turnaround." Tom said with urgency in his voice. "Can you bring in the FBI on short notice?

"Can we get the sheriff over here right away?" Bea asked. "I want him in the loop at all times." She ran her hand through her short gray hair as if sweeping away how pressured she felt. She pulled out a small notepad and a pen.

"Yes, of course. Rex has been informed of everything," Tom assured her.

"Now, tell me about all the civilian players. Who are the players at the ranch?"

"A father and two sons. I can't imagine the younger son, Cody, is a part of this. I've never had a problem with him, but Buddy, the older son is a different story. He's had petty crime problems, civil disturbance issues. Personally, I think he's crazy, in the true sense of the word, and he's mean as hell. I suspect he's the ringleader. I don't know how the father fits in, but he's letting this happen on his ranch. Money, I suspect, is his motivator. There may be a cop from The Dalles involved, but I don't know it for a fact. And then there are people who work out there, but we're thinking they are on the road most of the time picking up unsuspecting girls to traffic."

"Let's eat up and drive out there so I can take a look at the lay of the land. And, I want to meet all the civilians who you can trust to help, including the priests. Can we pull them together tonight? We need their information and their eyes."

Tom picked up his mobile phone to call Tiny and Matthew. When the conversations ended, he looked up and grinned at Bea. "It's done," he said. "Eight o'clock, here in The Dalles, in the sheriff's office."

Two steak dinners and two beers later, they left the restaurant. Plans would soon be underway, and Bea Sanders, one of the best FBI commanders in the country would be at the helm. But it was clear this would not be the "piece of cake" it had at first appeared to be.

CHAPTER FORTY-FIVE

Eighteen men and four women gathered in the back room of the sheriff's department. The space was cramped, but nobody complained. They wore somber faces, waiting for something to happen.

The door finally opened and Detective Marshall strolled in, followed by Sheriff Rex Tyson, and a woman. All eyes focused on Bea Sanders.

"Thanks for coming. We appreciate your willingness to be eyes and ears for this plan. Our goal is to bring Maggie and Dakota home safely," said Tom Marshall.

The room collectively inhaled. Some whispered, "Dakota?"

Tom said, "Yes, Dakota. She was found with Maggie. Now, I would like to introduce you to Bea Sanders. She is Commander of the Northwest Field Office of the FBI." Everyone watched the woman as she stepped forward. Dressed in a navy-blue pants suit, she immediately took control.

"First, I'd like to thank you for volunteering. I'm told that all of you searched five years ago when the twins first disappeared. Who is the mother?"

One of the four women stood and raised her hand. Bea said, "My sincere condolences for your loss. I want you available at all times to identify your daughter, if we are able to find her. What is your name?"

"Ananya. I'll do whatever it takes to find my daughter, Dakota."

Bea smiled, then turned her focus to the group. "What we need from you is the ability to observe. That means rotating shifts so no appointed observation post is left unattended. Tom and I drove out to the ranch so I could see how we might set up observation posts. There are four main locations that must be constantly observed. The first is the driveway onto the ranch. I saw a driveway almost across the highway. Is the owner of that land here?"

Black Hawk raised his hand. "Yes, ma'am."

"The team that volunteers there must be constantly alert. All night. No sleeping. If you get tired before your time ends, call in a replacement.

"The second place is Dinty's Café. You may get coffee-loaded, but if you see any of the people outside of the Garrity family that may be involved in this operation, you are to immediately call Tom. You'll know them by unknown trucks or cars. People that just don't seem to fit in.

"The third spot is the mission. Its value is that if the two women were able to escape, they would probably head for the church." Bea scanned the group. "Everybody, understand?" she asked. They murmured and nodded their heads.

"The fourth spot is the berm behind the house. It's an awkward spot, because anyone can be seen from the back of the house in the daylight. Those observers will have to be down behind the berm, with someone watching the house at all times.

"Fifty FBI agents are due to arrive in the morning, but if something happens before that, we'll know about it because of you."

"Thanks, Bea. We appreciate your help," Tom Marshall said.

She smiled and said, "Now, you all understand that you're not FBI agents. You are observers who call us to intervene. We need your eyes. You will start tonight, as soon as you get home. As soon as agents arrive, they will be posted with you, but until tomorrow morning you will be on your own. Now, who is Matthew and who is Tiny?"

The two men stepped forward.

Bea said to Matthew, "I'm so sorry about your wife."

Matthew looked at her. "Thanks" was all he said.

"And, I know you're Tiny. You've been described to me. Thanks for coming in."

Bea went on. "You two will play an important part. Should Maggie somehow free herself, you will be our first contacts."

"Then you know what happened to her and where she is," Matthew said.

"Yes. Tom told me as much as he knew. And by the way, no vigilante action. We want these bastards to stand trial, plus all accomplices."

Matthew nodded to Tom that he heard the message.

From the back of the room, a young Native man asked in a loud voice, "You mean like that cop, Art Camden, who threatened us five years ago, threatened to put us in prison for killing the twins? He harassed us for months."

Bea turned to Tom. "Fill me in later." To the crowd, she said, "We will investigate this, I promise you."

Bea stood ramrod straight, making it clear she was in charge and her instructions were to be followed. "This is how it will be. Do not take any action on your own. I do not want any of you in the line of fire. Now, divide yourselves into teams of four. Tom will supply each team with a radio phone, so we can be in communication at all times.

"Tiny, I want you and Black Hawk to man the driveway across from the ranch. Find two others to help. Be close enough to the road that you can see anyone that comes out of Garrity's driveway, but far enough back that they won't spend time wondering why different autos or trucks are sitting in the driveway. As much as you can, change rigs often.

"The café will be easier to deal with. Anyone's allowed to park there and drink a cup of coffee." Laughing, Bea said, "This team will have free coffee for however long it takes. My treat. And doughnuts and pie. Dinty's has agreed to make all the pies we'll ever need." The crowd laughed. Hands went up immediately. She chose several of them.

"Jasper, who knows who might want to cross your land? I want you to stay at your place but be alert and be ready to make a phone call if you see or hear anything strange. Matthew, your place is the mission.

"And finally, and here's the tricky part, no one is to shoot anyone unless, of course, you're being shot at. I don't want any of you going to jail for murder. Do we all understand?" Heads nodded. Matthew said to Tiny under his breath, "Maybe."

"And thanks again for coming." Bea held out her hand to Tom, turning the meeting back to him.

Tom held his hand up. People stopped talking. "Will you please leave me a list of who's on which team and all your mobile phone numbers? I'll copy the list for Bea, Rex, and myself. This op begins tonight. Don't know how long it will last, but thanks again for your assistance."

The men gathered into four groups and Tom dealt out the radio phones. Each team mapped out how they would rotate around work and family. The women turned to Ananya. "How can we help?"

"I'll bet Pauline at Dinty's will need our help making pies."

Eager chatter brought the four women to make a plan about where and how pies would be made and delivered. "Let's go see Pauline and let her know what we can do."

The plan had launched.

CHAPTER FORTY-SIX

Buddy stood in the upstairs guest room and watched his brother, with Toby, cross the lawn to the barn. His gut told him something wasn't right, but he couldn't put his finger on what it was.

His brother, Cody, was the straight arrow who loved, in Buddy's words, "a damn squaw," who wanted nothing to do with the family business, who refused to take a dime when the money rolled in, was an enigma. Buddy had talked to his father over and over about Cody. He'd said that at some point, Cody was going to have to be eliminated. Leo Garrity wouldn't hear of it. Cody was his son. But, when Leo wasn't around to hear it, Art Camden agreed with him.

Buddy hated Cody. He'd gone to college. He, Homer Garrity, had chosen not to go to college, but rather chose to stay at home and learn rodeoing and ranch management. He was going to have to take absolute control of the situation. But how, without upsetting his father? To hell with his father, he often said; he would do what needed to be done.

Buddy's gut sensed when something wasn't right, and something wasn't right with the woman they'd taken at the horse auction. She hadn't been afraid to whack Peanut in the name of self-defense. She'd forced them to get rid of the body. It was a mystery who she was and who might know her. Buddy would mull on this awhile and figure out what to do.

He watched as Toby ran to the barn door and pushed it open. Damn half-breed brat, Buddy called him. He could never figure out why his father loved that kid. Buddy didn't. Didn't want him around. Didn't want any of them around, his brother, that squaw, or the kid.

Dakota was waiting in the barn. She and Cody went to Maggie's door. "We're here, Maggie, Dakota said. "I got the message to Black Hawk.

Cody put his arms around Dakota. His face was full of foreboding. "Buddy watched Toby and me walk over here. I could feel his eyes on me, and my gut tells me he's getting ready to make a move. He's crazy. I'm scared for all of us."

"Okay, I have an idea," Maggie said. "There's an old guy, Jasper, who lives next door. He sometimes comes out to spy on you."

"That's true," Dakota said. "Remember the picnic we had a couple of weeks ago? He was watching over the berm."

Cody looked at her. "And you knew this? How?"

"I saw him."

Maggie intervened. "His property is on the other side of the berm out beyond the barns. When it is late and the moon is down, all of you, the six girls who come tonight included, can go over the berm to Jasper's house. There is a path. Everybody, including Toby, must not say a word or make any noise. You don't want to alert Buddy that something's going on in the meadow. Once you reach his house, you'll be safe for the moment." Dakota said, "Dogs. Buddy's dogs and Jasper's dog. They'll let everyone in the county know that things are not as they should be."

Cody said, "No problem. We've got tranquilizers for horse and steer injuries. I'll lock the dogs in the barn with sleep cookies. I'll have one for Jasper's dog."

"What about you, Maggie?" Dakota asked.

"Unless you can bring a key, I'm locked in. Gives me deniability of knowing what's going on. Buddy's bound to be pissed, but I can say I don't know a thing. As soon as you get to Jasper's he'll call Matthew. They'll come get you and take all of you to the church in The Dalles, where everyone will be cared for. Ask for Father Daniel. I'm sure he knows I was kidnapped and I know he remembers you, Dakota."

Dakota sounded skeptical. "We should do this late at night?"

"Do it when you think it's safe. No flashlights until you're over the berm. You have to hope everyone is asleep. Maybe, Cody, you can tell your dad that you and Toby are going to sleep in the barn with Dakota so if Buddy misses you, your father can tell him where you are."

"That's only as good as what hour it is. Buddy doesn't sleep deeply. He hears everything going on outside."

"I know this is a lot to ask of you two, Toby, and six girls we don't know, but I want you out of here before they kill you. Remember, move quickly and silently. When this nightmare is all over, many hugs will come your way."

"I'm scared," Dakota admitted. "I don't want to leave you, Maggie. How do we tell six girls that we're leaving and they must come, too, and that they must do everything they're told or they may be killed?"

"We will tell them exactly that. I know you have the courage to do this," Maggie said.

"Let's hope they cooperate without questions. When they're free, they'll thank us," Cody said. "I'm going back to the house to put some things in a backpack for me and Toby. You do the same, Dakota. No suitcases. They'll weight us down. I'll talk to Toby just before we leave and tell him absolutely no talking, yelling or crying. I'll carry him. Right now, I'm going to the bank to change accounts and get cash so we can travel." Cody grabbed her hands. "I love you, Dakota. Always remember that." He kissed her and left her holding Toby's hand. Together they watched Cody disappear through the door.

The way he said that, Dakota wondered if she would ever see him again.

CHAPTER FORTY-SEVEN

The van carrying the girls arrived a bit after nine. The sun had set. Six teenage girls arrived by limo and were taken to the first barn. Maggie was not out there to meet the girls. They milled around, not knowing what to say or do. Buddy arrived and told them to wait, that he would be back with a woman who was to help them.

"What are we going to do?" one girl asked. She was dressed in short-shorts and a short-cropped top.

"I'd like to know, too," said the girl who carried a brown teddy bear close to her chest. She wore a black tee-shirt and black pedal-pushers, her long blonde hair fell almost to her waist. Buddy stared at her, obviously wondering why a teen-aged girl carried a teddy bear. He knew that would appeal to some of the men.

"You'll find out soon. Step into this stall. There are chairs so you don't have to stand. Grab yourselves some lemonade and cookies." The girls obliged, softly talking among themselves.

"Who's going to talk to us? Is she nice?" The girl was dressed in a white jumper without a blouse. It hung loosely off her shoulders, indicating that she had come from someplace warm. In fact, as Buddy stared at each girl, they all appeared to have hot weather clothing on. Could be from just about anywhere except the southern hemisphere.

"I'll bring in the lady shortly." Buddy turned to Dakota who had just walked in. "See to them," he barked. Dakota nodded, but said nothing.

Shortly, Buddy returned with Maggie. "Tell 'em how to behave," he said. "Teach 'em how to act." He looked at Maggie. "I'll be back in an hour. Have 'em ready for Tuesday night. And be sure they know what happens when they don't do it right." The look on his face made her think of Peanut, and she felt a cold chill up her spine.

An hour wasn't going to be enough time to prepare them, Maggie thought. No time to think about things. She had to prepare the girls, but not for the men they were scheduled to meet in two nights. She had to ease into why they were here and then hope they would understand why they needed to leave in secrecy. She hoped Cody had taken care of the dogs. She hoped Buddy would be in bed. Time for a prayer to St. Jude.

"The reason you were brought here was to act as dates for men who paid a great deal of money to spend a few hours with you." She waited for a response. No one said a word. Maggie said, "You came here to be prostitutes." That got their attention.

"What?" asked one girl. "I was promised an opportunity to have a job earning good money."

"So was I," said another girl.

"That's not going to happen. This is about saving your lives," Dakota said. "We're going to escape. Sometime later, when we're gone from here, I'll explain everything to you, but right now you have to listen closely and do exactly what Dakota and I tell you. Anyone who screws up runs the risk that we'll all be killed."

"Killed?" The girl with the teddy bear stood up. "What do we need to do?"

Maggie was surprised that she was the girl who understood the consequences. She explained where they were going and what they were to do. "You are to be silent and do exactly what Dakota tells you to do. The man who brought you here will be back soon to make sure you're all okay, and he will take me away. Do not tell him anything. Do you understand?"

Eyes wide, six young girls nodded. Then they began asking questions.

Maggie answered them, keeping them calm as best she could. When nearly an hour had gone by, she began to tell them she was proud of them and she knew they would be brave and would do well, that they would be quiet and calm and do exactly what was asked of them.

As they listened to Maggie, Buddy entered the barn and nodded, approving of Maggie's pep talk. Exactly what he expected of her. He stepped in and said, "You girls ready? You know how to behave when you meet your dates?" They nodded but said nothing.

"Girls, you get some sleep," he said, pointing to the cots. "You, come with me," he said, grabbing Maggie's arm. She winced.

As they left, Maggie glanced back at Dakota. Dakota knew what she had to do. Maggie was now a sitting duck. God help us all if Buddy finds out what is about to happen.

Buddy took Maggie down the hall. "You may do, after all," he said. Then he locked her in her prison without another word.

CHAPTER FORTY-EIGHT

A t midnight, Cody entered the barn. He carried a sleepy Toby. Toby would have asked what was happening, but his dad had told him he couldn't talk, and he had promised. Dakota and the girls were fully clothed, waiting in the dark, ready to go.

Cody whispered to Dakota. "Let's go." Then he said to the girls, "When we get past the barn, walk by twos as fast as you can. Dakota will lead. Toby and I will bring up the rear. You probably know we are going to a cabin on the other side of the berm and across the fields. There'll be no flashlights until we are well away from the berm. Absolutely no talking. We don't want any dogs to know we're out here. Everybody understand?"

The girls nodded, silently.

Dakota led the way out the back door. They walked single file under the barn eave. When they could see the meadow, the girls teamed up and they walked quickly to the berm and crossed over to the other side. Away from the berm, Cody passed a flashlight to Dakota as she led the way.

The observers lying on the berm watched the procession in shocked silence. They could only see that eight figures were walking away from the ranch, and one seemed to be carrying a small bundle, maybe a child. They knew instinctively that the best thing to do was to lie still and keep quiet.

Within a few minutes they were at Jasper's cabin. Miraculously, the dog hadn't warned his master that people were there. He was in a deep, uncharacteristic sleep. Cody knocked, then opened the door and ushered the others into the little cabin.

"What the…" Jasper jumped out of his chair and went to the door, closing it behind Cody. Cody put Toby down, who stood close to his father's leg.

"Hi Jasper. Before I tell you what's going on, will you please call Matthew and tell him to call the police. He'll know who to call."

Jasper did as he was told and called Matthew at his post at the mission. "Matthew. Call Tom Marshall and tell him I have Dakota, Cody, Toby and six girls here. I think they need to be moved tonight."

"What's going on?" Matthew asked.

"Don't know yet, but I'll find out while you round up the police and some cars to transport them out of here. Tell them no sirens." Jasper turned his head to Cody. "Where to?" he asked.

"Maggie said the Catholic Church in The Dalles," Cody responded loudly enough for Matthew to hear. "She said Matthew would know what to say."

"I do, but why isn't she with them?" Matthew asked.

Jasper relayed the question. "Because she's locked up," Dakota said. "And don't try to rescue her now. Too many people with guns. The police need to do that."

Matthew hung up and called Detective Marshall. "Can you come get some girls, plus Cody Garrity, Dakota and their son Toby, and move them to the Catholic Church in The Dalles? They're at Jasper's. There are nine of them."

"Stay where you are," Tom said. "We'll go after them and I'll let you know if we learn anything new about Maggie.

Matthew sat in the chair, groggy, but manning his post as he prayed for Maggie's safety. At 5:00 a.m. the radio phone cranked off. Matthew grabbed for it, immediately alert.

"Don't mean to drag you away from the mission, but the white van just left Garrity's." Tiny's voice boomed from the crackling radio. "I'm going to follow. Want you to follow me as fast as you can. If the van turns off the highway, I'll pull in a few feet and wait for you. It's heading south. Hustle."

"As fast as it takes me to get there."

Matthew called Tom on the landline. "What?" Tom asked, in a not too cordial voice, as he had finally gotten back to bed after transporting nine people from Jasper's cabin in Bigg's Junction to safety at the Catholic Church in The Dalles.

"The white van just pulled out of Garrity's driveway. Tiny and I are going to follow it."

"Okay, but don't overstep your bounds," Tom shouted.

Matthew did not respond. He threw on clothes and boots and drove up the highway, finding Tiny pulled over on a dirt road a few miles south of Biggs.

CHAPTER FORTY-NINE

M atthew parked and jumped into Tiny's truck. "Thanks for the call. Do you know what's going on?"

"No, but I think any time that van leaves the safety of Garrity's ranch, and turns into the desert, I'm worried. The desert is where things are left to die." Matthew looked straight ahead, and it didn't take a mind reader to know he was thinking about how he would save Maggie, if she was in the van.

The sun gradually edged over the horizon. A pink-orange glow covered the sage brush. They drove eight or ten miles into the desert, when they spotted the van through a gap in the rim wall, down in a low ravine.

Suddenly, Tiny took his foot off the gas, easing the pickup over the low berm that defined the edge of the desert dirt road. "What are you doing?" By the time Matthew got to "doing," he was shouting.

"Well, there's a chance he hasn't seen us yet. And I'd bet good money that he's got a gun, and I think he's got Maggie. If we go down there and just drive up to him like a couple of morons, there's nothing good that can happen, to us or Maggie, if she's in that van." Tiny's evaluation calmed Matthew just enough to get him from raw panic mode to combat ready. Tiny drove slowly, negotiating the scab rock and sagebrush until he was as close to the ravine's edge as he could get without being seen by whoever was in the van. Tiny opened the driver's door, stepped out, and then turned back.

"Tiny, what the hell are we gonna do way back here? That van's got to be five-hundred yards away." Tiny said nothing, but reached over the pickup's seat and pulled a rifle out of the gun rack. He opened the bolt to confirm that there was a live round waiting in the magazine, and then he closed the bolt almost completely, the new cartridge making its chinking sound as it found its way into the rifle's chamber. With his right hand holding both the rifle and the not-quite-closed bolt, he was ready, but safe. He didn't need to worry about the rifle's manual safety. "I make it closer to four-hundred yards," Tiny said.

Matthew opened the passenger door and got out. "Don't slam that door shut," Tiny whispered, "Sound carries a long way out here." Matthew nodded and left the door ajar, a pistol in his hand.

Tiny blinked in surprise. A pistol in the hand of a priest who obviously knew how to handle it. "Matthew, a pistol won't do any good at this range. I have my coyote rifle."

As they walked toward the ravine's rim, Matthew looked at the rifle in Tiny's hands. A plain bolt-action rifle, with a banged-up stock. The rifle had the kind of soft shine that says this gun has never been without oil. The black scope sight looked big and serious.

As they got close to the edge, Tiny caught Matthew's eye and patted the air, at the same time lowering himself into a crouching walk. Matthew got the message and crouched also. They saw the white van on what remained of the old road, near an ancient cattle guard and a broken-down fence that had been built to guard it. A few feet in front of the van was Buddy, and he was, well, dancing. Back and forth and a hop. Back and forth and a hop . . .

Tiny tried to sync his sights to Buddy's movement. Tiny dropped to his belly down on the ground, and spread his legs to stabilize body rotation. He shoulder-supported the rifle, both elbows on the ground, moved his head until an image appeared in the scope lens, acquired the target with the scope and took two deep breaths, placing his finger lightly on trigger, inhaled a third breath and let half of it out slowly.

"Tiny, what the hell's he doing? What's happening down there."

"He's kicking something on the road, and I think it's Maggie," Tiny said with the last half of his third breath, "and he's moving so much, I'm not sure I can hit him."

"Maggie! Are you sure? Is she okay? Is she alive?" Matthew dropped into military mode. "Can you shoot him, maybe just wound him? Remember what the FBI lady said: we can't kill anybody. I've gotta get down there."

"Matthew, do not go down there! You'll be out in the open for a long time, and that's just crazy."

Tiny's eye lined up with the scope and almost immediately he found Buddy. Tiny could see Buddy moving in an ugly dance kicking Maggie's face. Tiny figured the range to be three-hundred fifty yards, maybe four-hundred. Buddy stood a lot taller than a coyote, so Tiny wasn't really worried about misjudging the aim. He'd won every shooting contest in the county since he was fifteen.

Tiny yelled at Matthew, as Matthew broke away and raced down the hill making no attempt to hide himself, screaming at Buddy to stop. "You sonofabitch. You kill her and I'll kill you. Stop."

"Stay the hell out of my line of sight. Last thing I want to do is shoot you." Tiny yelled, returning his attention to his breathing and trigger control. He had promised not to kill anyone, but no one said he couldn't maim someone who was trying to kill Maggie. And to make sure he could never walk again, Tiny would go for a shot that would hit both legs.

A few seconds later, Buddy's head whipped around to look straight at Tiny. He stopped kicking and raised a hand to shield his eyes from the early morning sun. When he stopped kicking, Buddy's legs appeared overlapped in Tiny's scope, forming a stable target maybe eight inches wide and maybe two and a half feet high. That height meant that Tiny didn't care about how accurate his range estimation was, because whatever the drop was, it would still hit Buddy in the legs. Tiny put the crosshairs about Buddy's hip level and started his trigger squeeze.

As if he'd made some decision, Buddy's body jerked and his right hand reached for the pistol in a belt holster, just as Tiny's fired. The rifle bucked against Tiny's shoulder and the scope lifted away from his eye. When the scope came back, Buddy was just hitting the ground, his legs sprawled at an odd angle. He seemed to have more leg joints than normal. The echo of the rifle's report from the rimrock seemed to go on forever.

Matthew could see that Buddy lay sprawled and apparently unconscious, no threat to him, so he rushed to Maggie. He could see that she lay on her side, not moving. Had Buddy killed her? Her face was pulverized. He had kicked her all over her head and chest. Blood oozed from her nose and eyes. Spots of red spread across her shirt.

Matthew lay down beside her. "Maggie, speak to me." She didn't move or respond.

As Tiny ran down the hill, Matthew yelled. "Maggie's badly injured. Will your radio work up there? I don't think there will be any reception down here. Call Francesco and tell him to get Lucas out here fast. He's a doctor and he'll be here a lot sooner than an ambulance. Then tell him to call an ambulance. Actually, we need two ambulances. I want Maggie in one with Lucas. I don't much care what they do with Buddy. I wish you'd killed the bastard, but thanks for making him regret everything he's ever done." Tiny scrambled back up the hill and did as asked. Then he descended into the ravine and stood by Matthew as he lay next to Maggie and prayed.

Lifting his head, Matthew said, "Tiny, go call Tom and tell him to call the sheriff and get some deputies out here. This is a crime scene."

Matthew whispered to Maggie. "Lucas is on his way." To no one he said, "I don't want to touch you in case you have internal injuries." He sat up and took off his jacket and put it over her. He softly and carefully touched her hand. She did not stir.

Tiny returned and told Matthew, "Lucas'll drive up here, ASAP. I told him to turn when he sees your truck. Francesco's taking care of calling ambulances and calling Tom Marshall. Do you think we should have water ready in case she wakes up? I have a canteen in the truck."

"No. If she has internal injuries, we don't need to make it worse. Why don't you move the truck closer?" Matthew looked at Buddy. "I suppose we should take a look at him."

"I already did." Tiny said. "He's unconscious. I put a tourniquet on one leg, so he wouldn't bleed out. I know you're supposed to loosen it every so often or he could lose the leg, but it looks like the bullet hit bone, so his leg is pretty much gone anyway. He'll live, but he won't bother anyone for a very long time, if ever."

A weak smile crossed Matthew's face. He rechecked Maggie's wrist again for a pulse. Her heartbeat was strong. She was still alive. To no one he said, "I really want to beat that guy to death."

"You know, it was really weird," Tiny said.

"What do you mean, 'weird'?" Matthew asked.

"Well," started Tiny, "I watched Buddy hopping and kicking for what seemed like forever, and I just couldn't get a shot, and all of a sudden, he stopped moving, turned, and looked right at me. And then he acted like he saw me, lying on my belly four-hundred yards away, and he reached for his gun. That's when I shot him."

"I'll be damned," blurted Matthew. "It was me he saw. You were two or three hundred yards behind me, but it was me, running like an idiot toward him with no cover at all. Well, low sagebrush, but basically no cover at all. He could've taken cover behind the van, or even Maggie, for god's sake, and shot my silly ass standing out in the open. I should've listened to you when you told me to stay."

"Well, you got him to stop moving so I could shoot," said Tiny. "And your silly ass is still alive. So, I guess it turned out okay."

"I guess," Matthew replied, but he didn't seem so sure.

Tiny said nothing. He sat on the rocky earth and waited, watching Matthew talk to Maggie. As the sun began to warm the desert floor, Matthew said, "I hope Lucas arrives soon. I don't want her to roast to death under this sun."

The words were no more out of his mouth, than Lucas's SUV bumped over the hill. The three bypassed formalities, as he got out of the car. He bent down, his stethoscope against her chest. "Did the other guy survive?" he asked.

"He did. Thanks to Tiny. Tiny shot him from way up there on the rim. Buddy kicked Maggie near to death. She hasn't moved or opened her eyes. I hope we're not too late."

Lucas checked Maggie, and said, "Her vitals are good. Everything's working, but she's unconscious, a result of the severe beating she endured." They sat staring at the rocky mesa overlooking the ravine. Matthew, his hand still holding Maggie's, said to Tiny, "I don't know how you made that shot. Some shooting. Have you given any thought to becoming a cop?"

"Yeah, when I was in high school, but I've never acted on it. We're not loved by whites and I feel like I'd always have somebody criticizing me for not doing things the way other cops do."

"I think you should talk to Tom Marshall sometime. I bet he'd be happy to recommend you to the police academy. You could always work on behalf of the indigenous population."

"Hmmm. Maybe."

Lucas did a cursory examination of Buddy. "Jesus, that leg looks awful! Bone splinters. Even some in the other leg, but I think he'll lose the one you hit first for sure," said Lucas.

"That sounds about right," said Tiny.

"What'd you mean 'about right'," asked Lucas.

"It's the leg that sonovabitch used to kick Maggie."

They could hear sirens off in the distance. Tiny noted. "Sounds more like three or four sirens. I suppose cops will come, too. Good. I want them to take pictures of what that asshole did to Maggie. They can nail him for attempted murder in addition to sex trafficking." He watched the rim for signs of the vehicles. "Can't help but wonder how they can get here in a hurry without breaking an axle."

"Let's hope they can," Matthew said. Then raising himself to an elbow, close to her ear and whispered, "Hold on, Maggie. Help is coming." He kissed her hand and held it to his face. "I love you so much."

CHAPTER FIFTY

Tom Marshall's car lead the procession of two ambulances and two sheriff's department cars. The cars came down the hill, careful not to hit any of the big rocks, leaving the ambulances to inch their way down like a herd of turtles. As Tom got out of his car, he saw Buddy on the ground and asked, "Is that Buddy? Is he dead?"

"No sir," Tiny said. "He's out because of pain. He'll be in a wheelchair for the rest of his life. It's Maggie who needs attention. He nearly beat her to a pulp. I hope you brought a camera, because I want a jury to see those pictures. I want to know they will hang him from the highest tree."

Tom walked to Matthew, still lying beside Maggie. "Is she conscious?"

"No," Matthew replied.

"The sheriff's deputies will take pictures and you and Tiny need to tell me what happened. I'm going to record it because I'll have to leave and get back to The Dalles. I spoke at length with Cody Garrity. There is to be another group of men and girls arriving tomorrow night. Bea is working on getting her men here and into assigned positions. Jasper is moving out of his cabin until this is over, so Bea can use it as a post. You need to be very proud of Maggie. She lined up everything from that locked room. She told them how to get to Jasper's, and you know the rest."

Matthew nodded, his eyes never leaving Maggie.

"Who shot Buddy?" Tom asked.

"I did," Tiny said. "You said not to kill anyone, but he was beating Maggie when we arrived, kicking her with metal-toed boots. I shot him so the bullet would damage both legs."

"That's some fine shooting," Tom said. "How did you know to come here?"

"I was doing what I was told to do. I was watching the Garrity driveway. Around 5:00 this morning, I saw the van leave, so I called Matthew and told him to watch for my truck, that I was going to follow the van wherever it went. My gut said something was wrong. Matthew caught up with me and we followed the dirt road into the desert. When we came over a hill and saw that piece of shit kicking Maggie to death, I stopped, grabbed my rifle, and shot him. Simple as that."

Tom didn't respond. He walked over to Maggie and bent down to see for himself her condition. He stared at her then looked away, bile rising in his throat. She would never look the same.

Tom straightened up and looked around the area. "This guy knew how to murder without leaving a trace. He'd leave Maggie to die in the desert, then he'd drive back home and get rid of the boots. What do you think, Doc? Will she live?" he asked Lucas.

"I took her pulse. It seemed strong, but I can't tell if it's strong enough for her to pull through."

The ambulances finally made it to the bottom of the ravine. Two medics got out of the first ambulance. Seeing Matthew, who was rising up from where Maggie lay, one medic asked, "I assume you haven't moved her?"

"No, except to lay my hand on her hand."

"Do you know what he used to beat her?"

Matthew turned away, unable to talk. Tiny said, "His boots. Steel-toed. When we arrived, he was kicking her with a vengeance."

"I'm a doctor," Lucas said. "She needs a hospital and x-rays to look at the damage. We'll have to lift her carefully to avoid damaging her further. Bring the gurney and I'll help you place her and strap her in. Then we'll take her out. Slowly." The medics wheeled the gurney to Maggie. Lucas helped strap her in, then watched as they lifted her and put her in the ambulance.

Lucas walked to the second ambulance. The two medics stood by, staring at Buddy's leg. One said, "Shit. That leg looks awful. Someone tied a tourniquet with barbed wire?"

"Yes," said Lucas. "It was tied with what they had available. Keep it there until you get back to the hospital. If he wakes up, give him a shot of morphine." They acknowledged his orders and Lucas moved aside while Buddy was loaded onto a gurney and placed inside the ambulance.

"Okay," called the medic from Maggie's ambulance. "We have room for one in here. Anyone riding along?" Everyone looked at Matthew.

"You're the doctor. Please take care of her, Lucas," he said.

Lucas could see Matthew's face was broken between fear and heartbreak. Lucas hugged him and said, "You know I will. I'll be with her at the hospital. Come as soon as you can."

"Matthew can ride with me," Tom Marshall said. He watched as Maggie and Buddy were taken away. He said to the deputies, "Treat the area as a crime scene. Pick up any evidence you find and bring it to my office." With those instructions, he got in his car and drove out of the canyon with Matthew in the passenger seat. He passed the ambulances and when they hit the highway, he turned on lights and sirens. The ambulances followed suit.

Tiny walked the area looking for anything that might explain what exactly had happened to Maggie. He didn't find anything, so he walked back to the van and looked inside. And there it was, lying on the floor in the windowless van, an empty needle. What was in it, he did not know. He left it there and called to the deputies who were searching the ground in a coordinated manner. "Look at what I found. It may have been used on Maggie." One deputy walked over drawing an evidence bag from his back pocket. He climbed in and bagged the needle.

"I'm heading for The Dalles," Tiny told the deputy. "Will it be faster if I take it?"

"We take it or it won't be admissible at trial. Hope it has something in it that knocked her out so she didn't know what was happening."

CHAPTER FIFTY-ONE

A rt Camden arrived at the Garrity ranch, climbed the steps to the house and didn't bother to knock. "Where the hell is Buddy?" he yelled at Leo Garrity.

"I don't know. We need to shut down tomorrow night's event."

"Bullshit. We can't shut down anything. No time. I'll be in charge. Everything will be fine. Where are the girls? I'll go talk to them."

Leo Garrity, head down, said, "They're gone. I don't know where they are."

"And the woman Peanut and Stud brought in? Give me the keys."

Leo Garrity shrugged his shoulders. "Buddy keeps them."

Art Camden raced from the house and down the steps. It was then he noticed that the white van was missing.

Tom Marshall sped back to The Dalles, the two ambulances close behind him. He called Bea Sanders and told her what he'd learned from Cody, that they had a thirty-six hour window before the next bus arrived. "I'm concerned that it won't happen because Buddy won't be there to lead the event. He's in serious condition in the hospital. I've told the hospital that neither his name nor Maggie's is to be released to anyone, including Leo Garrity, until after the raid. He is under police protection. He'll probably lose a leg. Cody says an ex-cop named Art Camden will probably take over, that is unless he figures out that we're looking for him, too. I'd really like to catch Art in the act. I know him. His history as a cop, makes him even more dangerous. He knows the ropes."

"Tomorrow? No sweat. I have agents on the way and will call in the rest when I hang up. They'll be in place by tomorrow morning. Do I assume that both men and girls will be there?"

"Yes. The girls usually arrive around eleven, the men around midnight. You can post men on Jasper's property. I just hope everybody waits for your signal."

"Tell me what happened."

"The quick story is that Buddy was in the process of killing Maggie. She's in the hospital at The Dalles, but as far as I know she hasn't regained consciousness. Now we have kidnapping as well as attempted murder to add to the list. I saw her face, Bea. Bashed in. I had to turn away before I heaved."

"Why was she being held at the ranch?" Bea asked.

"She was supposed to teach the girls how to behave, be sort of a den mother to the trafficked girls. They didn't have any idea who she was, or that she lived anywhere near Biggs Junction. She convinced Dakota and Cody to take the six girls and escape with them."

"Why didn't she go with them?" Bea asked.

"Buddy had her locked in a room with three locks and he had the only keys. She never had a chance."

"Do you think she'll live?" Bea asked.

"I hope to God she does. Everyone around her is a wreck. Matthew is between yelling and sobbing and Tiny has his hands full trying to comfort him and keep things moving. By the way, I want to recommend Tiny to the FBI. I don't think he'll ever become a state cop. There's too much bad blood between the local law enforcement and the Native community, but he'll be a real asset to the FBI."

Bea said, "Remind me when this is over. Tom, if Maggie dies, it's murder one. If she lives, but can't function, I'll charge attempted murder and felony assault, in addition to sex trafficking. Either way, Buddy and the cop are spending the rest of their lives in prison. Not sure how Cody and his father fit in."

"Hold on Bea, I have another call." He clicked over to the new call. He listened intently and said, "Make sure the vial gets to the evidence room under close scrutiny and then under lock and key. You are to stay with it until it's processed."

Tom clicked back to Bea. "Tiny found a needle in the van. One of the deputies bagged it. It's going straight to the lab under protective custody."

CHAPTER FIFTY-TWO

A gurney was waiting when the ambulance pulled into The Dalles hospital along with Tom Marshall and Matthew. A doctor and three nurses helped Lucas lift Maggie from the ambulance and wheel the gurney into ICU. The doctor asked Lucas about her injuries. "She was kicked in the head and chest. I think the first thing we need to do is examine her head. Since I'm not a resident here, you take over, but if it's okay, I want to assist and stay close to her. She's my sister. This is Matthew, her husband." The staff member nodded and began taking her into imaging.

Matthew withdrew to the ER waiting room. He picked up a magazine, read for a page, then picked up the next one. He knew Lucas would be out to tell him how she was doing, but the tension of not knowing, was tearing him apart. As if in a vision, Francesco appeared before him. Matthew poured out the story and what was in his heart.

"All I can think about is how I saw that scumbag kicking her in the head. I don't know how she can survive. I want to kill Buddy with my bare hands. But it's too late. My chance has come and gone."

Father Francesco listened to his friend without judgment. This would take time to heal, and Matthew would reconcile his feelings with God in due time. He left Matthew with a fatherly hug and a sign of the cross.

An hour and a half later, Lucas came out. "Let's get a cup of coffee and something to eat," Lucas said, directing Matthew towards the cafeteria. They bought a couple of sandwiches and took them to a window table. "I'm not going to lie to you, Matthew, she's in pretty bad shape."

"Has she regained consciousness?" he asked, hoping for a miracle.

"No. Matthew. She was badly beaten. The x-rays show skull fractures. Her chest is also badly injured."

Matthew put his elbows on the table and held his head in his hands. "Do you think she'll live?" he asked.

"Too early to say. If she regains consciousness, then I think she will. If not, I don't know. The one thing I do know is that Maggie is a fighter. After we finish this meal, we'll find out where she is in ICU. You'll be able to see her for a few minutes, even sit by her bed. And, Matthew, no kissing, not even her hands. Her face is a mess and you don't want to infect her injuries."

"I won't. Thanks Lucas."

They sat for a few more minutes, eating their sandwiches and Matthew asked, "Should we call your mother? I'm sure she would want to come down. We now have a place for her to stay."

"I'll call her," Lucas said. "She's going to take this very hard. I didn't hear the end of it last year when we almost lost Maggie in the fire. Mom just doesn't understand Maggie, why she's always getting herself hurt or getting herself in trouble. She always thought Maggie should marry and have ten children. Somehow, Maggie always laughed and said, 'Mother, I'm not made for raising children.' To which my mother said, 'Yes you are, you're always saving somebody or something. Think of all the puppies you saved.'"

Matthew smiled. "I wonder the same thing every single day."

When they entered Maggie's room, Matthew controlled the urge to run to her. She lay on her back, tubes running from her nose, mouth and left arm. Her face and chest were carefully bandaged, so he really couldn't see her wounds, but he had them fresh in his mind. He brought a chair close to her bed and touched her hand. Lucas stood in the doorway and watched, then stepped outside and called their mom.

CHAPTER FIFTY-THREE

Bea stood on the desktop so the agents could see and hear her. Tom Marshall, Rex Tyson, and Coyote stood next to the desk. Bea welcomed everyone and said, "This mission is now a hostage rescue mission. It appears this will be relatively easy, but don't assume that. One of the ringleaders, Buddy Garrity, is in the hospital with serious leg injuries. He'll never walk again."

A quiet murmur filled the room.

"This is our mission. We will set up between eight and nine crews. You three agents," Bea said, pointing to three of the women, "will get in position behind the barn closest to the road. When it's pitch black, enter that barn and wait. If someone is in there, neutralize them so they can't warn others. This is where the girls will come in first, before the men arrive. Once they're in, keep them there. Tell them they are in protective custody. The girls aren't going to know what to do, so your major job will be to reassure them and keep them calm."

One officer asked, "What if one tries to bolt out of fear of going to jail?"

"Explain to them that they are not the subjects of the raid. Tell them that when this is over, you want to hear all their stories, that you will help them find their parents or custodians.

"The rest of you are to form six teams, of six agents each, including a sniper. Geographically, the first team will be behind the berm on Jasper's side. The second will be on the hill behind the barns, the third will be directly behind the house. The fourth will enter from the road. Five and six will be in the open area behind the house. Local officers will be on the road controlling traffic. You will be down the hill in Bigg's Junction. We don't want bus drivers and the limo drivers to sense something is wrong."

"What about the dogs?" Jasper asked. "I'll keep my dog inside, but they have two nasty dogs."

"Beware the dogs," Bea said. "They're Rottweilers. They may give us away, which will be unfortunate, but if we're quiet, hopefully they'll lose interest."

"Ma'am." Coyote Marshall stepped forward. "I believe I can control the dogs from Jasper's house."

Bea looked at the man in jeans, denim shirt, leather jacket and Stetson hat. "How?" she asked.

"Well, I'll call them in to Jasper's house and feed them go-to-sleep meat."

"And, just how do you plan to do that without people in the house knowing?" Bea asked.

Tom couldn't help watching his brother mess with Bea. He knew what Coyote would say.

"Well ma'am, I'll call them in. I'll sound like a jackrabbit in trouble and they'll come flyin' in for the kill."

Bea looked at Tom for confirmation. He smiled and nodded.

"Okay," she said with a smile. "Now, back to business. You are to bring in Leo Garrity and Art Camden. In cuffs. Art is a dirty cop, so we especially want him so he can tell us how this sex ring started, and how it has maintained itself without the community knowing about it."

"Remember, this is a raid, not a kill," Tom said.

"Yes," said Bea. "There'll be an hour, maybe two, of waiting. It isn't really dark until after ten. The girls arrive at eleven, the men at midnight. The men will be dressed in tuxes and should be carrying a lot of money that they plan to give Art."

"Talk about guns, Bea," Rex said.

"I do not expect anyone to be carrying, but you never know who has a small gun hidden on their person. I do expect a gun on Art Camden, so be ready. I want all of them brought back to The Dalles. As far as the men go, Tom has organized rooms to be available to talk to them and take information. Get names, addresses, social security numbers, and how and why they got involved. Find out which ones have had past problems with the law."

Tom said, "I don't expect anyone to try run behind the barns. If that happens, teams, you are to nab them. They're going to ask you to not tell their wives, that they have children. As you cuff them, tell them they should have thought about that a long time ago. If anyone tries to run or scream, you have permission to stick a gun in their ribs."

Bea wrapped it up, saying. "Okay everyone. You are the cream of the crop. I don't have to tell you how to do your jobs. I expect this mission to be wrapped up in about four hours. Oh, and on the lighter side, be sure your boots are laced tight, this is rattlesnake country."

CHAPTER FIFTY-FOUR

The next evening, FBI crews pulled out of The Dalles at 8:30 p.m., moving separately and far apart. Off the freeway at Biggs Junction, each group took the road to their assigned positions. One truck pulled into Dinty's Café. They looked like a bunch of hunters, on their way to a campout. They drank coffee and ate pie.

It was now 10:00 p.m. and time that everyone moved into position. The café group was the road crew; thus, they were to hang back until the men's limos pulled in. The women had come out separately and were already in place behind the barn.

Bea asked each group to call in and they did in rapid succession.

Suddenly, Detective Tom Marshall radioed from the berm in front of Jasper's place. "Attention, there is a car approaching the entrance and turning in. Do not approach it. Let's see who he is and watch him." The car pulled up to the house. A man got out of the car, climbed the front steps and entered the house.

"Do you know who he is?" asked Jasper.

"Yeah, his name is Art Camden," Tom answered.

"Where is everyone?" Art Camden yelled as he stepped into the living room. He stood, feet apart and hands on his hips, waiting for Buddy to respond. When Leo Garrity came from the kitchen, Art growled, "Where's Buddy? The bus will be here in half an hour."

"I don't know. He never came home last night. I guess you're on your own."

Art stared at the old man. "What kind of bullshit is this? He knows what's coming down tonight. This is a big night. Twenty girls, twenty men. Should I go look for him?" Art paced in circles.

"I already looked. It's too late. I took care of the food." Leo didn't tell Art there weren't any girls in the first barn. There should have been six. He hadn't bothered to check on the woman in the second barn. Buddy had the only keys. For all Leo knew, she might be dead behind that locked door. But worst of all, Cody and Dakota were missing. And Toby. He suspected that Buddy might have had something to do with that. But Buddy was gone, too. Everything was crumbling around Leo Garrity.

"Well old man, you're going to have to meet the men. Big smiles and handshakes all around."

"I'd rather not. You know I don't like this."

Art Camden stood very close to Leo Garrity, his finger pointed at his chest, "What I know is that you like the money. Now, get going."

Leo Garrity didn't move. In his soul, he felt impending doom, and he didn't care.

"I'm going to the barn." Art walked out, headed for the barns. He went into the barn closest to the house, inspecting the stalls, expecting to see girls. None. "What the hell is going on?" he muttered. The barn was dark. He grumbled, "Guess they aren't here yet." He started to go look for the six who had come in Sunday but turned toward the party barn instead. He found everything in order. At least that much had been taken care of.

The three FBI women behind the barn carefully opened the back door and slipped in. Each wore a Kevlar vest under her jacket. Whispering to each other, they wondered if they should turn on a light. Better not until the bus arrives.

Bea radioed. "Are you in place?"

The three women responded, "Yes."

Ten minutes later Bea and Tom saw the bus coming up the hill. Bea radioed, "Everyone on alert. Here comes the bus. Remember, you don't move until the limos arrive and all the men are deposited."

The FBI women could hear the bus as it pulled around the circular drive and stopped in front of the big wood door, lights out. They heard the driver open the door and help each girl out, then listened as the girls shuffled inside.

"Hey, where's the woman who's supposed to be here to help us?" someone asked. "It's dark in here," said another.

Once they were all inside, the door closed, the lights came on, and the girls saw three women waiting for them.

"Hi!" the speaker had grey hair and a nylon cap pulled close to her ears. "I'm Jackie. My friends and I are here to help you. Please move against the back wall while we talk to you."

The girls looked at each other but did as they were told.

Another woman raised her hand. "We're here to rescue you. My name is Mimi. Stands for Maria Magdalena, but that's too tough to say and too long to remember. We're FBI." The girls grabbed hold of each other, not sure what to do or what to believe. "We're here to help you. We call it a rescue mission. Right now, we don't want your names."

The girls tentatively nodded and huddled closer together.

"We want you to trust us, even though you don't know us. I'm Barb. Listen carefully and do as you're told." The speaker was the tallest and the youngest of the three women. She looked like she was maybe two or three years older than the girls. "How many of you know why you were brought here?"

Two girls raised their hands. The others stared at the two.

One of the older girls said, "We're being trained as escorts. Translated, that means we'll be prostitutes for very rich men."

One girl started to sob. Through tears, she said, "My older sister told me not to go to the photography studio, but I wouldn't listen. I thought I'd make my way to Hollywood."

Barb smiled and nodded, acknowledging that to be a common story. "How many of you have had a similar experience?" She asked. All but two, raised their hands. "And you?" Mimi asked the black girl who looked to be sixteen or seventeen.

"I was kidnapped in New Orleans. No photography studio. They picked me up off the street."

"Me, too," said the girl with long blond hair. "I was taken in Chicago. I haven't been able to speak to my mother for more than three years. I miss her so much. I tried to escape, but each time I was caught, they beat me. I finally stopped trying. I just hoped that someday, somebody would help me." She sounded resolute, but bitter. "I'll help any way I can. I believe you."

Mimi spoke. "Thanks. We really are FBI. This is how it's going to work. When the men arrive, we'll be back against this wall. When the FBI moves in, we are going out this door and onto the road. There will be vans waiting and we will take you to the Catholic Church in The Dalles. At that time, officers will learn your names, where you came from, and your parents' names. We will begin the process of reuniting you with your families."

"What if I don't have a mom and dad?" the black girl said. "My parents were killed maybe two years ago. I was living on the streets when I was kidnapped."

"Do you have relatives, an aunt, uncle, cousin?"

"I have a cousin my age. We used to play together, but I don't know where she is."

"We'll try and find her," Mimi said.

Jackie looked at her watch. "They should be arriving soon. Our commander will let us know when they are at the driveway. If you have to talk, talk quietly."

Barb turned to the young girl next to her. "So, you didn't know who took you?" she asked.

"No. Two men. They were strangers to me."

"Do you remember what they looked like?"

"One was tall and one was short. The tall guy called the small guy Peanut."

"Interesting. What's your name?" Barb asked.

"Joann," she answered.

"Later, I want a statement as to how you were kidnapped and where you stayed. How did you get here? The whole story. When we're back at the church, I want to talk to you. We may ask you to be a witness. The name, Peanut, has come up before."

Joann looked at Barb, eyes wide.

At exactly midnight, five limos pulled into the circular drive. Twenty-one men exited the vehicles. One asked, "Where's Buddy?"

Leo stepped forward, "Buddy's away tonight. I'm Leo. I'll help you." He took them into the festive party room.

Leo Garrity walked among the men, watching. It was clear he was uneasy about doing Buddy's job, and some of the men began to look disgruntled. Then a bull horn boomed into the night, "Do not move. You are under arrest." Agents swarmed from the darkness, descending on the group of men.

The men, in their fine tuxedos, stumbled over each other trying to find a way out. One man bolted for the highway but was blocked by two agents carrying rifles. "What the hell is happening?" one man bellowed. "Where's Buddy?" another asked. "Oh my God. I'll be in a divorce court over this," said another. As the circle of FBI agents surrounding them began to tighten, some men asked for permission to leave, saying they'd never do this again. The agents said nothing, just marched the tight circle of handcuffed men to the road and into the waiting trucks

In the tack room, Art wiped dirt from the window so he could see. Cops. FBI. The men surrounded. "Shit!" The look on his face said it was time to move on. He ran through a door out behind the barns. Sticking close to the wall, he opened a door at the back of the barn closest to the house, pulled out a motorcycle he had stashed there and leaned it against the wall. He went back inside the tack room and carried a bale of hay into the middle of the aisle, then poured an entire gallon can of gas on the hay. He ran back into the tack room, pulled out a file full of papers, and threw them along with the desk chair on the hay. He wadded a roll of papers, lit it, and threw it on the hay. Evidence began to go up in flame.

The explosion knocked him down, but he was able to crawl to the door and take off on the motorcycle. "This is a token of my esteem," he yelled as he headed for the dirt road that ran between the back berms.

The sniper, located on the berm to the left of the road, covered his eyes. Art was gone before he could see him, but he pulled off one round in the direction of the motorcycle. He radioed to the field team, "Subject on motorcycle coming your way. I missed my shot due to the explosion. Barn on fire."

"Shit," said Bea. To Tom, she said, "That has to be Art. I saw Leo enter the first barn." "Field agents," came Bea's voice, "one suspect has gotten away on a motorcycle. Into the back field. See if you can bring him down. If you can, bring him in alive."

Bea directed another order to the women. "Your first responsibility is to get those girls out. NOW. There's a fire in the barn closest to the house. Don't wait for the vans—a bus awaits you on the highway." Bea watched as the girls fled the barn and raced towards the highway, the three FBI agents keeping close to them. Bea watched until they reached the highway and were safe and then turned her attention to the men.

The men, in their black tuxedos and bow ties, sat in the truck, heads bowed. Some muttered and complained about ruining their tuxes. One agent said, "A dirty tux is the least of your problems. No crap from you. Get in and shut up."

"Shit," said Bea. She notified the men. "I've called the fire department. Get your trucks off the road and turned around. We don't want fire trucks having to dodge our trucks."

Tom Marshall looked at the house. Somehow, Leo Garrity had been able to sneak back into the house. In the upstairs window he saw Leo looking out over the destruction of his life's work. What was he thinking? He would be talking to him very soon. Tom drew his gun and headed for the house.

CHAPTER FIFTY-FIVE

Three days passed in near silence. Matthew sat with Maggie, constantly reviewing what Lucas had told him. She was in a coma until the swelling in her head went down. The fourteenth day, Maggie made moaning sounds, but did not regain consciousness. Another five days passed with moaning, but no recognition of sounds or people. In the fourth week, Maggie opened her eyes. She did not respond to anyone or anything. Matthew never left her side. He slept in a recliner chair, waking at every sound made by the machines monitoring her life signs. Visitors were not allowed in, so only messages of love and encouragement connected Matthew to the outside world. Lucas monitored it all, as much for Matthew's sake as Maggie's.

A month later, her bandages, which had been replaced almost daily, were finally removed. Both Matthew and Lucas were stunned at the condition of her face. She had healed far better than anyone expected, but the left side of her head held deep gashes that would probably never go away, and it would take years of reconstructive surgery to replace the bone structure that was shattered.

Matthew watched the nurse gently remove the bandages from her chest. Another miracle. The major scar was across her collar bone and shoulder were barely visible. Lucas pulled up a chair beside him.

"Matthew, I'm pretty sure that she will recover, but it may take at least six months before her brain will return to normal. It's going to be a very long recovery. I have some news that will shock you, so I think you should hold her hand while I deliver this message." He watched Matthew move his chair to her side and take her hand.

"Matthew, Maggie is pregnant."

"What?"

"I didn't want to tell you unless I was absolutely sure the baby could survive and absolutely sure that there was a good chance that Maggie would eventually open her eyes and actually see what's going on around her. I want you to take her home, now. You have a lot of people who are eager to help out. You can set up around-the-clock care. I am putting together a list of what I want done and how you should do it. Three nurses will take turns going to your house to make sure everything is going well. I've asked for an ambulance to come day after tomorrow."

Matthew was speechless. Stunned was an understatement. "Are you sure she can carry a baby to term?"

"I'm sure. If Buddy had kicked any lower, I doubt whether she or the baby would have survived. She's about three plus months. I'm guessing she never told you."

"No. We had so much going on, she kept it to herself. Or maybe she didn't know, yet." Matthew wiped his eyes. "Don't think I've ever cried as much as I have over Maggie. These are tears of joy."

"Tom has asked to talk to you, as has every female in the valley wanting to see her or know how she is. I haven't let them in, but when she goes home, I'm going to suggest that they be allowed to visit, maybe two or three at a time. I want Gabriella there. Her parents have given her permission to stay here, with you and Maggie. She loves Maggie and will be a great help. Ananya will help. She will bring her friends and daughter to help."

"Has Dakota met her mother?" Matthew asked.

"She has. The two are best friends, as if Dakota had never been away.

Ananya loves her grandchild. She wants to do a special Sioux service for Maggie when she has recovered. And Tiny is a wonder. He's been at the mission every day to help Francesco, and Sasha's been there, too."

Matthew smiled ear to ear.

"They all love you, Padre. You'll have a built-in parish."

"What about Francesco? I haven't been very good about talking to him."

"He's fine. He, too, has a surprise for you," Lucas said. "The guy who has had a lot of trouble staying away is Detective Marshall. Seems there's already a trial date. There is so much evidence against them, they will have a lot of time to contemplate their sins."

"They got Art Camden?" Matthew asked.

"Yes. This is new. Art tried to escape by burning down the barn closest to the house. A sniper picked him off as he tried to navigate the meadow on his motorcycle in the dark. Pulled off a hail Mary shot and figured he'd missed. Turned out he hit Art in the leg but they didn't find him until the next day, pretty near death. Almost bled out, but he pulled through. The bastard will stand trial."

Matthew shook his head slowly, back and forth. "I didn't know any of this."

"I just wouldn't let the law talk to you. You had enough to cope with. Now you're ready to retake the reins. I'm going to call Tom and Francesco and tell them they can check in. Then they'll let the others in when Maggie's moved home." Lucas smiled at Matthew. He finally saw life in Matthew's eyes.

"Lucas, I can't thank you enough for everything you've done. I know staying here has been hard on the you. And I'll thank this hospital for giving you privileges here."

Lucas smiled. "I just might transfer down here. I love The Dalles. They told me to call when I'm ready."

Matthew hugged his brother-in-law. "Maggie and I will love it."

"By the way, Mom will come down when Maggie is alert. She'll stay as long as you need her. I'm on my way to call Tom."

"She knows everything? You've told her?"

"Yes. I didn't want her calling all the time or getting a bee in her bonnet and driving down. She cried straight for a week, but she's okay now and is willing to help out. I told her about the baby and she's on a binge buying spree for baby clothes and whatever else new babies need. When Maggie's home, keep Mom posted as to Maggie's progress."

"I will. I'll ask Francesco to call her. They seem to get along really well. And thanks, Lucas. You're the best."

Tom arrived a half hour later. He entered the room, a smile on his face, and shook Matthew's hand. "I hear she is finally gaining on it. Two months have been a long time, for all of us. It's been tough staying away, but that's what Doc Lucas wanted us to do. I want you to know that Buddy, Leo, and Art are in jail. No bail for any of them. Bea filed first degree attempted murder charges against Buddy, plus running a nation-wide sex trafficking operation which includes kidnapping, a federal crime. Art is charged with kidnapping and running a sex trafficking ring. Leo's charges are less serious, but he, too, is charged with allowing his home to be used for sex trafficking. Art and Buddy will live out their lives in a federal prison. Cody is a cooperating witness, and there's plenty of evidence that he was an unwilling participant, so I think he'll be given a lenient sentence, if any."

"I don't know if Maggie is going to be able to handle a trial any time soon, emotionally or physically," Matthew said.

"We don't need Maggie's testimony. Those three men did it to themselves long before Maggie came into the picture, and there's a long line of evidence against them. Not worrying about a trial will take a lot of stress off her. And you. Bea can't wait. She wants this FBI bust known around the world."

Two days later, Maggie came home. Everything was cleaned and ready. A big urn of flowers sat by the door, welcoming her. Matthew waited as the ambulance brought Maggie home. Maggie would be so happy to learn the surprise Francesco had arranged. Maggie's horse watched from the corral.

"That will bring Maggie around," mused Matthew. "That will be the best therapy available. May I wheel her out every day, even though she may not be aware?" he asked Lucas.

"Yes. That's your job, Padre. Take her to church. Don't make her clean walls until she's ready. Matthew, let me know when she is close to delivery. I want to be here. Be sure she sees an OB/GYN regularly. We want this baby to be happy and healthy. I guess that's it for orders. You have my list of things that must be done on a regular basis. I'll be going home tomorrow, but you can call me anytime. And, Matthew, I want you and Francesco to do what you do best. Pray every day, several times a day, for her recovery."

"We will. Can you possibly give me an idea of when she might come back to us?"

"I believe within the month her eyes will see the world around her. But I don't want to give you false hope. Her brain's been badly injured. We released pressure on her brain, but that doesn't mean it's fixed. Sending her home is a gamble. When she wakes up, you and everyone around her, must not expect that she will jump up and pick up where you last knew her. There may or may not be permanent brain damage. Promise me that if she isn't coherent when she wakes up, you will take her back to the hospital and call me ASAP. And, Matthew, she's not going to be able to walk for a while, and she may have trouble speaking."

"How can we help her?" Matthew asked.

"All of you, when you're on duty, talk to her. Tell her stories that will help her remember how she knows you. We'll be very lucky if she knows the people around her, so it's very important that everyone talks to her all the time. In a low voice. Keep the curtains open during the day. She's going to need physical therapy. She'll need a wheelchair that she can maneuver by herself at first. Later, she'll need a walker. I've asked a physical therapist to keep in touch. She can lay out exercises that you will need to help her with so she can regain her strength. This will not be an easy road, but I know everyone will pitch in. This is an incredibly strong community."

"We'll all be ready. Safe journey, Lucas. Our love to your mother."

Matthew turned away, and for the first time in two months, he felt like they had finally reached the end of the dark tunnel and the sun was shining.

CHAPTER FIFTY-SIX

As Maggie lay in a fitful but unconscious state, it was Gabriella who cared for her during the day when Matthew worked. On a bright, sunny day, Maggie opened her eyes, looked around and said, "I'm so tired, I think I need a nap."

By the time Gabriella had called everyone in, Maggie had already gone back to sleep. "And she said those words in a clear voice?" Matthew asked.

"Yes. It was only a few seconds, but it sounded like Maggie. What does it mean?" she asked.

"It means she's going to wake up."

It was another two weeks before Maggie woke up again. The day nurse was with her when she opened her eyes and said, "I have a really bad belly ache."

Matthew came as soon as he got the nurse's call. He pulled a chair close to the bed and carefully took her hand, holding it to his face. She did not respond. He took off his shoes and climbed up on the bed beside her, putting his arm around her, pulling her close so he could talk to her. He lay beside her, continuing to talk to her about their hopes and plans for the future, hoping for a response. When none came, he lay next to her for another hour, finally deciding she wasn't going to wake up.

As he lifted up to swing his legs off the bed, Maggie's hand tightened around his. He swung back to look at her face. Her eyes were closed, but she turned her head toward him. "Maggie," he whispered. He wanted to talk to her but remembered what Lucas had cautioned.

"Take things very slow when she wakes up." he had said. "She'll be confused. It may take a while before she knows you and the others. Hold her as often as possible. We want her to feel safe."

"My stomach hurts," she said, again pulling at Matthew's hand. Matthew put his hand on her belly and slowly rubbed it. "Why does it hurt?" she asked.

She squeezed his hand and opened her eyes, stared at him, then closed them again.

Disregarding his own previous desire to keep the news from her until she was fully awake, he said, "About your belly ache. You are with child, Maggie. Lucas says the baby is fine and will be born healthy. All I want is that we may live out our days watching sunsets, holding each other, laughing, and watching our child grow strong. I want you to know the depth of my love and what you've given me. Please wake up, beautiful lady."

Matthew made the sign of the cross over her and smiled.

CHAPTER FIFTY-SEVEN

Another false alarm. But he already had Lucas on the phone.

"Hey, is Maggie really awake?" Lucas asked.

"No. And being the fuss budget that I am, I'm worried. She wakes up and then goes back to sleep.

"Matthew, I've told you that when the swelling is gone, she'll be back."

"I know. That's what Juanita, her nurse, keeps saying, but it's been nearly three months. And her belly is enlarging. Is she getting enough nourishment for two?"

"Yes. Ask the gynecologist and a pediatrician to come look at her. To relieve your stress, know that if all her organs are functioning properly, and I believe they are, the baby will be fine. Granted, there aren't many cases of a woman in a coma giving birth, but there are some."

"Don't know what I'd do without you, Lucas."

"You'd find somebody else to ask," Lucas laughed. "I believe we're getting very close to when she wakes up and asks for food or you, not necessarily in that order. She's really going to wake up, Matthew. You need to be thinking about how you're going to help her get back on her feet. Do not let her confine herself to the wheelchair. That will not help her regain her strength. In the beginning, she will have to take many small, slow steps, but she'll get stronger. Get her out to her horse. You'll figure it out."

"What if she asks how she got this way?"

"Tell her. She needs to know everything that happened. She needs to know that she's lucky to be alive. She should be dead. Getting kicked in the head is not easy to survive."

"Thanks, brother."

Matthew put down the phone and walked to Maggie's bed. He folded a blanket and walked to the door. "Matthew." Her voice was almost unheard.

Matthew turned. "Maggie?" He looked at her eyes as he walked back to the bed. "Maggie?"

"I'm so tired, Matthew. I don't understand what's happening to me. And I don't understand why I'm so hungry."

"When you're totally awake, I will tell you everything. What would you like me to do?"

"Take all these tubes out so I can sleep."

"I'd like you to sit up. We'll start with raising the bed." He grabbed the handle and slowly lifted her head. "If this works, we'll go outside in the wheelchair. Let's get you upright. I'll call the Juanita and see if any tubes can be removed. And, what would you like to eat?"

"How about a grilled cheese sandwich, no crusts? I'm starving."

"At your command." Matthew kissed her cheek and left the room.

"Juanita, Maggie is awake and I believe this time she'll stay awake. She wants a grilled cheese sandwich and her tubes removed. Is that okay?"

"Better than okay. Most of the tubes can go. Get Gabby to make the sandwich." The nurse went into the room. Matthew called Gabby and asked for the sandwich.

Gabby's eyes got big. "She's back?"

"I believe so. Before you start the sandwich, no crusts, please, go find Francesco and give him the news." Gabby ran for the front door.

"Father, Father," Gabby yelled. "Come quick. Maggie's awake."

Matthew called Lucas who did not answer. Matthew left a message. "She's awake and this time it's for real. She wants a grilled cheese sandwich."

When he got back to the bedroom, Juanita had unhooked most of the tubes, but left the nutrient drip hooked up.

"We'll see how she does with the sandwich. She may not digest it well. I'm calling the obstetrician and her doctor and asking them to drive out as soon as they can to look at her. Tomorrow, if she handles the food well and passes the doctor's exam, we'll get her in the wheelchair." Juanita's smile was at least as big as Matthew's.

Francesco bustled into the room and went straight to the bed. He raised his arms above her head and blessed her. Then he bent down and kissed her cheek. Matthew waited to see if she would know him and his name. The response was immediate. "Francesco, how are you?"

"I am well, lovely lady, how are you?"

"Tired. I need to rest, but first I want to eat."

Juanita poured water into a paper cup and set it by her bed. "Someone needs to help her with the water. We'll see how she handles the sandwich. And, everyone, stay here. Real stimulus will show us whether she is slowly coming back to normal. The sooner she can get up and move around, the healthier and safer she and the baby will be."

"Baby? Who's having a baby?"

"You are," Juanita answered.

"Is that why my belly aches?"

"Yes. Now let's get this sandwich into you and get you drinking lots of water.

Maggie sat there, fear creeping across her face. She couldn't understand her sudden anxiety. Matthew knew exactly what concerned her. He went to her, pushing her hair aside, and whispered in her ear, "The baby's fine. Don't worry." Maggie immediately relaxed, but she no longer talked. She ate half the sandwich then lay back and pulled up the covers, staring at the ceiling.

Months passed and Maggie grew stronger. She could manage the wheelchair and loved to visit her mare. She was learning how do small chores. She prepared food for dinner, snapped beans, and ate a tree full of apples. On a particularly sunny day she asked Matthew what they should name the baby. She was close to her due date and they had never discussed names, let alone the sex of the baby. "What would you name a little boy?"

she asked.

"Lucas has to be in there somehow, first name or middle name. How about you? Any preferences?"

"Let's name him Matthew Lucas, but call him Luke."

"Done. And a girl?" he asked.

"I've always liked Rebecca," she said. "And call her Becca."

"Mary Rebecca?"

"Had to get that good Catholic name in there," she laughed.

"But of course."

"Done. I'll bet that was the fastest baby naming session anyone's ever had."

Matthew laughed. "Come on, let's get you up out of that chair and walk you to the fence. Your mare is waiting."

As she stood, Matthew holding her arm, she said, "I just remembered something. Weren't we supposed to look for the mare that was stolen from here?"

"Guess that got lost in the kidnapping."

"Was there ever any sign of the horse?" Maggie asked.

"No, but I admit I wasn't looking."

"As soon as the baby is born, let's see if we can find that horse.

Two days later, Mary Rebecca Brannigan was born. Mother, father, daughter, and all the community, doing fine.

CHAPTER FIFTY-EIGHT

SENTENCING

After the trial in Federal District Court in Portland, Oregon, the three defendants appeared once again for sentencing. All three defendants had been convicted: Leo Garrity, Art Camden, and Homer "Buddy" Garrity.

The evidence against the three men had been overwhelming, even without Maggie's testimony. Attempted premeditated murder and sex trafficking, and sexual abuse of young girls and women, sealed their fates. Because of his youth, the fact that he had not participated in the nefarious operation, and his cooperation in bringing the others to justice, charges against Cody Garrity had been dropped.

People slowly packed the courtroom until there was standing room only. Ananya sat with Dakota and a very somber Cody in the far back of the room. Tiny and Sasha sat mid-room, surrounded by a large contingent of tribal members who had taken part in bringing these men to justice. Jasper sat in the second row, hoping he could whisper to Father Francesco and Father Daniel in the front row. A third place was saved next to Francesco, for Father Matthew to slip into. Bea Sanders stood with detective Marshall. Beside them, Gabriella stood with her mother, both of them dressed in Mexico's bright colors. They had all traveled a long way to share this momentous day.

The polished mahogany furniture and judge's bench made the room seem smaller than it was.

The crowd buzzed in soft tones and then went silent as the bailiff called for them to rise. The judge entered and the gavel came down, signaling them to be seated again.

The three defendants sat, staring up at the high bench: Judge Kate DeLaney presided.

Maggie wore a long, green silk dress, her mahogany curls tamed by her hair cut short. The crowd inhaled when Matthew wheeled her in. He could see the shock on the faces of the convicted men. Maggie was there, to face them.Matthew, in his priestly black suit and white collar, wheeled Maggie to the ramp, then picked her up and placed her in the witness chair. The judge waited until she was settled. "Thank you, Father Brannigan," she said as Matthew stepped away.

"Mrs. Brannigan?" Judge DeLaney addressed her. "I'm happy to see you're doing well." The audience came alert. "She is married to Father?" A loud buzz ran through the audience. "Did you know?" "How can that be?"

Judge DeLaney turned to the three defendants. "This hearing is to determine a sentence for each of the charges for which you have been convicted. For the record, Mrs. Brannigan, please give us your name and address."

"My name is Mary Margaret Callahan Brannigan, known to all as Maggie. I live in Biggs Junction, Oregon."

"I understand you would like to address the defendants. Please tell the court what happened to you." Maggie told the entire story about being kidnapped at the mustang auction, and then taken to the Garrity Ranch, followed by Buddy's brutal attempt to murder her and her long road to recovery from her injuries. People waiting in the hall crowded into the courtroom despite the bailiff's efforts to dissuade them, as Maggie told her story.

"The one positive thing I learned when I woke up, was that I was pregnant. The happy result is our daughter, Becca, who was born a happy, healthy baby." She sat back, signaling she had finished.

The judge waited a few seconds to let the story settle in on the observers and the defendants. "Thank, you. I can't help but notice that your face is badly scarred. Is that the result of Mr. Garrity's attempt on your life?"

"Yes. My face will undergo surgery sometime in the future." Maggie rubbed her hand over her face emphasizing the deep-rutted scars. "I did not want to risk any harm to my unborn baby by having surgery."

"One more thing, Mrs. Brannigan. I notice you had to be carried up to the witness chair. Are you not able to walk?"

"Yes and no. Yes, I can walk short distances. No, I can't walk for any prolonged amount of time. I'm in therapy to help stimulate my brain to function properly with the rest of my body. It's a long process."

Silence blanketed the courtroom for a long moment. Then Judge Kate DeLaney, her face showing the revulsion she'd felt as Maggie laid out her story, looked down upon the three defendants. "If I were allowed to take the law into my own hands, I would sentence all three of you to the gas chamber. It would be no loss to humanity."

Heads down, the three men stared at the table.

"But since I can't," she went on, "Mr. Leo Garrity, you are sentenced to fifteen years in prison. Your home and land will be sold to pay Mrs. Brannigan's extensive medical bills and any legal fees incurred." Leo Garrity stared at the judge his eyes unflinching.

"Mr. Arthur Camden, I have a question for you. Do you think becoming a dirty cop paid off?" Art Camden did not respond. "You are hereby sentenced to life in prison."

"And, finally, Mr. Homer Garrity, I consider you an adult bully. I suspect you were always a bully. Didn't get your way, you resorted to violence. You are hereby sentenced to life in prison without the possibility of parole. Any problems within the prison system, and I will bring further charges against you." The courtroom was silent.

Judge DeLaney pivoted in her chair. "You wanted to say something, Mrs. Brannigan? I am truly sorry you had to face this ordeal."

Maggie lifted herself from the chair, slowly moving to the rail. She held on tightly, her knuckles showing white. She looked out over the audience in the courtroom. "First, I would like to thank all the local law enforcement and the FBI for all they did to save me and the many girls who were these men's victims."

Then, turning to the defendants, Maggie said, "What you did to me is unconscionable, Homer Garrity. But what you all have done to hundreds of young girls and women is even more unconscionable. Yours are perverted minds that believed you had a right to kidnap and use these girls for your own sexual fantasies and personal wealth. You took untold thousands of dollars, probably millions, from hundreds of men willing to pay you to indulge their fantasies.

"I consider all of you to be predators and pedophiles, preying, through fear and intimidation, on young girls and women who are terrified and unable to extricate themselves from the situation forced upon them."

Maggie felt like she might fall but stayed upright and turned back to the audience.

"Across the world the insidious nature of human trafficking must be stopped. A group of young women who were able to escape these men's depravity have made it their mission to work with me to bring services to victims of this crime. We will start with local efforts to rehumanize victims, and then our efforts will grow. We will work with law enforcement to find sex trafficking and prostitution and bring their perpetrators to justice. We will educate communities to recognize this heinous crime that takes place all around us, often in plain sight."

She turned back to the three. "Gentlemen, sex trafficking is modern day slavery and we will put a stop to it just as we have put a stop to you."

Maggie watched the three men. Two sat stoic. Leo Garrity, his head between his hands, sobbed. Maggie stood erect, pulled her shoulders back and took small, grueling steps down the ramp. Pain enveloped her face with every step. No one in the courtroom moved as they watched her walk down the ramp, into Matthew's waiting arms. He smiled and gently helped her into the wheelchair.

He leaned down and whispered, "You won. You were magnificent and I love you."

She whispered back, "We won, and I will always love you."

ACKNOWLEDGMENTS

I would like to thank the first readers for their gracious input into the story: Sherry Lien, Patti Bruneau, and Nancy Thompson, your input helped the story fall into place. Nancy, your background in working with young girls in trouble was invaluable. Special thanks to Beta reader Jenny Read, for her input regarding Native American culture. And to Avis Rector, who read and reread the story and made suggestions that helped the story move forward. Without you, this book would not have happened.

Thanks to my two writing groups for their input into how the story should unfold: the Whidbey Writers Group, a long-standing and prolific group of writers, and the Honchas, seven women in search of the muse and a glass of wine.

I am grateful to so many people for their wisdom and skill in actually bringing this book together. I would like to thank Dorothy Read, my editor for keeping me going in the right direction and for believing in the story. And thanks to Terry Hansen for the beautiful book cover and interior design, and to Grace Hansen for her super proofreading.

And finally, I thank my patient husband, Bob, and my good friend, Mike McNeff, for providing the details into how guns work and how the FBI does its work.

I love you all.

Pat

A NOTE FROM THE AUTHOR

Sex trafficking, as the topic for this book, is very important to me. I spent thirty some years in education as an English and competitive speech teacher, librarian, and school administrator. Girls would come to me and tell their stories. Some told of becoming prostitutes because they had been thrown out of their homes and needed to support themselves. Many stories were about being sexually abused by their fathers or other family members and they wanted help to deal with it. Every girl was crying for help, but didn't know how to ask for it. They were afraid; afraid of jail, afraid of those who controlled their lives, afraid their parents might find out, and fear their mothers would find out, because they knew their mothers would never believe them.

Three told me the horrors of being trafficked; one girl murdered. These girls were from different parts of the Northwest, but basically told the same story. This book shows the dark and criminal side of trafficking and how even the people who try to help are themselves abused. In researching this book, I learned a great deal about how trafficking is hidden deep in the criminal world.

I want to explain that I did a great deal of my research online. I do not list those resources, but if you want to know, research the horrors awaiting young girls and often young boys.

Today there are a large number of organizations to go to for help. Even on our small, island community there is an organization that helps abused girls. One of those workers read my book for accuracy and helped me understand this criminal world.

RESOURCES

FURTHER READING

Bales, Kevin. The Slave next door.

Belles, Nita. In our Backyard: Human trafficking in America and what we can do about it.

Birrell, Nani. Witness: One Woman's Story From Human Trafficking to Freedom, A Memoir.

Enrile, Annalisa, Phd. editor. Ending Human Trafficking & Modern-Day Slavery, Freedom's Journey

Farrow, Ronan. Catch and kill.

Federal Government Tribal Justice

Holler, Clyde. The Black Elk Reader.

Nichols, Andrea Theory, Research, Policy, and practice.

Parker, RJ. In chains: the terrible world of human trafficking.

Patterson, James. Filthy Rich: The Billionaires Sex Scandal and the Shocking True Story of Jeffery Epstein.

Siddhartha, Kara. Sex Trafficking: Inside the business of Modern Slavery.

Truer, David. Rez Life.

Vachess, Alice. Sex Crimes, then and now: My Years on the front lines Prosecuting Rapists and Confronting their Collaborators.

Yates, Travis. The courageous Police Lea

WHERE TO SEEK HELP

Indigenous Women's Resource Organization. This organization is available to assist all indigenous women. There are ten organizations under this umbrella.

CAST (Coalition to Abolish Slavery and Trafficking)
1.888.539.2373 https://www.castla.org

National Children's Advocacy Center
1.800.422.4453 https://www.nationalcac.org/

National Center for Missing and Exploited Children
1.800.843-5678 https://www.missingkids.org

National Sexual Violence Resource Center
1.877.739.3895 https://www.nsvrc.org/

Office for Victims of Crime
1.800.422.4453 https://ovc.ojp.gov

Shared Hope International
1.866.437.5433 https://sharedhope.org/

THORN
info@wearethorn.org https://www.thorn.org/

The Urban Justice Center's Sex Workers Project
1.646.602.5617 https://swp.urbanjustice.org/

National Children's Advocacy Center
1.800.422.4453 https://www.nationalcac.org/

United Nations UNICEF, USA
1.800.367.5437 https://www.unicefusa.org/

Violent Crimes against Children
1.888.407.474 https://www.fbi.gov/investigate/violent-crime/cac

BOOK DISCUSSION QUESTIONS

1. Do you know someone who has been pulled into prostitution or sex trafficking? Did they ever seek help? Why? Why not?
2. Who is at risk of becoming involved in a sex trafficking ring? Why?
3. Do victims see themselves as victims?
4. How easy or difficult is it to leave trafficking?
5. Has anyone you know ever helped their trafficker find victims?
6. What circumstances lead to trafficking? Name at least 4.
7. Discuss the fact that trafficking is both a national crime as well as an international crime. Why?
8. How does trafficking affect families?

ABOUT THE AUTHOR

Patricia Kelley experienced every rung of the ladder in her education career. She taught speech, writing, and theatre arts and served as a media specialist before she became a school administrator and retired as a district superintendent of schools. An award-winning poet, she now teaches all ages about the art of writing, the art of public speaking, and the art of giving an outstanding book signing. She has co-directed writers' conferences and retreats and enjoys mentoring young writers. She describes herself as "a writer helping writers."

Poetry from the Desert Floor, is a collection of photographs and poems reflecting Patricia's love of the southwest desert and the people, places, and things that inhabit it. Her first novel, *The Last Confession*, launches the Father and Wife Series featuring Maggie Callahan and her surprising love interest as they solve intricate mysteries and pursue justice.

Made in the USA
Las Vegas, NV
24 February 2021